AZRAEL

BY

MICHAEL J BENSON

CHAPTER 1

IRAQ 2003

Al-Qadir was sixteen when the second Gulf War broke out in March of 2003. His father Abbud was a police officer with the rank of general in the town of Miqdadiyah, Northeast of Baqubah in Iraq. Abbud Hadi was a well-known and respected general in the police. With twenty-five years of service, he had seen everything that Iraq and invading forces could throw at his town. He was respected by the local Mayor, Baravan Laghmani and the city council. The mayor may have respected him, but he didn't respect the mayor or the city council cronies the mayor had put in place. Every part of the mayor's office and city council was infected with corruption. Every contract that was issued by the City council had a percentage taken off for bribes to the mayor and his cronies. In his early career as a general he'd experienced the corruption firsthand when the mayor tried to give him a bribe. The police department was due to get ten new vehicles and uniforms for fifty officers. The mayor offered him the equivalent of one thousand US dollars to turn a blind eye as only seven vehicles would be delivered to the police and twenty uniforms. The three missing vehicles would be given to the mayor, his brother, and the accountant for the city. He refused and started to raise a stink as it was an insult for them to think that he would accept a bribe.

A week after he refused the bribe his best friend, also a general came to his house. He tried to get him to accept the bribe, but he still refused. It was at this point that it got physical between the old friends. His friend pulled his sidearm out of its holster and put it to Abbud's head. He was told to stop his investigation of the mayor, or he and his family would suffer for it. He took the warning for what it was, a death threat. He was not scared of his friend or the mayor and his corrupt council, but he had to protect his family. He was physically removed from his home and taken to the mayor's office the next morning for a meeting. After it was made clear to him that he would be kicked out of the police and arrested for corruption, which meant prison, he came to an agreement. He would not talk about the corruption, bribes, or threats if he and his family were left alone. He just wanted to do his job and be a police officer. The mayor agreed but let him know that he would be on a short leash and watched closely. After the meeting he never spoke to his friend again except when he was performing police duties.

After the threats by the mayor, he trained all four of his sons in the use of side arms and rifles. He was an expert in the Persian martial art of Varzesh-e Pahlavani. He tutored his sons in the art, but Al-Qadir was the only one that took it seriously. At eighteen Al-Qadir had become as good as his father and ran a small class for his friends without anyone knowing. Varzesh-e Pahlavani was frowned upon by the religious mullah's and elders. In their eyes it was a sin to take part in the ancient Persian art form.

Al-Qadir was talented with his hands and made his own wooden Meels, that looked like bowling pins with a round handle in the top. He exercised with these daily in a series of swinging motions that went into hundreds of sets.

Meels dated back hundreds of years and were introduced to the Indian continent during the Mongol invasion of 1256AD. They had a short wooden handle attached to a conical shaped body which resembled a club. Traditional Meels would range in size and weight from ten pounds to as much as sixty pounds. Professional Meels were adorned with ornate carvings or paintings.

His brothers trained very rarely as they did not have the interest or enthusiasm as their father and youngest brother. With the threat of another invasion by the USA, the three eldest sons were drafted into the Iraqi army. Their father tried to persuade the local military General to allow them to train as police officers, but he refused. The only one spared by the army was Al-Qadir, he had to report to the police station to enlist for police training.

It was the first invasion by the US and allied forces that changed everything for Al-Qadir and his family. His father was trying to keep control of law and order in his sector of Miqdadiyah. Locals were looting and fighting amongst themselves as the news of another invasion was imminent. Quietly the people hoped for the foreign troops to come into the country again as things had worsened since the previous invasion. Poverty had increased, jobs were exceedingly rare, and rebels were running rampant in parts of the country. Feeding families especially children for fathers had gone to desperation levels. Crime was growing on a weekly basis, with stores and market holders being the main targets of the starving people.

The police were recruiting as many young men as they could but were under constant attack from the militants. Even though the threat was high, and their lives were in danger they still lined up at recruitment events at local police stations. Most of the young men were joining in the hope that they could help their fathers put food on the table for the family. In recent days in Baqubah there had been three attacks by suicide bombers on police stations that were trying to encourage new recruits. Thirty-two men died and twenty-one were injured in the attacks. This did not deter the potential recruits as they were well below the poverty level in their community. They had to do something to find a way of helping provide a basic life for their loved ones.

Al-Qadir was halfway through his police training when he was sent to serve in his father's sector. He proved to be an excellent student and extremely strong and agile for his five-foot eight-inch height. He spoke not only his native tongue but English and French fluently. This was thanks to his mother who taught all four sons to speak French and their father taught them English. He was excited to join his father in fighting crime and keeping the peace. The timing of him joining his father could not have been worse as it was the first day of the allied bombing raids. The smaller towns and cities were being flooded by Iraqi military forces as they ran from the main cities that were being bombed by the allied forces.

General Hadi sent his son Al-Qadir and twenty other young police recruits to one of Saddam Hussein's palaces closer to the Iranian border. He sent them off in the middle of the night with one of his most seasoned sergeants. The sergeant had their story straight before they left for the palace. The general's idea was the young recruits were at the palace to stop anyone looting or damaging it. This would take his son and many of his friends' sons away from the rampaging and abusive Iraqi soldiers that would most certainly arrive. The sergeant and young recruits would be safe away from the city, or so he thought.

CHAPTER 2

GENERAL MUTAZ

Just hours before the young recruits arrived at the palace it had been occupied by a group of Hussein's Republican Guard special forces. The soldiers had orders to protect one of Hussein's daughters that lived in the palace. By the time the soldiers arrived at the palace the only occupants were the caretaker, his family, and garden staff. Hussein's daughter and family had already left the palace and fled across the border to Iran with their personal security guards.

The two open backed police trucks were half a mile from the palace when four soldiers stopped them. After explaining who they were they were allowed to continue to the palace. The police vehicles stopped a hundred yards from the palace walls. To the right of the palace there were several military vehicles parked in a row. The sergeant in charge of the recruits and his driver got out of the lead vehicle.

"I'm Sergeant Ali, we have been sent to provide security for the palace," he said to the soldier that was blocking their way.

"Wait here," said the soldier abruptly.

The sergeant waited five minutes when a huge soldier walked towards him with four other soldiers.

"What do you want?" asked the soldier.

Ali saluted the soldier when he saw that he was a general.

"I'm Sergeant Ali, we have been sent here to protect the palace from any potential looters," replied Ali.

"I am General Mutaz. You don't think we can protect the palace?" said the general.

"We didn't know you were here; we were told the palace was at risk," replied Ali.

"We are here now. Get those police officers out of the trucks and tell them to stand in a line," he replied.

"If you are here to protect the palace we don't need to stay," replied Ali as he saluted the general and turned away.

Ali had a bad feeling about the general. His twenty-five years as a police officer gave him something of a sixth sense for certain situations.

"Get them out of the truck," shouted the general to his men.

The four soldiers with him ran to the vehicles and pointed their guns at the recruits.

"Everybody out," shouted Ali.

"I give the orders around here," said the general.

Ali turned towards the general and saw a fist coming at his face. The blow to his head was massive breaking his nose and right eye orbit. Ali crashed to the ground unconscious, blood flowing out of his nostrils and eye.

Al-Qadir and two of the recruits ran towards Ali to help him, they did not get far. The soldiers brutally smashed the butts of the weapons into their heads. They did not stand a chance against such well-trained soldiers as they were kicked and beaten by them.

"Stop, stand them with the others in the line," shouted the general.

Al-Qadir was shocked at the ferocity of the attack, he did not expect to be assaulted by his own countrymen. He stood in the line as blood ran down the side of his face. He could hear his two friends coughing and spitting blood. He knew they would be no match against the soldiers in a fist fight. He only weighed one hundred and fifty pounds and was the biggest in the group. The soldiers all looked to be at least two hundred pounds and the general had to be two hundred and fifty of solid muscle.

The general walked to the line of recruits inspecting them as he walked.

"Stand to attention," shouted Ali as he recovered from the punch. He was now on his feet and staggered towards his recruits.

The rest of the soldiers in the palace gathered in a mob behind the general. They were laughing aloud as Ali stumbled to the line of recruits.

Al-Qadir broke away from the line when he heard Sergeant Ali shout the order. His sergeant needed help and he was not going to stand still and watch him struggle to walk.

The general smiled when he saw the recruit break away from the line. One of the soldiers was walking towards him with his weapon raised to hit him in the back with the butt. The general put his hand up to stop the soldier. There was something about this young recruit he liked but he would have to teach him a lesson.

"Thank you," said the sergeant as they rejoined the rest of the police recruits.

"Stand to attention until I return," said the general.

"It is eleven in the morning and extremely hot, they need water," said Sergeant Ali.

"They will get water when I say so," barked the general.

"I will get the water bottles out of the vehicle," replied Sergeant Ali.

"Stay in line," shouted the general.

"I'm getting them water," he shouted back.

"We don't need water," said one of the recruits with fear in his voice.

A soldier stepped forward and punched the recruit in the stomach for speaking out.

Ali walked to the first truck that he rode in and lifted out a case of water. He carried it to the line of recruits and started to tear open the plastic that was holding the bottles together.

The general walked up to him as he knelt in the sand. He was tearing at the plastic trying to free the bottles.

The general was furious and took out his sidearm and shot Sergeant Ali in the head at point blank range. Ali's body slumped onto the bottles as his blood soaked into the sand around the case of water bottles.

The recruits all shouted out in shock and anger, several including Al-Qadir ran to the sergeant's side only to be beaten to the ground by the soldiers.

"Get up and stand in a line," shouted a sergeant.

"Sergeant Talabani, leave them where they are," said the general as he walked away.

Sergeant Ahmad Talabani was the general's right-hand man. Al-Qadir noticed a purple mark on his right hand.

They were all made to stand in the sun as their sergeant's body lay in front of them. The general just walked away back into the palace as his soldiers watched the recruits from the cool shadows of the palace wall.

It had been five hours since the sergeant was brutally murdered. Four of the recruits lay in the sand unconscious from the heat and exposure to the sun.

Two soldiers and the sergeant from earlier approached the line of recruits.

"Into the palace," said Sergeant Talabani.

"What about our colleagues?" asked Al-Qadir.

"They can lay in the sand," replied the sergeant laughing.

"Pick them up," said Al-Qadir to his friends.

He was punched in the stomach for his trouble.

"I said leave them there," said the sergeant.

The two soldiers escorted them into the palace courtyard where they drank water from the fountain in the center. The water tasted foul as it had chlorine in it. They drank as much as they could before the soldiers pulled them away from the fountain.

"Please let us help our friends outside," pleaded Al-Qadir.

Just as he asked, he heard a series of gunshots outside. He bolted out of the palace followed by the recruits. The soldiers did not try to stop them this time they just stood watching and laughing.

They all stopped in their tracks at the sight that was in front of them. The general stood over the beaten bodies of their friends with a pistol in his hand.

"This is what happens to the weak," he shouted at the recruits.

A soldier was pulling at the hair on the head of one of their unconscious and beaten friends, he yanked at the hair to show his face. This pulling of the hair woke him out of his unconsciousness, and he squinted at the general.

The general stepped forward and shot him in the head twice. The cries and shouts of rage and fear from the remaining recruits were loud and passionate. Al-Qadir stared at the general and the soldier and showed no sign of emotion. He looked through the two men and swore under his breath to get revenge for his friends, if he survived.

That night the recruits were all tied to different columns in the palace. Across from them there were the bodies of the palace caretakers and gardeners. They were all shot in the head by the general, the man was a sadistic animal.

CHAPTER 3

GENERAL ASHKOURI

Al-Qadir's father General Hadi knew from previous invasions by allied forces that soldiers based in Baghdad would run to the smaller cities and towns. The Republican Guard where the ones that he worried about most because of their reputation for being brutal. They had the protection of Saddam Hussein and they used that to loot, pillage, and rape. Many wealthy Iraqi families had already left the country for fear of what was to come. They were not worried about the allied forces but their own.

It had become apparent that many of Saddam Hussein's inner-city palaces were being targeted by the coalition forces. The more remote palaces known to be occupied by the female members of Saddam Hussein's family were not bombed.

General Hadi had to move quickly before troops from the Iraqi Republican Guard arrived.

To try to protect the women and children in his area he put the word out for them to stay indoors. A group of police officers that worked for General Hadi set up safe houses for over fifty women and young girls. The local Mayor through one of the corrupt police officers found out where two of the safe houses were located.

A section of Saddam Hussein's Republican Guard under the command of General Ashkouri traveled through Baqubah a day after the initial bombings by coalition forces. They had targeted

Miqdadiyah as a place for them to lay low for a while or until the bombings stopped. As in the past they were like an infestation of locusts, swarming over everything and everyone.

General Ashkouri left two of his soldiers and two motorcycles in Baqubah to spy on any foreign troops coming into the city. Their job was to let the general know if the invading forces headed in his direction. His forces and General Mutaz had decided to separate before they reached Baqubah. Both had a reputation for being extremely violent, as did the troops under their command. General Ashkouri headed towards the city of Miqdadiyah, while General Mutaz headed east of the city, where he was going nobody knew.

General Mutaz had stashed millions of dollars and gold in different Palaces around Northern Iraq over the years. He had safes placed under the floors of the palaces and then concreted over them. The workers that dug out the holes and installed the safes at each palace were taken out into the desert and killed. He did not want anyone knowing about the safes or their contents.

When General Ashkouri and his troops arrived in Miqdadiyah he took control of policing and security. He put the local police in control of roadblocks and security for the hastily arranged military camp. Ashkouri's soldiers stole all the food and drink from local stores leaving nothing for the local people. If store owners resisted, they were shot or beaten severely.

Even though they had only been in the town a few hours they had created havoc. The soldiers abused the local women and young girls, killing or torturing any man that tried to protect them. Many homes of families that tried to defend their loved ones were set on fire or destroyed by the soldiers as an example to others that might resist.

AZRAEL

Mayor Laghmani, cow tailed to General Ashkouri and gave him whatever he wanted, including his own office in the city hall building. A few days after their arrival word had reached the generals ears that the mayor was corrupt and had stacks of money hidden away somewhere.

The mayor was at home eating dinner with his wife and three daughters when Ashkouri's soldiers burst in.

"What is the meaning of this. You cannot just kick the door down on my home, General Ashkouri will hear of this," he shouted at the soldiers.

"He sent us to escort you to his office," said the lead soldier.

"I will come when I have finished my dinner," he replied arrogantly and turned to continue eating.

The soldier walked up to him and slammed his face into the plate of food in front of him. His wife and daughters all screamed and immediately started sobbing.

The force of his face smashing into the plate of food had broken his nose and it was bleeding profusely. His wife jumped up to help him only to be knocked to the floor by another soldier, her head catching the edge of the dining table giving her a nasty cut.

"Put him in the car and his wife," ordered the soldier to his colleagues.

Two soldiers lifted the mayor to his feet and dragged him outside. They returned and did the same to his wife.

"I will be out in a few minutes," shouted the lead soldier as he looked over the mayors three daughters.

The mayor's wife was screaming at the top of her voice inside the car.

"Please don't hurt my children, please," she shouted over and over, it would not help.

The front of the mayor's shirt was covered in blood by the time they reached his old office. He was dragged up the flight of stairs to his office, along with his wife. He was now sobbing on his knees in the presence of General Ashkouri, the man who he thought was protecting him.

The general did not waste any time as he stood over the weeping mayor.

"Where is the money?" he asked loudly.

"What money?" replied the mayor.

He received a boot to his right side for his reply.

"The money you have been squeezing out of deals with contractors doing work for the city," he said.

"I don't know what you're talking about," sobbed the mayor.

"One more time I will ask you, where is the money?"

"I don't have any money," he replied.

"Tell him," Screamed his wife.

"Shut up," he yelled at her through his bloody mouth.

"Your wife is obviously a lot smarter than you. You don't want any harm to come to her or your daughters, do you?" asked General Ashkouri.

"She is talking about our savings in the wardrobe in our bedroom," he replied.

"No, this is more than savings, at lot more."

"That is all the money we have," he said looking up at the general for mercy.

"Tie him to his old office chair," said the general.

Two soldiers picked him up off his knees and tied him to the chair.

"Please," said the mayor.

"Strip her," said the general pointing at the mayor's wife.

As the soldiers grabbed her, she turned into a screaming banshee and fought them with all her might. It did not take them long before she was naked in front of everyone.

"Put her face down on the desk. Last time, where is the money?" asked the general.

The mayor cried but did not answer as he looked at his wife's terrified face. The money meant more to him than his wife.

"Tell him you bastard," she screamed.

"I will be first and you four can be next," said the general to his soldiers as he started to undo the belt on his trousers.

"OK, OK, it's in a box buried at the back of our home, I will show you," he sobbed.

"Good, now I will have my fun," he replied as he continued to undo his belt.

"No, please don't. I can tell you where more women and young girls are hidden. Don't hurt my wife," wept the mayor.

"Something else you've been hiding from us?" asked the general.

"No, but it came to my attention that some policemen had put women and girls in safe houses."

"And you know where they are?"

"Yes, I will show you," he replied.

"You have just saved your wife but if you are lying to me, she will enjoy the whole barracks. If what you say is true, she will not be harmed."

As they sat in the back of the truck the mayor's wife lashed out at him with her feet cursing him for what he had put her through.

The money was recovered very quickly from the rear garden of the house but not soon enough to save his daughters from being abused by the soldiers.

So far, the general kept his word and the mayor's wife had not been touched. But he had other ideas for the mayor.

The mayor and his wife were taken into their home where they could hear their daughters sobbing upstairs. A soldier walked into the room with blood pouring down his face from where one of the daughters had clawed him with her nails. The wounds were deep and ghastly.

"A child did this to you?" said Ashkouri.

"Yes sir, the bitch can fight," he replied.

"I don't expect a young girl to get the better of one of my soldiers," he replied and shot the soldier in the face.

The soldier dropped to the floor dead.

"What have you done to my girls?" screamed the mayor's wife.

"It's been a long time since some of my soldiers have had a woman," replied Ashkouri.

"You animal, God will send you to hell for this," she shouted as she lunged at Ashkouri.

The mayor didn't do or say anything as his wife clawed at the general trying to rip his face with her nails. A soldier stepped forward and knocked her to the floor where she lay sobbing.

"Do something, you coward," she shouted at her husband.

He didn't reply, he just sat on the floor crying.

"I gave you my word your wife would not be hurt, but not you. Strip him," said Ashkouri.

For the first time the mayor gave up a fight, a pathetic attempt but a fight no less. Once stripped he was held by his arms by two soldiers.

"You let your wife be stripped in your office, you never fought for her, you just let it happen. This time it is you that will be bent over a table," said Ashkouri.

The soldiers put him face down on the dining room table.

"You can go to your daughters."

The mayor's wife didn't need telling twice and she ran up the stairs as fast as she could.

"Some of my soldiers have a liking for men not women. You are about to see how many," said Ashkouri as he left the room.

The mayor's wife was in a bedroom upstairs consoling her daughters and trying to cover their ears as the sounds of her husband's screams filled the house.

After he was raped several times, the mayor went with the general and pointed out the safe houses that he knew about. In a vein hope of stopping the rape the mayor gave up the names of two police officers that spied on the police generals for him. They were the ones that new the addresses of all the safe houses. They were picked up by soldiers and thrown into the bed of a pickup and taken to the mayor's house.

The convoy of pickups and canvas backed military vehicles left the mayors house with the police officers and the mayor in the bed of one of the pickups. In the back of the pickup, they had nowhere to hide as the people watched the vehicles drive past them.

The mayor cried and begged for his life on the way to the safe houses vowing to give the general any information he wanted. He shouted out that General Hadi was the one who organized the safe houses for the women and girls. Ashkouri sat in the front of the pickup listening to the crying and shouting. When General Hadi's name was called out it interested him. Ashkouri stopped the convoy and gave the two police officers a beating until they confirmed that the mayor was telling the truth.

CHAPTER 4

POLICE GENERAL HADI

After the visit to the safe houses the mayor was unceremoniously dumped in front of his home, still naked and bleeding.

The general and sixteen men returned to the first safe house which had two police officers outside. Without thought or hesitation they shot both police officers as they walked towards them. Inside the house were twelve women and girls who were all taken away.

The same thing happened at another safe house with no mercy for the police officers on guard. It didn't take long for the word to get around about the killing of the police officers. General Hadi was to be the next target.

Soldiers kicked open the door to General Hadi's home. After a quick search they realized the house was empty, so they trashed it. They threatened his neighbor next door who told the soldiers he was in work at the police station. That would be their next stop.

General Hadi was standing outside the police station smoking a cigarette when the troop vehicles pulled up. He didn't flinch, he just kept on smoking his cigarette.

"We are looking for General Hadi," said one soldier.

"I'm General Hadi, what is it you want?" he asked, even though he knew.

The soldiers had clear instructions to treat the general with respect.

"General Ashkouri wants you to come with us," he replied.

"Where am I going?" he asked.

"You'll go wherever we take you," snapped the soldier.

Two police officers stood to the left of their general stepped towards him as if to protect him.

"I will be back soon," he said to the two police officers holding his hand up to stop them.

If he didn't move quickly the soldiers would shoot his police officers as an example.

As the troop vehicles left the two police officers quickly reported on the radio what had happened to General Hadi. There were many responses to their radio call and not just from their own police officers but calls from the city of Baqubah. The groundswell of emotion and anger from police officers on the streets to the high-ranking police generals was like a rumbling volcano.

The corrupt police officer working for General Ashkouri went straight to the mayor's office. The general wasn't going to see the police officer at first but when the soldier told him what it was about, he was intrigued.

The police officer was marched into the mayor's office. He saw the general sitting back in a high-backed leather chair behind the desk. He had his feet resting on the desk and a huge expensive looking cigar in his mouth. He went to sit down in the chair on the opposite side of the desk.

"I didn't say sit," said the general.

"Sorry, I wasn't thinking. There is a lot of chatter on the police radios that soldiers have taken General Hadi," he said.

"So what?" he replied.

"General Hadi is very respected by all ranks of the police force here in Miqdadiyah. Just before I came in here, I heard that there is a high ranking general in Baqubah asking questions. He wants to know why he was taken and where?"

"Do you see this as a problem?" asked Ashkouri.

"It might be as General Hadi trained many of the police officers serving today. Many of them are extremely loyal and some hold high ranks. He is extremely popular with not just our police force but with the city of Baqubah."

"What do you think the police will do?" he asked.

"They will find out where he is and most probably demand his release," replied the police officer.

General Ashkouri laughed aloud when he heard this.

"You think that a group of low life policemen could take me on?"

"No, you would squash them, but they can make things difficult. They will most probably start by putting up roadblocks and demonstrate outside the town hall. They know you are here and will make this office the center of their protest."

"Let them come and I will kill all of them. It will be a lesson to any other police officers that try to defy me. What do you say Sergeant Qasim, shall we kill them all?" he asked his right-hand man.

"We could kill them easily, put them down like dogs," replied Qasim.

"I sense you are holding something back Qasim?"

"We won't be staying here much longer but we need to keep gunfire down to a minimum whilst we are here. We don't want the American troops hearing about us killing policemen, it will only bring them here sooner."

"You make a good point. Is General Hadi here yet?"

"Yes, sir he just arrived."

"Good, you can leave and if I hear that you have repeated anything that was said in here, I will cut out your tongue and eyes," said Ashkouri to the police officer.

"I won't say anything," he replied.

As the police officer left the office, he walked right past General Hadi who was standing between two soldiers in the reception area. He hung his head and didn't even acknowledge the general.

"Salute your general when you pass him," barked Hadi.

The police officer jumped in fear and gave him a half-hearted salute. He scurried out of the building; his head hung even lower. General Hadi now knew that he was working with General Ashkouri, and he would be punished for it. He had to get out of Miqdadiyah before word of his treachery got out to other police officers.

One of the soldiers grabbed General Hadi by the arm to march him into the office. He pulled his arm away with force.

"Don't put your hands on me, I'm a general in the Miqdadiyah police," he said with authority.

The soldier was about to hit him with his rifle when Sergeant Qasim stopped him.

"Stop," Qasim shouted. "Bring him into the generals office."

The soldier was furious but did as he was told and marched the general into the office.

General Hadi didn't fear these soldiers or their general, he had dealt with many men like them in his career. Out of respect for his rank General Hadi saluted General Ashkouri when he stopped in front of the desk.

General Ashkouri was still sitting with his feet on the desk and did not return the salute. He just glared at the police officer, he considered him to be beneath him even though they held the same rank. However, this police general had a fire in his eyes, and he hadn't dropped his hand from the salute yet.

"Sit," said General Ashkouri.

General Hadi ignored the command to sit and kept his hand to his head in the salute. He was being disrespected by not receiving a salute in return.

"You are a stubborn one. Sergeant, you can leave us alone," said General Ashkouri.

Sergeant Qasim left the office and closed the door.

General Ashkouri gave the police officer his salute but not until they were alone. If he gave the salute with Sergeant Qasim in the office, it would be taken as a sign of weakness.

General Hadi had won the first round and sat in the chair.

"I understand that you and other police officers put many women and girls into safe houses. Why is that?" he asked.

"It is important that we protect the women and children in our community, I'm sure you agree," he replied.

"Yes, but who are you protecting them from?" asked General Ashkouri.

"Anyone that would do them harm," he replied.

"Why didn't you come to me, I would have helped you protect them?"

"It is your soldiers that are abusing them," replied General Hadi.

He could see that he had overstepped the mark with the general accusing his soldiers of abuse. He watched, evaluating General Ashkouri and his reddening face.

"Tell me the names of the soldiers and I will punish them," he replied.

It was now a game of chess and General Ashkouri knew that he had to keep his temper in check.

"I don't have any names," he replied.

"You call yourself a policeman?"

General Ashkouri was laughing as he relit his cigar that had gone out.

"Yes, I am a good policeman, but I cannot arrest your soldiers because you would have my officers and the women and children killed," replied General Hadi.

"Well, you don't hold any punches, do you? What if I just shoot you now," he replied pulling out his sidearm and pointing it straight at General Hadi.

He noticed that the police officer didn't even twitch when he pointed the gun at him. It was quite the opposite he went even calmer; this was no ordinary policeman.

"We aren't here for the niceties of life we are here to try to resolve the problem of ongoing abuse," replied General Hadi.

"I don't like you, but you are a man of principle as am I. You're standing up for your people and I admire that but if I say something happens to them it happens and there is nothing you can do about it."

"You are correct I cannot stop you, but you don't need any more trouble or attention being brought to this city whilst you're here. The allied forces are spreading out across many parts of Iraq now and you cannot afford to be trapped here by them."

General Ashkouri jumped up from behind the desk and cocked his pistol placing it hard against General Hadi's forehead.

"Do not make the mistake of underestimating me, I can kill you right now and nobody will help you. I can then send my troops to your home, the homes of your family and neighbors and burn them all down. I would then let my soldiers do what they wanted to the women and children."

Again, he noticed that the police officer didn't flinch, even when he put the gun to his head and threatened his family.

"As I said earlier there is nothing, I can do to stop you," he replied.

General Ashkouri could tell he was not going to be able to intimidate this man. He holstered his sidearm and returned to his seat. He stared at General Hadi for five minutes as he enjoyed his cigar. Likewise General Hadi stared right back without so much as a blink. The silence was broken by a knock on the office door and Sergeant Qasim walked in. He walked up to the general and whispered something in his ear and left the office.

"It would appear that you have friends in the police. There are police vehicles gathering in numbers in various parts of the city. They will most probably head here to negotiate your release. When they get here, I will have my troops on the roofs of every building that leads to this office. They will wait until the police vehicles arrive and block the streets. I will then give the order for my men to shoot everyone that is a police officer or that is close to the vehicles. They won't have time to fire back and defend themselves because they will be trapped. Bullets and grenades will rain down on them until every one of them is dead. I will then drive out of here with my troops and be long gone before any allied forces arrive." General Ashkouri let the words hang in the air for a minute.

General Hadi knew that what he was saying was not only doable, but he feared that this would happen. He had to give the general something to help him save face with his men, particularly his sergeant. If he played hard ball too much it would end badly for many people.

"I cannot stop you and I know that you will kill me before any of this takes place. I may have a solution which would give you what you want and what I want," he said.

"I'm listening," he replied.

"Allow a group of police vehicles into the square outside. Request that senior generals are present and some of my men from the police station that I control. When they arrive here, we will go to them together. You will let them know that we discussed the abuses that have taken place and you will make sure that they stop. I will tell them that you have been very cooperative, but you are still in charge until you leave the city."

General Ashkouri liked this idea as it saved face for him with his sergeant and his immediate security. They would still hold some of the women they had already taken for the soldiers.

When the two generals walked out of the town hall building, they saw four police officers standing on either side of the square. General Hadi waived one of them over to him.

As the police officer got to where the generals were standing, he saluted them, they returned the salute.

"Your radio, please," he said.

The police officer handed it over with a little confusion on his face. With his message relayed for the meeting at the town hall all they had to do was wait for the arrival of a select number of police generals. It only took thirty minutes for them to arrive, gathering in the square.

General Ashkouri made the announcement as agreed about stopping the abuse. It wasn't received well by some of the police generals, but they knew they couldn't do anything about it. During his speech General Ashkouri humiliated General Hadi as often as he could in front of his colleagues and police officers.

General Hadi knew it was futile to defend himself from the verbal abuse, he had to remain calm to protect his family and the people of the town.

With General Ashkouri's speech over the police officers all went back to their duties, including General Hadi.

It had only been three days since General Ashkouri's arrival with his troops. It had been three days of hell for the residents of the city. If truth be known, the people in the city were praying that the invading troops would come quickly as they could see the situation getting even worse under the Iraqi military rule. The same thing was happening in many small towns and villages throughout Iraq as the troops fled from the invading forces. On the way out they were looting and pillaging the homes of wealthy Iraqi families and Saddam Hussein's own palaces. Many of the troops abused women, children, and boys. Some of them were taken with the troops when they left the towns and cities. The murders committed would add into the hundreds.

This pattern of violence and carnage had occurred during the first Desert Storm in Iraq. Unfortunately, only a few of those responsible were arrested or taken to court. Politicians, city leaders and Judges in a lot of towns were not only corrupt but were for sale to the highest bidder.

US dollars were handed out like confetti to town and city leaders after the initial invasion. The money was to help rebuild the infrastructure of the towns and cities. But like most places in the world that are corrupt the money did not go to the right cause. The corrupt officials opened personal bank accounts in Iraq and European city banks. The preferred banking systems were overseas in the likes of Switzerland and the Bahamas. These tax haven banks also had extremely strict policies about giving out their client's details or information on their accounts.

The money would eventually end up in various accounts in France, Germany, and the United Kingdom. Small transfers at a time didn't normally catch the eye of the government agencies watching for terror money. In most cases less than ten thousand dollars went under the radar.

CHAPTER 5

HUSSEIN PALACE

It was the third day after no food and little water when things were about to get worse for the young police recruits. The smell of the rotting corpses in the courtyard was overwhelming. The soldiers walked around with cloth wrapped around their faces to keep out the smell.

Sergeant Talabani came out of the palace with four soldiers.

"Untie them and have them take the dead bodies outside in the desert, they are stinking," said the sergeant.

The soldiers immediately untied Al-Qadir and his colleagues. They tried to stand but their legs were not strong enough at first. They helped each other stand as the soldiers kicked at them to get up. The dead bodies were buzzing with flies which swarmed into the air as they were dragged outside. It amazed Al-Qadir that they were in the middle of nowhere, but flies always appeared as if they were summoned by the dead and dying.

The soldiers pushed the young recruits back inside the palace courtyard. They were told they could drink the rancid water in the fountain again. Al-Qadir resisted as he knew it would only make him even sicker. Some of the young police officers hobbled towards the fountain.

"Don't it will make you sick," shouted Al-Qadir.

Laughing the sergeant then threw bottles of water at them. There was a scramble for the bottles as the police officers pushed and shoved each other to get to them, but not Al-Qadir.

The general came through a doorway he only had on his pants and boots. He looked even bigger as his muscular body glistened with sweat. He was dragging a young girl along by the hair. She looked like she had been through hell at the hands of the general, which she had. She was only thirteen years old and the daughter of the gardener whose body was amongst those the recruits had dragged outside. The general pulled her along until she could see the bodies.

"Look," said the general pushing her to the ground.

The girl struggled to her feet and looked straight into Al-Qadir's eyes. She was pleading for help he knew it and there wasn't anything he could do. This was when she realized what the general wanted her to see, the pile of dead bodies outside. She screamed aloud when she saw that one of them was her father and ran to his corpse. The flies swarmed again but it didn't stop her from hugging her father.

"She's yours, we leave in four hours," shouted the general to his soldiers.

A group of soldiers ran towards the girl pushing each other out of the way to be the first to get their hands on her. The first soldier that reached her pulled her up and threw her over his shoulder.

"She's mine first," he said.

The group of police recruits were helpless and ashamed, they held their heads down but not Al-Qadir. He watched everything that was going on he was making notes of faces. He saw the girl once again look into his eyes as she was slumped over the soldier's shoulder.

She smiled at Al-Qadir and pulled a knife from the soldier's belt. With speed she plunged the knife into the man's left kidney three times. He screamed out in pain and dropped the girl. Another soldier ran to his aid and pulled the girl to her feet. She let him lift her and slashed out at his face with the knife. The wound was deep from his ear across his eyes. A second strike and she opened the other side of his face. Soldiers ran at her as she smiled plunging the knife into her own throat.

Al-Qadir watched as she fell to the floor with blood squirting everywhere. She gave him one last look before her eyes closed in death.

The general heard the commotion outside and ran out to see the girl collapsing to the floor. He walked to the wounded soldiers on the floor who were screaming in pain. He shot them both once in the chest and then brutally kicked the dead girl in the head.

"Bring the policemen outside, I want some exercise," said the general.

The soldiers marched the police recruits outside the palace standing them close to where their friends' bodies lay.

"You want to hurt me for what I have done to them," said the general pointing at the bodies. "Then come and punish me, first in line come forward."

Al-Qadir was on his feet in a flash, he had rage and hate in his eyes.

"No, you will be the last one," said the general smiling.

One by one the recruits were thrown into a human circle formed by the soldiers. The general punched and kicked them as they were pushed forward by his men. A couple of the recruits did manage to get to punch the general, but they paid for it as they were held by the soldiers as the general beat them mercilessly. There was only one left Al-Qadir.

"There is a vehicle coming," said one of the soldiers.

In the distance they could see a cloud of dust and sand being kicked up by the wheels of a vehicle travelling at speed.

"It's our scout vehicle, ignore it," said the general

Al-Qadir knew he could not beat the general, but he was going to try to get as many punches in as he could. His father had taught him how to box and the art of Krav Maga the Israeli Defense Forces special fighting technique. His father was extremely good at boxing and trained at an elevated level in Krav Maga.

He was thrown into the circle of soldiers to face the general. The man was sweating profusely and smelt badly of body odor. He got the exercise he wanted beating defenseless men in their late teens. He was to become his next victim but not before he got a couple of punches in.

Al-Qadir took a boxing stance and started to move in a circular fashion around the general. He didn't move lightly on his feet as he wanted the general to think he wasn't particularly good. He had to wait for an opening to move in quickly. He was about to make his strike when he was held from behind by two soldiers. They held his arms as the general walked up to him.

Al-Qadir knew he had to move fast and threw his feet out at the general's chest. He used the man's size and weight to walk up his chest and somersault backwards. This forced the soldiers to lose their grip on his arms. He landed flat on his feet facing the backs of the two soldiers that were holding him. He swung a fierce right-handed chop to one soldier's neck and a right kick to the side of the knee of the second. He heard the leg crack at the knee where the maximum amount of force was placed. They both fell to the floor as more soldiers rushed in to grab Al-Qadir.

"Stop, he's mine," shouted the general.

Al-Qadir knew that he had given away his agility and had to move in quickly on the general. He rushed at him like he was going to body tackle him, screaming at the top of his lungs.

The general was surprised when he felt the power of the young man's feet on his body as he flipped backwards. The strikes on his soldiers were timed perfectly with power and precision. This youth could fight but he was going to teach him a lesson.

The young man ran at him roaring like a lion. He smiled and placed one foot slightly back to brace himself for the impact. He knew that the youth wouldn't be able to knock him down, but he wanted him to realize he had hit a brick wall when he smashed into him.

At the last second Al-Qadir dropped to the ground and slid between the general's legs. As he went through, he interlocked his fingers and swung his double handed fist upwards as hard as he could. His target was the general's balls and he hit them with full force.

The general was surprised when the lad dropped to the floor and grabbed at him. He was too slow just missing him. He felt a searing pain in his groin as the strike hit home hard. He dropped to his knees and held his crutch.

"Get him," shouted the general.

The group of troops rushed forward and lifted Al-Qadir to his feet.

The general slowly stood up with fury in his eyes he glared at the young recruit.

The vehicle seen earlier was now careering to a stop remarkably close to the group of soldiers. A soldier jumped out before the vehicle had stopped, his legs could not keep up with the motion of his body at it was propelled from the passenger side of the vehicle. He stumbled and fell flat on his face. He quickly recovered jumping to his feet he saluted the general.

"General American troops are coming," he said in a panic.

"How far away are they?" he asked.

"Around nine or ten miles," he replied pointing into the desert.

The general calmly scanned the desert and could see a faint cloud of dust towards the horizon.

"Collect everything, we leave immediately," he shouted to his men.

The general jogged slowly towards the palace entrance gently rubbing his balls at the same time.

"What do we do with this one?" asked the soldiers holding Al-Qadir.

The general stopped and turned slowly. He saw two of his men helping the soldier with the damaged knee to his feet. Another soldier was holding up the lad that had just punched him in the balls. He took his pistol out of its holster and fired once. The bullet caught the injured soldier high on the chest. The bullet tore through his collar bone where it joined the chest and exited through the back of his neck. The soldiers dropped their comrade and stepped away from the body in shock.

"He would only slow us down, run boy, run," he said to Al-Qadir.

He didn't need telling twice and ran as fast as he'd ever ran in his life into the desert. He heard the shot and crashed to the desert floor.

The general smiled as the young man ran for his life. He lifted his pistol slowly and squeezed the trigger. The pistol gave a slight kick pushing the muzzle of the gun upwards. The bullet was on its way quickly it found its target and slammed into Al-Qadir's back. The general watched as the body crashed into the sand. After a short skid it came to a stop in a crumpled heap.

Within a couple of minutes, the cowardly Iraqi special forces vehicles raced off into the desert in the opposite direction to the oncoming US forces.

CHAPTER 6

US TROOP ARRIVAL, MIQDADIYAH

The line of US military vehicles had left the city of Baqubah and headed northeast. Intelligence had been received from the police that Republican Guard special forces were entrenched in the city of Miqdadiyah fourteen miles away. They had already experienced resistance on route to Baqubah but nothing serious. A few short exchanges of fire had taken place with the quick surrender of poorly trained Iraqi soldiers.

They were approaching the outskirts Miqdadiyah when they came upon a large and well-organized roadblock. A lone police officer stood in the middle of the road. A hundred yards to the rear of him at the side of the road was a white police pickup with a police officer stood by the open driver's door. The police officer in the road held up a white flag and gently waived it at the convoy.

The lead vehicle of the US military convoy stopped closely followed by the remainder of the convoy. Soldiers jumped from different vehicles fanning out into the desert and on the road. They were taking up defensive positions against a potential sneak attack.

General Abbud waived the white flag in the hope that the US soldiers would see that they were not a threat to them. He had lost enough of his police officers to the Iraq Republican Guard already, he didn't want to lose any more to the invading forces. The convoy of military vehicles stopped, and soldiers jumped out of them. He walked slowly towards the lead vehicle holding the flag high. He was thinking of his sons and his wife and daughter who he had not seen for four days. If he were going to die this day, they would be the last thing he would remember. He was saying a quote from the Quran under his breath, guide us to the straight path. He was fifty yards from the lead vehicle when two soldiers walked towards him.

"I am General Abbud head of the police for this town," he shouted.

After a short greeting, the soldiers offered him a bottle of water and asked him to explain what the situation was in the town. They talked for ten minutes as General Abbud explained what had happened since the arrival of the Republican Guard elite forces. The cowards had run when they heard that the US army were coming, leaving death and devastation behind them.

The US major was surprised but not shocked to hear about the mistreatment of locals by the Iraq military. In his pre-deployment briefings, he'd been told of such abuses in the first invasion of Iraq. He also knew that this police officer could be leading them into a trap. He agreed to let the police vehicles escort them into the town.

A part of the US military convoy followed General Abbud and his police vehicle. As they entered the town the people slowly came out of hiding. General Abbud was using a megaphone to tell people that it was safe. He was telling them to come out of their homes and businesses to meet the American troops. It didn't take long before the streets were heaving with men women and children all cheering the arriving troops.

After a couple of hours of searching the town, it was obvious the Iraqi military had left. The American troops were told of the abuse and murders committed by the Republican Guard troops.

Many of the families had not only lost their husbands, fathers, and brothers but their homes. The tales of rape and abuse of the women and boys disgusted them all. There were dead bodies scattered inside and outside of homes and businesses. The American troops helped the families of the murder victims and assisted in their burial per Muslim protocol.

CHAPTER 7

General Abbud told the Major about the palace where the daughter of Hussein was in hiding. The same palace that he had sent the young recruits to. He agreed to lead the Major and a small contingent of troops to see if the Hussein family members were still there. As they got closer to the palace, they could see a cloud of sand and dust in the distance moving away from the palace. They did not know that it was General Mutaz and his cowardly troops escaping. The major called in air support to get eyes on the vehicles that were in the distance.

As they approached the palace, they could see bodies lying in the sand and by the smell they knew they were dead. The Major stopped the convoy and sent his troops to search the bodies and palace for booby traps. General Abbud could not wait he had a bad feeling about this. His son and the other recruits should have come out to greet them by now. He started to walk towards the bodies in the sand. As he got closer, he saw not only the uniforms of Iraqi soldiers on the bodies but police uniforms also. He started to run towards the police uniformed bodies and recognized his sons bloodied body. He shouted his sons name at the top of his lungs. He didn't hear the major and other troops telling him to stop. They were trying to get him to be cautious as they did not know if the dead bodies were booby trapped.

The general dropped to his knees and rolled his sons body over to see his face. Tears were rolling down his face as he cradled him.

"My son, my son," he said repeatedly.

A US soldier walked slowly up to the general to comfort and help him, that was when he saw one of the young policeman's feet twitch.

"Medic, medic," he shouted as he pulled the general off the body.

"What are you doing? Leave him alone," said the general.

"He's alive, his foot moved," he replied.

"What, alive," said the general laying his son's head gently on the sand.

A medic arrived and immediately went to work on the general's son.

"Check each body see if anyone else is alive, be careful of potential booby traps," shouted the major.

"Soldier alive here," shouted one of the US soldiers.

The general jumped to his feet and ran to the soldier.

"Who did this, who murdered these young men?" said the major shaking the dying soldier.

The soldier was trying to say something so the general leaned closer to listen.

"General Mutaz, he killed all of them," said the soldier as he exhaled his last breath.

"Mutaz, who is he?" asked the major.

"An animal, I have heard many horrible stories about him. He was responsible for the attacks on the Ma'dan marsh people in the South after the first Gulf war. He killed hundreds of the marsh tribe people on the orders of Saddam Hussein. The marshes were a good hiding place for activists that were against the Hussein regime. After the war he was sent to the marshes to eliminate anyone that did not support Hussein. He butchered hundreds of people," said the general.

"I've heard about the marsh people, an ancient tribe," said the major.

An hour later the American troops moved out of the palace and the general returned to Baqubah with the bodies of his police recruits. On the journey back the general didn't leave his son's side. He only regained consciousness once and spoke briefly with his father.

"Father, I will avenge my brothers, I promise you," said Al-Qadir.

"Rest my son we can talk about this later," he replied.

His father took him directly to the hospital in Baqubah and sent word for his mother to join him.

A police sergeant who was close to the General and his family volunteered to go to their home and transport her to the hospital. The sergeant was not looking forward to seeing the General's wife as he knew she would push him for answers about her son.

As he pulled up to the house in his police pick up a group of women were talking to the General's wife. They all turned when they saw the police vehicle.

The sergeant walked towards the group of women, but they didn't wait for him to reach them. They were the mothers of the police recruits that had been sent to the palace by the General. They all started shouting at the sergeant asking where their sons were. Before he could answer a beat-up pickup raced towards them with several men in the rear. The sergeant drew his sidearm when he saw that they were all carrying automatic weapons.

"It's our husbands, it's Ok," shouted one of the women.

The sergeant immediately relaxed but wondered what the men were doing.

All the men jumped out of the vehicle and walked towards the women with horror and sadness in their faces.

"Hussein's murdering soldiers have killed all of our son's," shouted one of the men.

The women all erupted into screaming and whaling at the news, including the General's wife.

The sergeant walked towards her to give her the news that at her son was alive. She was screaming and crying at the top of her lungs and collapsed at the sergeant's feet before he could say anything. She had a massive heart attack killing her instantly.

The sergeant and one of the women tried to resuscitate her but she was gone. Now the sergeant had to return to go to the hospital and tell the General that his wife was dead. He grew up with the general and his wife since they were small children. He lost a good friend in the general's wife as did his wife. At the hospital the general did not really take in the news of his wife's death, he went into denial. The news only got worse for him when he was later told of the deaths of his other sons in the military. He waited for

Al-Qadir to regain consciousness before he left the hospital to see his wife. He had lost everything except his son Al-Qadir.

His wife's funeral took place the same day, attended by his friends and neighbors and his son in a wheelchair. The doctor at the hospital gave him permission to attend the funeral on the grounds that he returns immediately to the hospital as his wounds were serious and he didn't want them to become infected. He was wheeling his son into the hospital when he had a stroke. Al-Qadir tried to get out of the wheelchair to help his father and fell to the ground. He tried with all his might to help his father, but he was too weak. He had ruptured several stitches that were keeping the bullet wound closed. Internal bleeding had started but the doctor had trouble locating where it was. He knew that the US military were setting up a field hospital two miles away, he took a chance and sent Al-Qadir in an ambulance to see if the American doctors could help. They had a lot more experience with wounds like his and hopefully they could save his life.

It took Al-Qadir's father two weeks to die from the stroke. His body was paralyzed down the left side, and he'd lost his speech completely. His right hand was still working but it was very weak. A nurse who was trying to help with his physical therapy was trying to get him to print his name. She left a writing pad and pen on the bed next to him each time she visited. He tried to write but it was difficult. On one visit the nurse noticed that he'd scratched something on the pad, but it didn't make sense. However, she was still excited that he'd done something, it showed improvement. Al-Qadir was on one of his daily visits to his father in his wheelchair and she showed it to him. The note read, Safe Jassim home sg. It did not make sense to him and the more he read it the less sense it made. He knew that his father was trying to say something but what? He had pushed his thirty-minute visit to forty-five when the nurse told him he had to leave and give his father some rest. He agreed and said his goodbye's. As he was leaving the ward, he had a light bulb moment. He wheeled himself back to his father's bed and held the pad in front of his father's face he could see it.

"Father, this writing did you mean to say, 'Sgt Jassim, safe house?" he asked.

"You must leave, he's very weak," said the staff nurse sternly.

"Please, one moment. Father blink once for no and twice for yes, is this Sgt Jassim and the safe houses?" he asked.

He stretched out of the wheelchair as far as he could to see his father's eyes, he blinked twice, there was no doubt.

"Did he give away the safe houses?"

His father blinked twice again.

"I will find him," he said to his father as the staff nurse wheeled him away from the bed.

Al-Qadir was angry and excited all at the same time. His father had given him the name of the man responsible for revealing the location of the safe houses to General Ashkouri. However, he didn't know that the sergeant had given the safe house locations to the mayor. It didn't make any difference to him; he was going to find him one day and kill him.

A week later Al-Qadir was on a visit to his father when he took his last breath. He repeated his vow to his dead father, not only would he avenge his fallen police colleagues but his mother, father and those betrayed by the sergeant.

He knew Sergeant Jassim; he'd been to his home and had dinner. The sergeant was also the recruitment officer for their local police station. He signed his papers when he volunteered to be a police officer and had been involved in his basic training. The thought that he would betray not only the family members of the woman and girls taken but his colleagues in the police force sickened him.

CHAPTER 8

MUTAZ ESCAPES IRAQ

After they left the palace General Mutaz managed to illude the allied forces with twenty of his men. He had split his military convoy into two, sending one much larger convoy northwest towards Chamchamal, which was east of Kirkuk. His small convoy headed northeast towards the Zagros mountains across the Iranian border. There were twelve soldiers in his convoy seven of which he trusted completely. He had trained all of them when they'd been recruited for the Republican Guard for Saddam Hussein. Sergeant Ahmad was like an army brother, and he knew that he would keep the men in line. The men respected Ahmad more than the general, they just feared the general. They called Ahmad Wasmeh, translated meant stain or blemish due to a large purple looking birthmark on his right hand. They used this name only between themselves, but they meant no disrespect to their sergeant.

Mutaz did not have any remorse or feeling for the young police officers or his own soldiers that he'd killed. Some of his men were starting to question why they were heading towards Iran and not home to their families.

The general stopped in a small farming town and took four pickup style trucks from the local farmers. Two died after they resisted, the rest complied and gave their vehicles up without a fight. His soldiers loaded up the vehicles with additional fuel, water, and food supplies for the journey. From the rear of one of the military vehicles Sergeant Ahmad had a large wooden box transferred to the vehicle he was sitting in. Two smaller boxes were placed in the rear of the tail vehicle in the care of soldiers he trusted.

"Gather enough clothes from the villages for eight of us. We will need to stay in our military uniforms until we cross the border." said Mutaz to Ahmad.

"Eight?" questioned Ahmad.

"Yes," he replied.

Ahmad knew that this meant that five of the soldiers were not going to make the full journey to Turkey. Once again, he did not question his general, he did as he was ordered, no matter what happened.

With everything loaded into the vehicles, the convoy of four farm trucks drove towards the Iranian border.

The first stop was just over the border on the Iranian side in a box canyon where Mutaz and Ahmad had meetings with Kurdish gun smugglers from Turkey in the past.

Mutaz had stolen hundreds of weapons and explosives over the years from the Iraqi military arsenals and sold them to the Kurdish rebels, known as the PKK, (Kurdish Workers Party). He admired the Kurds especially for their brutality against the Turkish military. The Turkish government had banned people from speaking the Kurdish language. The military had ransacked many small villages in the southeastern portion of Turkey which were Kurdish. Hundreds of people were killed by the Turkish military, and their homes burnt to the ground. Food and basic day to day living supplies were blocked from getting to the same areas of Turkey. The government-imposed embargos on the Kurdish people

47

especially after they started to fight for their own state. War with the Kurdish rebels had gone on for decades with the Turkish military outposts and convoys being the targets of the Kurdish fighters.

Over the years the PKK had attacked cities in Turkey, especially Istanbul. Bombings and armed assaults had become expected in Istanbul because of the governments stand against giving them an independent Kurdish state. Even though the PKK had announced a formal end to the war the previous year there were still militant strongholds that refused to recognize the ceasefire until they got an independent state. It was these groups that Mutaz was feeding with weapons and explosives. He had made a small fortune with these transactions and his greed for money had gotten out of control.

They small convoy was approaching the foothills close to the Iranian border. A mile away they saw military vehicles heading towards them. The vehicles were driving down the center of the road with no way of passing except by going off the road. They had obviously seen the general's convoy as the lead vehicle stopped and soldiers jumped out. They were all aiming their weapons at the general's convoy as they approached.

"They look like our soldiers," said Ahmad.

"They do. Drive slowly towards them, I will hold a flag out of the window," he replied.

Mutaz pulled an Iraqi military flag out of his duffle bag that was behind his seat. He leaned out of the window and waived it back and forth. It didn't appear to have worked as several bullets hit the road close to the general's vehicle.

"Stop," said Mutaz.

Ahmad immediately stopped and pulled to the side of the road. To his surprise the general got out of the pickup.

"Stay in the vehicle," he said to Ahmad.

Mutaz, now held the flag above his head so that the group of soldiers two hundred yards ahead could see it clearly. He kept walking towards the military convoy.

A colonel in charge of the convoy ordered his soldiers to fire shots at the oncoming pickups to make them stop. Someone was hanging out of the passenger door of the lead vehicle waving a flag. He couldn't see what kind of flag it was as it flowed backwards in the wind. The flag waiving passenger got out of the vehicle and walked towards them.

"You four follow me," he said to the group of soldiers that had just fired their weapons.

As he got closer to the man walking towards him, he could see that he was wearing an Iraq military uniform. He still did not trust him as anyone could have stolen the uniform. It wasn't until he was within thirty yards that he recognized who it was.

"Drop your weapons drop them," he shouted at the soldiers.

The soldiers did as they were told but were ready to raise them again at any sign of danger.

"Which of your men fired at me," said General Mutaz with arrogance.

The colonel saluted, "I gave the order to fire warning shots, I didn't know it was you general," said the Colonel with fear.

The four soldiers had followed the colonel's example and saluted as soon as he did even though they didn't recognize the general.

"At ease," said Mutaz.

"I'm sorry general, if I'd have known it was you."

He stopped talking as the general held his hand up.

"How would you know; I am in civilian vehicles. You have not seen me or my men we are on a special mission, do you understand?" said Mutaz.

"Yes, Sir," he replied.

"How do you know me?" asked Mutaz.

"You came to our barracks in Kirkuk and gave a demonstration of hand-to-hand combat using a knife,"

"Yes, I remember," said Mutaz.

"We haven't seen you," he reiterated.

"Good, I will walk back to my vehicle make room for us to pass," he said arrogantly.

Mutaz walked away with a smile on his face, he knew that the colonel was terrified of him. He did in fact remember the demonstration at the barracks as he took on three soldiers in the demonstration. They were all young soldiers with only a year in the army. Mutaz slashed one of them across the face leaving him with a savage looking scar after it was poorly stitched by an inexperienced field doctor. The other two soldiers did not fare much better, one was stabbed in the shoulder which impaired him from raising his arm above his shoulder and the third had a permanent limp due to the damage caused to his thigh muscle.

He climbed back into the pickup and smiled at Ahmad.

"Go," said Mutaz.

They could see the military vehicles all pulling off the road to allow him past. Soldiers stood by the road and in vehicles all saluted as they drove by. Mutaz saluted the soldiers back as they continued their journey.

"Was that General Mutaz?" said one soldier to the colonel after they had driven past.

"Yes, I am lucky to still be alive. I felt sure he was going to shoot me in the head," replied the colonel.

"I've heard about him from my cousin, but would he really shoot you?"

"Believe me, he would shoot his own mother if it meant he got what he wanted. He has shot many recruits and soldiers in the head. He has a reputation for it, a sickness. You said your cousin told you about him, how would he know?" he asked.

"My cousin was one of the men at the barracks in Kirkuk, the same time you saw him, two years ago," he replied.

"Who is your cousin?" asked the colonel.

"Sergeant Amir Faiz," he replied.

"Amir with the scar?" he asked.

"Yes, the general gave it to him."

"The scar has given him a terrifying look, but he has become a real warrior. I know your cousin; he was taken under the wing of one of the generals after the attack by General Mutaz. His brother who was also a general, he reported Mutaz to the President on a visit to the palace in the hope that he would be punished. It did not work, the President told General Mutaz about the complaint and told him to apologize."

"Did he apologize?" asked the soldier.

"We will never know; the general was found in the river Tigris a month later with many knife wounds in his body. There was talk amongst the other generals that were close to the President that General Mutaz had done it, but nobody wanted to have the murder investigated."

"I will tell my cousin that we saw him," said the soldier.

"Don't be a fool, didn't you hear him, we never saw him."

The soldier did not care he was going to tell his cousin because he knew how much he hated the general.

CHAPTER 9

THE IRANIAN BORDER

The small four vehicle convoy drove off the main highway into a dead end in a gravelly shaped half-moon area. The sergeant driving the lead vehicle drove through a narrow gap in the rocks which was hidden by a giant bolder and two Persian oak trees. The other vehicles followed as they all narrowly made it through the gap. Half a mile later after several very tight squeezes between rocks there was an opening the size of half a football field. This time it was a dead end with a cliff face blocking the way.

"Everybody out," shouted the sergeant.

The soldiers got out of the vehicles and walked to the sergeant.

"Why are we stopping?" asked one of the soldiers.

"This is where we will stay for a couple of nights," shouted Mutaz.

"Why?" asked the same soldier.

"Do you wish to question your general's decisions?" asked the sergeant.

"No, sorry," said the soldier realizing the stupidity of his question.

The other soldiers looked at him as if he had lost his mind, surely the general would make an example of him.

Mutaz walked up to the soldier. The fear was already creeping into the soldier, and he could smell it.

"You have a question soldier?" asked Mutaz.

"No, sir," shouted the soldier in reply as he snapped to attention.

"Good," he replied.

"Make a fire. It will be cold soon," shouted the sergeant.

They were far enough inside the canyon that the fire could not be seen from the road. The soldiers slowly settled around the fire and ate.

Mutaz waived to the sergeant to follow him as he walked over to his vehicle.

"Bring three men with you. We need to go back to the road to steal new vehicles. Our Iraqi plates will stand out if we are seen in the daylight. There is a place two miles down the road where we first met the Kurds three years ago. It is a popular stopping place now for drivers taking a rest," said Mutaz.

"Yes, I remember it well," replied Ahmad.

"Side arms and knives only, we need to keep them hidden," said Mutaz.

"Yes, General," he replied.

Sergeant Ahmad quickly selected the men to go with them and left instructions for the rest to stay alert. As he walked past his vehicle he climbed into the back and checked that the lid on the large wooden box was secure. Although the box had ammunition stamped on the side in Arabic it was obvious to a couple of the soldiers that there was something much more important inside. Their curiosity would eventually get the better of them.

The road crossing the border was busy with people fleeing Iraq into Iran to escape the war. This gave the general a terrific opportunity to steal Iranian vehicles that were smuggling Iraqi people out.

Mutaz, sergeant Ahmad and three soldiers were only gone thirty minutes when they saw the first opportunity, as they came out of the pass. Mutaz and his men almost gave themselves away as they came out of the pass from behind a giant boulder. It was getting dark and two canvas backed trucks had stopped just off the edge of the dirt road that led into the pass.

Mutaz and his men watched from the cover of the rocks. Three men were sat on the ground with their backs to them. In front of them was a campfire that was just getting to full flame. To the right of the campfire fifty yards away was a group of about sixteen people, men, and women. They were huddled together by the front of one truck their bodies soaking up heat that was left from the truck's engine. They were directly between the truck and the rocks about ten feet away. The people were obviously being smuggled across the border from Iraq.

A man with a Kalashnikov rifle slung over his right shoulder was standing at the rear of the second vehicle relieving himself into the dirt. When he had finished, he waived his penis at the women in the group sitting on the floor. They all turned away in disgust. The man laughed aloud and said something that Mutaz and his men couldn't hear. He walked over to the campfire and joined his colleagues.

Mutaz knew that they had to be incredibly careful as people smugglers were known to be very capable fighters and vicious. They could not go into the camp firing weapons as they were too close to the main road and passing vehicles would see or hear them. He had to be patient, but the chilly night air was quickly setting in and he had to make a move soon. They watched as one of the smugglers reached into a metal pot hanging over the fire and dished out what looked like stew into a metal bowl. He did this until all four of them had a hot steaming bowl. Within five minutes they had devoured the contents of the bowls.

One of the men at the campfire walked towards the group of Iraqi's being smuggled. He grabbed hold of a young girl and pulled her to her feet. She started to struggle and scream for help. A teenage boy jumped to his feet only to be struck on the head with the butt of the man's rifle.

Several Iraq's stood to help when one of the men by the fire shouted at them to sit down. They all reluctantly sat as he was pointing his rifle at them. The man dragged the girl into the rocks with the intent of abusing her. She was a fighter and Mutaz admired this and got a little excited at watching her fight back. She was punched on the jaw by her assailant knocking her out.

Mutaz pointed to two of his men to stay and watch the others around the campfire. He and Ahmad crept through the rocks to where the man was dragging the girl. In the fading light he could see the man placing his rifle against a rock. He was now totally focused on the girl as he readied to abuse her.

Mutaz dropped a small stone behind the man to get his attention.

The smuggler was beyond excited at the thought of the girl when he heard a noise behind him. He ignored it; she would have his full attention.

Mutaz moved silently behind the man and slapped his hand over his mouth. His knife slid across the man's throat slicing deep into his neck. He then pushed the man onto the girl as the blood sprayed out of the wound. The man falling onto the girl woke her up. She thought that he was about to attack her and opened her mouth to scream. Mutaz put his hand on her mouth just to muffle the cries slightly.

The three men around the fire heard the cries of the girl and smiled. They thought that their comrade was having a fun time. One of them shouted that it was his turn and walked towards the location where his friend had taken the girl.

Mutaz moved his hand from the girl's mouth and allowed her to scream twice more before he stabbed her in her right eye forcing the blade through the brain killing her instantly. He would have stabbed her through the heart, but the body of the smuggler was on top of her. He slipped quietly behind a large rock and looked towards the campfire. There was another man walking towards him, obviously intent on having his fun with the girl. He had his rifle over his shoulder with the sling across his back. He saw the man approach the crowd of people that were huddled together in fear. They had paid a lot of money to be smuggled out of Iraq only to be treated like animals. The smuggler growled loudly at the women with his hands raised and fingers curled like he was imitating a tiger. He laughed at them as they all cringed, he walked behind the rock to have his fun with the girl.

The smuggler saw his colleague laying on top of the girl but there was something strange they both looked motionless. Before he could see what, the problem was a man dropped in front of him from a high rock to his right. He was a huge man with a knife in his hand. He reached for his own knife but was too slow.

Mutaz climbed onto a rock which was directly above the dead bodies of the girl and her rapist. He waited for the smuggler to get close enough to see the two bodies. It was already dark, and the man would have to get close before he would know that there was a problem. When the man stopped next to the bodies, he jumped down from the rock landing with both feet firmly in the dirt. His knife was in his right hand, ready to attack. The surprise in the man's eyes excited Mutaz as he could see the fear, even in the dark. As he reached for the knife in his belt Mutaz swiftly and expertly stabbed him once in the throat just below the Adams apple. The knife was in and out of the throat in a split second. The man grabbed his throat with both hands when he felt the knife cutting into him. Mutaz watched as the man sunk to his knees in the dirt and struggled to get air. He kneeled in the dirt with him his face inches away from the man's. He was enjoying the man's useless effort to stay alive as blood oozed between his fingers.

The Iraqi soldiers watching the men at the campfire knew that at some point they had to kill the two men. A second man walked towards the rocks where the girl was taken leaving the last two at the fire with their backs to them. As the man disappeared around the rock they moved quickly. They were only a short distance between their hiding place behind the rocks and the campfire.

The men at the campfire heard movement behind them and turned to see what it was. One of them did not stand a chance as the soldier's blade plunged straight into his throat. The second man was a little quicker and managed to get his knife out and slashed at the figure behind him. He was no match as the Iraqi soldier slashed his knife hand followed by a quick stab to the chest. The wounded man fell backwards onto the edge of the fire. He jumped up quickly screaming as the flames burnt the hair on his head.

The Iraqi soldier watched the man fall onto the fire and swiftly jumped on him as he tried to get up. He lifted the man up only to spin him around to face the fire. With a swift and expertly placed boot to the legs he plunged him headfirst into the flames. The screams were unmerciful as the soldier put his boot onto the back of the man's head holding his face down into the white-hot embers.

Mutaz was pleased how he had taken out the two men with such expertise. He did not give the girl a second thought as he walked around the rocks towards the group of Iraqi's being smuggled, they were all standing. He pointed his rifle at them and told them all to sit down, he was quickly joined by the rest of his men. They now had a problem, what do they do with the prisoners?

Mutaz quickly calmed down the panicked Iraqi's and told them they had nothing to fear, he would help them continue across the border into Iran.

"My daughter was taken by the smuggler," said one of the men.

"I'm sorry but he killed her," replied Mutaz.

The man and his wife and two remaining daughters started crying.

"Go to her, my men will show you where she is," said Mutaz waiving two of his men to walk with them. He gave them a signal to kill the rest of the family.

The mother and daughters were crying loudly as they disappeared into the dark.

A plan quickly formed in his sick and evil mind as he split the remaining men and boys from the women and girls. The sergeant had dragged the dead and burning body off the fire and moved it into the rocks out of sight of the road in the distance.

Mutaz sat the women and girls close to the fire showing that her cared for them as they were all shaking with the cold. The smugglers had blankets and a carpet by the fire. He gave a blanket to one of his men and kept one for himself. He then told the Iraqi men to follow him to see if there were any more blankets in the back of the trucks that would keep them warm. He split them into two groups, one group with him the other with his sergeant.

As the men walked ahead of Mutaz he wrapped part of the blanket around the end of his pistol, his sergeant followed suit. As they got to the rear of the vehicles, they quickly fired a bullet into the head of each man.

Back at the fire the women and girls were enjoying the heat of the flames but were still very scared. They had right to be scared as their lives were soon to end.

"We will use the smugglers vehicles," said Mutaz to Ahmad.

"What do we do with the bodies?" asked Ahmad.

"Put them in the back of one of the smugglers vehicles. Take it and two soldiers with you to where we left our trucks. Dump the bodies and move our boxes and weapons from our vehicles into the new truck. Stay there until we join you." said Mutaz.

"Yes, general," he replied.

Ahmad and two soldiers spread dirt on the bed of the vehicle as well as clothing they took off the bodies. He hoped that this would soak up any blood that was on the bodies and they could easily clean the truck out when they dumped them.

"What shall we do with the women and girls?" asked Ahmad.

"Put them in the other truck, we will take them into the canyon for the night," replied Mutaz.

Ahmad was no fool, he knew that the women and girls would not come out of the canyon alive. He walked over to the fire where they were grouped together.

"Into the truck," he shouted. They did not move. "Now," he yelled.

The women held onto the girls and scurried towards the truck.

"You will join your men, it is too dangerous here so close to the road," said Mutaz smiling.

The women and girls did not look up they just helped each other climb into the truck.

The truck was much bigger than the pickups, but Ahmad still managed to squeeze it into the canyon.

The soldiers loyal to Mutaz and Ahmad had moved the bodies of the men from the truck to a place behind some rocks so they could not be seen. One of them went to look for a place to use as a toilet and spent several minutes trying to relieve himself of his constipation. As the wind gently rolled into the canyon, he could hear someone talking. Their voices were being carried along by the breeze and it sounded like they were within a few feet of him. A strange phenomenon of box canyons as sound traveled very easily.

"Did you get chance to open the wooden box?" asked the first voice.

"Yes, the box is full of money, US dollars," said the second voice.

"US dollars, so what is in the two smaller heavy boxes?" said the first voice.

"I don't know, and I don't care. As soon as we get close to a town, we will steal the money and run," said the second voice.

"If he catches us, he will kill us," said the first voice.

"Then we can't get caught," replied the second voice.

The soldier pulled up his pants and quietly worked his way towards the voices. He could see two of the soldiers standing together discussing the boxes. He knew they were talking about the ones in the pickup trucks. He also knew that there was money in the large box because he helped steal it from one of the Presidents palaces. He kept quiet as he did not want them to know he had heard their conversation. The money was to be shared amongst the general's trusted soldiers and these two were not part of that group, nor were their three colleagues. He would have to wait to talk to Sergeant Ahmad about what he had heard.

The soldier only had to wait a couple of minutes before he made his way back around to the camp. He crept through the rocks to come in from the opposite side to the where the two soldiers talked about the boxes. He did not want them to get suspicious.

Mutaz and Ahmad arrived at the canyon camp in the second smugglers vehicle. None of the soldiers moved from the fire until the general got out of the vehicle.

"Get out two at a time, now," said Ahmad to the women.

The first two got out to be escorted by Mutaz towards the other side of the farm pickups. He waived over one of the soldiers to follow him which he did. The soldier saw the general pull out his knife and he knew what was about to happen. He did the same and walked up behind one of the women. As soon as they got alongside the vehicle both men put their hands over the mouths of the women and slit their throats. This went on until all nine women and girls were dead. Each of his trusted soldiers took a turn in murdering them. They didn't even flinch when they killed the three girls. With the women out of the picture the soldier that heard the conversation about the money approached sergeant Ahmad.

"Sergeant, can I have a quick word?"

"Yes, what is it?" he asked.

"Something personal, can we talk over there?" he said.

The sergeant was getting concerned as he thought the soldier was getting a conscience about what they had just done. He could not have been more wrong.

"What is it?" asked the sergeant as they stepped behind one of the smugglers trucks.

He repeated everything he'd heard that the two soldiers had said about the money.

"I will tell the general, wait here," he said.

It didn't take long before he returned with Mutaz.

"They definitely discussed the American dollars," said Mutaz.

"Yes, general. They intend to steal it when we get to a town," he replied.

"OK, we will kill them and the other three, we cannot trust them. Get them to join us by the women's bodies, say we are going to move them," said Mutaz.

"I will get our loyal soldiers to join us, and we will kill the five of them and the traitors can rot with the women," said Ahmad.

The five soldiers had no idea what was about to happen, and they were all dispatched within seconds of each other.

The men hadn't been dead more than a couple of minutes when Mutaz gathered his remaining trusted soldiers together. They were back to his original trusted group of seven and the sergeant.

"Let's eat and then get some sleep, we will leave as soon as the sun gives us light in the morning," said Mutaz.

Mutaz had arranged to contact his Kurdish allies as soon as they left the canyon. He used a satellite phone for all communications with them and the calls were always short and cryptic. He knew that the Americans and Europeans were always scanning calls in and out of Iraq and Iran. He would only switch on his phone when he had to make a call and turn it off immediately following the call. If the Kurds needed to contact him, they had a prearranged time to do so each day.

Mutaz had already arranged for a meeting place which was in a valley in the Zagros mountains Northwest of Zarivar lake in Iran. Although he did not trust the Kurds completely, he needed them to smuggle him into Turkey. If they tried to double cross him, he had his sergeant and seven of the best fighters he had ever known with him. The Kurds knew of his reputation, so he did not anticipate any real problems. They also had to avoid the Iranian military and their surveillance systems. The Kurds were experts at this, another reason he needed them.

The call was less than a minute with the Kurdish contact. Mutaz did not like what he was told but he had no choice but to do what he was told, something he wasn't used to. The meeting place in the mountains had been changed to one much closer to where they were in the foothills at the base of the mountain range. He received information that the Iranian military had increased their activities closer to the Iraq border because of the invasion by the US and allied forces. Even though the meeting place was closer it did not give Mutaz any more comfort.

They had only been traveling for four hours when they were close to the Kurdish smuggler's location in a small group of trees and shrubs just off the road. Mutaz had met them at this location in the past handing over weapons and explosives. He did not like the meeting point as you could hide a sniper or attackers anywhere in the shrubs and brush easily.

"Stop here," Mutaz said to Ahmad.

"Is there a problem?" he asked.

"I do not trust the Kurds. Send Ismail and Ali across the hill on our left where the road bends around it. Give them a radio each to communicate, two clicks we are clear to go in, three clicks it is an ambush. It will take them about twenty minutes to get to the meeting place. I want them to make sure we are not walking into an ambush," he replied.

"Yes, but we cannot sit here for twenty minutes. If an Iranian military patrol comes along, we will not be able to avoid them. What if we pull into the shrubs on the side of the road? We can cut some of them down as camouflage for the trucks?" replied Ahmad.

"As always you think like me, do it," said Mutaz.

Ahmad gave the two soldiers their instructions and they were up the side of the hill like a couple of goats. Both men carried Tariq pistols, Norinco Type 56 rifles with folding stocks and extra magazines. Mutaz took a position where he could see the road in both directions watching for Iranian military vehicles. Ahmad and his men quickly drove the two vehicles into the brush and covered their tracks with branches they cut from the bushes.

It took Ismail and Ali longer than expected to get over the hill. By the time they had done a security check of the meeting spot it had been almost forty-five minutes. They could see two vehicles both cream colored Toyota Landcruiser's hidden from the road. There were four men next to the Landcruiser's, all were kneeling on prayer mats.

Ismail mumbled a verse from the Quran under his breath and waited until they had finished praying. He turned on the radio and pressed the button twice indicating it was clear to come in. If there were any other men around, they could not see them.

Mutaz was getting impatient, and Ahmad could see it. He was not known for his patience and the lack of it normally led to violence if somebody let him down or didn't do exactly what he'd asked.

"They will contact soon," said Ahmad.

"It has been too long," he replied.

"You know those soldiers, they won't say it is safe until they are absolutely sure," said Ahmad.

"Yes," he replied.

Just as they had finished talking the radio clicked twice.

"Time to go," said Mutaz with a spring in his step.

They watched the road to make sure nothing was coming and drove out of the bushes. The followed the road until they saw the dirt track that would lead to the meeting point. As planned two more soldiers got out of one of the vehicles and scurried into the bushes. Their job was to provide cover fire for Mutaz if they were ambushed. The windows were down on the vehicles as they drove along the short dirt track. Mutaz and Ahmad both had there Norinco rifles at the ready. They quickly came upon the two Landcruiser's and were greeted with waives by four men.

"Slowly," Mutaz said to Ahmad.

They stopped fifty yards short of the four men and got out of the vehicles. Mutaz, Ahmad and the soldiers all scanned the bushes and the area around the men and their vehicles. Everything looked good so Mutaz walked towards them.

"Good to see you again my friend," said the lead man.

"And you," replied Mutaz.

"You have our agreed payment?" asked the man.

"Yes, you will get it when we are in Turkey," replied Mutaz curtly.

"I must see it first," he replied.

"You don't trust me after all these years of dealing with me?" asked Mutaz.

"It's not that I don't trust you, I just like to see my reward for getting you to Turkey safely," he replied.

"Follow me," said Mutaz.

All four men started to walk towards Mutaz.

"Only him," said Ahmad with authority.

The lead man gave him a disapproving look and indicated that his men stay where they were.

Satisfied that the gold and explosives were all there they sat down and went through the plan and route that they were to take to get to Turkey. After they finished going through the plan they sat, drank hot tea, and ate. The first part of the journey was only about six hours after which they would stop at an almond and pomegranate farm hidden from the road. They were only going drive at night and with over five hundred miles to cover before they arrived at Bitlis, Turkey it would take three nights.

Both Land cruisers would lead the way closely followed by Mutaz and his vehicles. It was getting very cold as the vehicles left and the four soldiers that were hiding in the bushes were glad to jump into the back of the trucks. The men in the Land cruisers didn't have a clue that they'd been hiding the whole time. They thought that there were only four men with Mutaz. Ahmad had bread and hot tea waiting in the back of the truck for the men as he knew they would be cold and very hungry.

Mutaz turned on his satellite phone again and made his next call.

CHAPTER 10

SYRIA

After General Ashkouri left Miqdadiyah and the devastation he had caused behind him, he headed due North with his troops for two hours and then northwest towards Tikrit. After skirting the city, they Headed northeast towards the Syrian border. Unlike General Mutaz he included his soldiers that were close to him to join him in deserting the army to find a new life in Syria. Only three took him up on his offer. Most of the soldiers had wives and families and they could not leave them behind.

Like Mutaz he had hidden a substantial amount of money in three different countries, Syria being one of them. The other bank accounts were held in London, and Zurich in Switzerland. He did not have the same amount of wealth as Mutaz, but he knew he could have a good life with the three million he had stashed away. He also had the cash he had stolen from the mayor of Miqdadiyah which amounted to just over twenty thousand dollars.

He and the three soldiers with him took one vehicle, a pickup that had no military markings, just a plain sand color. At sunrise they drove out of the small encampment they had made with the other soldiers, nobody really cared that they were leaving. The general's initial target would be the town of Al Qamishli on the Syria-Turkish border. It was a good safe place in his mind and allowed a quick exit through Turkey by vehicle or by plane from the airport to Damascus where he had friends.

The sun was rising fast across the desert giving it an almost golden glow. He was enjoying the sight when they heard a series of loud explosions behind them in the distance. They stopped the vehicle and looked in the direction of the sound. On the horizon, they could see plumes of black smoke rising towards the sky. They all knew that it was most probably missiles sent down by the Americans.

"That's where our camp is," said one soldier.

"I think that's where it was, the Americans must have been tracking us by satellite," replied the General.

Instinctively they all looked up at the sky, it was just a beautiful blue sight as far as the eye could see.

"What do we do?" asked one of the soldiers.

"We get back in the vehicle and drive but drive slowly like we are not in a hurry to go anywhere. With luck they will not target us for fear that we are locals and not military. Quickly change into civilian clothes in the truck. Don't be looking at the sky, keep your focus ahead of us. Let's go," replied the general.

Within a couple of minutes, they were all dressed in rough looking civilian clothes. They did not look up even when the urge to was too great to ignore. After thirty minutes of driving, they knew that they were not going to be the target of another missile attack. They took an old desert road that was used by illegal traders and gun runners. It was rough terrain and terribly slow going especially as they had over two hundred miles to go. As they got closer to the border, they came across two abandoned vehicles, one with Syrian license plates. The vehicles had obviously been there for a long time as scavengers had stolen the wheels and important engine parts. They removed the license plates from the derelict vehicle and put it on theirs. They drove another five miles and made camp for the night. The desert driving had bounced their bodies around in the vehicle making them sore and tired.

They could not drive at night especially in this part of Iraq. There were sink holes everywhere, many you can't see in daylight until you're right up to them. They would have the same problem when they crossed the border into Syria.

The next morning at sunrise they continued their journey. With slow and cautious driving through the desert they crossed the border into Syria four hours later. Once they found a road with a decent surface, they picked up speed stopping at the first gas station they came to. They filled up the vehicle with gasoline, purchased water, food and had a black coffee before they left. They were all in high spirits as they drove to the city of Al Qamishli. Each one of the soldiers thought that their life would improve now that they had left Iraq and the fighting. They had families back in Iraq, Mothers, Fathers, and siblings but none of them were married.

He liked Al Qashmili city with its green trees and palms, there was a hustle and bustle about the place. The fact that it was connected to the Turkish city of Nusaybin made it even more attractive. He gave the three soldiers one thousand US dollars each when they reached the city and told them to spend it wisely. They found a cheap hotel to stay in and started their new life by finding a place to enjoy women.

The general had his own agenda and after a wash went straight to the bank from the hotel. He had spoken to the manager on several occasions by phone about his account which he had opened two years earlier. It was not long before he bought himself plain clothes for his journey to Latakia the main port city of Syria and capital of the Latakia Governorate. He would leave the three soldiers to their own devices and left without telling them where he was going. They were on their own now.

He was in no hurry as he drove to Latakia stopping occasionally to enjoy some of the roadside cafes on the route. He spent one night in a small run-down hotel which he didn't mind, it was better than any military tent.

As he approached Latakia he was amazed at the amount of greenery. The area was very popular with the farming community and had a wealth of produce growing. He had the address of the apartment that he was supposed to go to. It belonged to his old general from the military who'd left Iraq after the first Desert Storm conflict. He was looking forward to seeing him as it had been five years since they had last met. After asking for direction twice, as there weren't any street signs, he found the apartment.

The building looked new and in good condition, unlike his old, rented apartment in Baghdad. On the first floor he saw the red door and knocked on it twice. He could hear movement inside and stood slightly to one side as the door opened.

"Welcome," said Mohamed.

"It's been a long time," replied Ashkouri.

They hugged and walked inside the apartment.

After he was shown around the small two-bedroom apartment they sat down to eat and drink tea.

As they ate, the two men reminisced about the early days and both of their careers. Mohamed talked about not having a family of his own and having no family in Iraq left. His parents were long gone, and his siblings had all died during the bombings of the first desert storm. As he did not have any family left, he surprised Ashkouri and told him that he would leave his apartment to him when he passed away. The attorney that helped him when he bought the apartment lived in the top floor apartment in the same building.

Mohamed was in extremely poor health and did not have long to live. He had been diagnosed with a rare blood disease that the doctors could not fix. His pale white skin showed that he was not well and not long for this earth. The old man promised to take Ashkouri down to the harbor the next morning to show him around. He had developed many contacts over the years in Latakia. It was getting late, and Mohamed was starting to fall asleep in the chair.

"I could do with some sleep," said Ashkouri.

"Me too," he replied.

They had a very enjoyable walk around the harbor the next morning with Mohamed introducing Ashkouri to several fishermen. He told them that they could trust him if he asked them to help him with something. One of the fishermen offered to take Ashkouri fishing with him, which he accepted.

They had lunch at a small fisherman's café and talked about the situation in Iraq. When Ashkouri brought up General Mutaz he was told not to use his name again. The hatred in the old man's eyes was like fire. He did not ask him why he was angry with Mutaz, he just left it alone.

The next morning Ashkouri was up early and made a pot of Turkish coffee on the stove. He stood for fifteen minutes at the living room window of the apartment looking at the city outside. After two hours his friend was still in bed, so he decided to wake him up with a strong black coffee. He gently tapped on the door of the bedroom but there was no answer. He slowly opened the door and called out his friend's name.

He could see his head still on the pillow, he was fast asleep or so he thought. As soon as he saw his face, he knew that he had died in the night.

Ashkouri took care of the funeral arrangements and burial that evening, it was the least he could do for his friend. He told the attorney on the top floor that Mohamed had died, and he was genuinely upset. He found the papers showing the ownership of the apartment and gave them to Ashkouri promising to file all the required documents to legally hand over ownership.

Over the coming months Ashkouri made the city his home. He spent a lot of time down at the fishing harbor conversing with the locals. He was surprised at how many Iraqi people lived in the city. Many of the Iraqi's had run away from the conflicts in Iraq and from Saddam Hussein's tyrannical rule. As he got to know the geography he liked the harbor proximity to Cape Apostolos Andreas in Cyprus, it was only 68miles away.

He had found the new life that he wanted and had even found a woman that he liked a lot. It was his intention originally to live in Damascus because it was such a huge city and easy to hide in. The more he got to know Latakia the more he realized that it wasn't as small as he'd originally thought. This is where he would stay and build a completely new life, leaving the old behind.

CHAPTER 11

BETRAYAL OF KURDS

After three long nights of driving on rough roads and at times off road the Kurds and Mutaz's vehicles crossed the border into Turkey. Within a couple of hours, they would be in Bitlis ready to rest before they started the next leg of the journey to Istanbul.

Everything had gone well so far with only two sightings of the Iranian military. They had only crossed the border an hour earlier when they came upon a military check point. The sun was just starting to rise, and it was directly in front of them. It made it difficult to see as the checkpoint was on the rise in the road with the sun directly behind them.

Mutaz was watching the Landcruiser in front of them and one of the men was waiving through the rear window telling them to slow down.

The satellite phone rang which made Ahmad jump.

"Yes," said Mutaz when he answered the call.

Ahmad watched the general as he listened to the caller on the phone, he didn't say anything else and turned the phone off.

"There are only about eight soldiers, we could kill them if they don't let us through," said Ahmad.

"Stay behind the Landcruiser's but not too close," replied Mutaz.

Again, Ahmad didn't question his general and did as he was told.

They both watched as the Turkish soldiers surrounded the two Landcruiser's. Both drivers looked like they were handing over documents to the soldiers at the driver's door.

"It looks like they are checking their identification documents. We don't have any," said Ahmad.

"We don't need them," said Mutaz.

Ahmad was not only confused but was worried what the general was going to do. Was his renowned lack of patience going to rise and make the situation worse? He slid his Norinco rifle onto his lap.

Mutaz smiled as he watched his sergeant move his rifle into a position where he could quickly fire it at the soldiers if he had to.

"You won't be needing that," said Mutaz with a rare smile as he placed his hand on the rifle.

"OK," he replied placing the rifle back in its place alongside the seat.

"I'm going to talk to our men, make sure they stay calm. You stay in the truck and don't do anything no matter what happens," said Mutaz as he got out.

Ahmad as always was the good soldier and followed orders. He watched the general in the rear-view mirror walking to the vehicle behind. He saw him talking to the men and then walk back to him. He tapped on the driver's door gently as he walked past. He was walking towards the Turkish soldiers.

Ahmad was really concerned and feared that the general was going to throw his weight around with the Turkish soldiers. He wasn't in Iraq anymore and his stature and reputation in Iraq meant nothing here in Turkey. He slid out of the vehicle and stood by the driver's door with his hand on the rifle.

The Turkish soldiers had now surrounded the Kurds vehicles but paid no attention to Mutaz and his vehicles. The Kurds were ordered to get out of the vehicles, which they did. They all looked incredibly angry and argued with the lead officer, their complaints were ignored as they were all lined up at the side of the road. Behind them was low crash barrier protecting vehicles from a steep drop of about forty feet. The Kurds were all shouting, protesting, and arguing as to why they had been stopped.

A heavy truck came up the hill towards the roadblock, it slowed down considerably as it got closer. Two of the Turkish soldiers stepped into the middle of the road and waived at the driver to continue through. The driver did not hesitate and picked up speed past the roadblock and disappeared down the hill.

Letting the truck through without checking it, incensed the Kurds and they were now really agitated. That was when it all went wrong for the Kurds.

The lead Turkish soldier held up his hand and dropped it. His soldiers starting firing at the Kurds, they riddled them with bullets, all but one, their leader. He stood shocked at what the soldiers had just done as his comrades lay dead around him.

Mutaz walked past the Turkish soldiers and up to the Kurd leader.

"You remember when we first met, we had an agreement for me to deliver weapons and explosives to you for a set price?" said Mutaz.

"Yes, and I gave you the money, American dollars," he replied.

"No, you only gave me half the money agreed. This, I wasn't happy about which resulted in me punching you. You retaliated by putting your pistol against my face and threatened to shoot me. Your men then pointed their weapons at me and my sergeant, something we remember well. I told you at the time that you would never point a gun at me again."

"That was three years ago, we have done many deals since then," he shouted.

"Yes, but you still went back on our original deal and demanded a lower price for the future weapons. This I agreed to because I had weapons and explosives and you had dollars. I'm a patient man when it comes to exacting revenge, quite the opposite to what I'm normally like. Now the gold I was going to give to you will go to the Turkish soldiers that helped me today." Mutaz pulled out his pistol and shot the Kurdish leader point blank in the forehead.

Ahmad was watching intently as his general walked up to the Kurd leader. He knew that the general would have something up his sleeve to get through the checkpoint, but he didn't see this coming. From where he was standing, he couldn't make out any facial features and didn't know that it was the same Turkish Colonel that he and Mutaz had worked with in the past. Shooting the man in the head was typical and just added another one to the general's count.

Mutaz called Ahmad and his men over to meet the Turkish colonel and his men. Mutaz's soldiers all carried their automatic rifles loosely by their side. Ahmad was the first to see the colonel and now recognized him. The phone calls the general had made must have been to the Turkish colonel to set up the roadblock.

The Turkish soldiers gathered around and all exchanged greetings.

"Come, I will show you the gold," said Mutaz to the colonel.

"Wait I have your travel papers to get you through any police or military roadblocks or inspections," he replied.

After retrieving the documents, he gave them to Mutaz as they walked to his truck to inspect the gold. They were within a few feet of the truck when Mutaz pulled out his pistol for the second time that day and shot the colonel three times in the torso.

The Turkish soldiers and Mutaz's men heard the shots and saw the colonel falling to the ground. Before the Turks could respond the general's soldiers raised their rifles and killed the remaining Turkish soldiers.

Ahmad was taken by surprise as he hadn't been told about this part of the plan. It all happened so fast he didn't even get to raise his weapon.

The general's soldiers immediately started to move the dead soldiers' bodies. They put one in a Turkish military vehicle and scattered the others around. They picked up two of the Kurdish bodies and tossed them over the side of the crash barrier where they fell into the ravine below.

"Finish quickly," shouted Mutaz.

His soldiers have recovered the automatic weapons from the Kurds and sprayed the Turkish military vehicles. The bullets punched dozens of holes in them.

Ahmad now realized what was going on. The general was making this look like an ambush by the Kurds on the Turkish military, a common occurrence in this region. If the Kurds bodies were found on their own, it would look wrong as there wouldn't be a report by the police or military of a conflict with them. By making it look like a fire fight between them both nobody would be looking for them.

He watched as his soldiers fired round after round into the vehicles the Kurds were driving and then into the crash barrier with the Turkish military weapons. It was all over in a matter of minutes then they were back in the vehicles driving deeper into Turkey. Istanbul would be their destination. Mutaz did consider switching vehicles and using the Kurds much faster and more comfortable Landcruiser's, but they would stand out more than the regular pickup vehicles they were already driving.

Mutaz could tell that Ahmad wasn't happy with him as they drove. He was unusually quiet and had a stern look on his face.

"What is wrong?" he asked.

"Nothing, sir," Ahmad replied.

"We are no longer soldiers Ahmad, we now call each other by our first names, all of us," he replied. We are in Turkey and soon we will be in Istanbul and then on to Europe to start our new life as free men. You are upset with me because of the situation at the roadblock, I don't blame you," said Mutaz.

"Why didn't you tell me what your plan was? My men knew but I didn't, this tells me you don't trust me," replied Ahmad.

Ahmad knew he was treading on dangerous ground with the general, but he couldn't hide his feelings and the general could see it. He wanted to reach for his pistol to protect himself, but he couldn't, it was trapped on his hip between him and the center console. This was the first time in twenty years that he felt that his life was truly in danger from the general.

"I'd been thinking about the roadblock for several hours and realized that if the bodies of the Kurds were found too quickly the Turkish military or police or even both would be looking for their killers. When I got out of the truck and walked over to tell the men to stay in the vehicles a plan quickly formed in my head. I didn't have time to stop and tell you as I knew that the Turkish soldiers were about to shoot the Kurds. I had to act quickly so I told our men to kill the Turkish soldiers and rake all the vehicles with each other's weapons to look like an ambush. You should be happy because we now have the gold that I was going to give to the Turks. You and the men will get a huge bonus when we sell the gold."

Ahmad wasn't happy as he didn't even know about the roadblock not just the false ambush, but he made it look like he was.

"This is good, a bonus. It will give the men something to look forward too," he replied with a smile.

"We will have a different life soon, a life of luxury, a life of tasty food and soft beds not a military barracks. We will be starting a new business and I want you to be a big part of it," he replied.

"What business?" asked Ahmad.

"I've been thinking about it for some time. I have a contact that left Iraq after desert storm, Riadh Al Musayyib. He left Iraq when he was sixteen with nothing and now, he is an exceptionally good businessman and very wealthy, he is richer than you could imagine. He has several businesses in Europe and has told me that I can make a lot of money with him," replied Mutaz. "I want you to be my business partner Ahmad."

It wasn't missed by Ahmad when the general said I was going to make a lot of money, not we.

"I will be by your side in whatever you do my general," he replied.

"Again, we use our real names now not rank," said Mutaz.

"Yes, Haider." It felt so alien for him to call his general by his first name.

CHAPTER 12

Al-QADIR RECOVERY

After the US military doctors repaired the internal bleeding and his wounds, he stabilized quickly. The military doctors then sent him to the civilian hospital for observation and day to day care. It took a month of rehabilitation before Al-Qadir could function properly. It was another three weeks before he was fully fit and ready to fulfill his promise to his father. The doctors were amazed at how quickly his body healed and how he responded to the rehabilitation and physical therapy he received. If they knew that he wanted to avenge his father and mother, they may have understood. He didn't discuss it with anyone, he had a score to settle with General Mutaz for the death of his parents and that was between him and Mutaz.

As part of a program to obtain the trust of the Iraqi people the US government set up programs to assist in local hospitals. One of these programs was for the rehabilitation of wounded Iraqi civilians and police officers. During his rehabilitation he would converse with the military personnel that were helping the hospital staff. He interpreted for them when some of the Iraqi's they were trying to help didn't understand what they were trying to say. The doctor's language skills were basic to say the least.

Arabic spoken in Iraq is Mesopotamia Arabic which is a part of the Aramaic Syriac dialect. The old Mesopotamian languages of Akkadian and Sumerian strongly influence it. This same dialect of

Mesopotamian Arabic was also spoken in Iran, Syria, and Southeastern Turkey.

As part of the program a US general visited the wards where civilians and police officers were being rehabilitated. He had a small entourage of US and Iraqi officials with him. It was a public relations exercise that he had been tasked to do and not one that he had chosen. He wanted to get back to the war zones and direct his troops.

Towards the end of his visit, he asked a US doctor who the young man was that was interpreting for the doctors. The doctor explained what had happened to the interpreter and that he had completed his rehabilitation in record time. They kept him around to assist with the language barrier. The doctor also told the general what he knew about the young man's family and what had happened to them at the hands of the Iraqi Republican Guard. He had become a real asset in the hospital and had the trust of the foreign doctors and nurses that were working there. The general saw something in the young man and requested a meeting with him before he left.

The doctor did the introduction.

"Al-Qadir this is General Hart of the US Army," said the doctor.

"Pleased to meet you sir," he replied extending his hand for the general to shake it.

"Good manners, I like that," replied the general shaking his hand.

"My father and mother taught me and my brothers to always be polite," he replied.

"A good lesson to give any child. Your English is excellent, where did you learn to speak it?"

"My mother and father taught me the basics. My mother also taught me French and thanks to her I speak it fluently," he replied.

"His English has improved immeasurably since he came to the hospital," said the doctor.

"French as well, that's impressive. We will speak again very soon," he replied shaking his hand.

Al-Qadir watched the general walk away and wondered why they would meet again; was he coming back for another visit?

The next day a man in street clothes came into the hospital and asked to meet Al-Qadir. The man offered him a job interpreting for the US military, which he quickly accepted.

At first, Al-Qadir was just interpreting around the military camp where he was living. It quickly became apparent that he had the ability to learn things quickly.

As his skills grew, he was assigned to another young Iraqi that had been interpreting for the military and had experience in the battlefield with soldiers. He trained Al-Qadir in the basics of not just the interpretation but how to move around soldiers when they were on maneuvers. His first trip out with soldiers and his trainee was not only interesting but fascinating. He watched how the soldiers moved with ballet like precision around each other. The interpreter moving in their shadow just as quickly or slowly depending on the situation. He knew after the first day that this was what he wanted to do. It was a couple of weeks before they gave him a firearm. He felt slighted by this but understood, they did not know him or trust him.

CHAPTER 13

ISTANBUL, TURKEY

The escape to Istanbul didn't go as easily as Mutaz had planned. After the discovery of the dead Turkish soldiers the military was on the hunt for more Kurdish fighters to exact revenge for their fallen brothers. This caused Mutaz and his men to hide in the day and only travel at night when they thought that it was safe to do so. Instead of taking the main roads they were now taking the smaller roads and old transport routes. These roads and off-road areas were slow going due to the condition of the roads and terrain. However, they did manage to get to Istanbul without detection.

Mutaz, Ahmad and the seven soldiers had spent four weeks in a safe house in Istanbul before moving to another safe house. Riadh Al Musayyib, the man soon to be in a business venture with Mutaz provided all the safe houses.

They had spent two weeks hidden away from the public eye in the second safe house only venturing out for cigarettes, food, and water. Ahmad and the soldiers were starting to become restless. It was OK for Mutaz as he went out every day to have business meetings or so he said. The distrust of Mutaz was growing in the men and especially in Ahmad. After not including him in the arrangement to meet the Turkish military and the ambush he felt that he could not trust him like he did before. If he excluded him once he would exclude him again.

Mutaz returned to the safe house on numerous occasions smelling strongly of alcohol. It did not go unnoticed by any of the men. In the first week he was only gone for an hour or two for the business meetings. But in the second week he was stretching it out to all day and now all night.

The men were all sitting around the living room of the safe house with Ahmad smoking cigarettes and drinking tea. They had discussed their dislike and now distrust of what Mutaz was doing. They were all being very vocal to Ahmad and wanted to know when they would get their money. They knew that the two small wooden crates held gold bars and the larger crate was full of American dollars. The weapons and explosives they had smuggled across the border into Iran for the Kurds had already been sold.

Ahmad was getting extremely nervous about the new distrust in Mutaz, he had to do something to calm the men.

"I will talk to Mutaz and ask him when we are going to get our share of the money? I also want to get out of here. You know he wants us to go with him to Europe. He said yesterday that he was going to give us the details today," said Ahmad.

"No, he said he would give us the details last night when he returned. Where is he?" asked Ibrahim.

"I don't know where he is, but I promise you all I will get answers from him as soon as he returns," he replied.

In the last week Mutaz had spent every day and now night at a local brothel with one of Riadh Al Musayyib's contacts. He had had his fill of women, alcohol, and a taste of the good life. It had not occurred to him that Ahmad and his men would be getting tired of staying indoors. It had been six weeks since they had arrived in Istanbul. His arrogance and hammer style control of his men when they were soldiers was clouding his judgement. They were no longer soldiers, his words, but he had already forgotten them.

He had a huge hangover from the previous night and walked slowly up the concrete stairs to the apartment on the third floor. Even though it had four bedrooms it was feeling increasingly closed in as the days went on. He was about to put the key in the lock when he heard raised voices inside. He put his ear to the door and listened to every word that was being said by his men inside. He was getting angrier and angrier as the conversation went on. Those ungrateful bastards were whining. If it were not for him, they would still be in Iraq, locked in a military prison run by the Americans. He quietly walked back down the stairs to calm himself down. He could not let the men know that he had heard their conversation. He still needed them and realized that he had neglected them because of his partying. He had to give them something to cheer them up, the promise of money and a night at the brothel would do the trick. In his eyes he could not trust them, he had to find a way to get back at them. As quickly as the thought of punishing them came into his sick mind a plan started to form.

He walked back up the stairs coughing and stamping his feet in the concrete enough for them to hear in the apartment. As he got halfway up the last flight of stairs Ahmad opened the door.

"Mutaz, we were getting worried about you," said Ahmad.

"Nothing to be worried about, we are in business. Inside and I will tell all of you what it is about," replied Mutaz.

He was boiling up inside with anger and wanted to shoot each of them in the head. The fact that he had a hangover helped hide his anger.

"Mutaz is back," said Ahmad feigning excitement.

The men sat around the living room could not hide the fact that they were angry and frustrated.

"I have great news," announced Mutaz. "We will be leaving this place in a couple of days. We will have an escort provided by Riadh who will get us to Paris, France. I have money for all of you. Two thousand Euro's each when we get to the ship and more when we arrive in Paris. Once you are there, we will all have our own apartments in a building that Riadh owns. He will also arrange for each of us to have a bank account opened in our own names. You will be able to access your own money whenever you want. But tonight, I have a surprise for you, we are all going out to a restaurant that also has women for us to enjoy. This is my way of thanking you for your patience."

Mutaz hoped that this news would settle the men down for a time, but he would not forget what he had heard through the door.

"That is excellent news," said Ahmad with a genuine smile.

"Now I need to get some sleep as I been working very hard on the arrangements for Paris," he replied.

The men now knew that he had been partying and by the sounds of it visiting a brothel. Now they did not care, they were to get out of the building and soon travel to Paris where none of them had been before. Their trust in Mutaz had gone thanks to his own actions. They wondered what else he had been up to while they were hiding in the apartment.

Ahmad had been a truly loyal and obedient sergeant to his general for twenty years. It wasn't until they planned the escape from Iraq that he started to question his general's loyalty back to him. He had planned the route out of Iraq with him including the stopping point at the box canyon. He knew that they were to meet up with the Kurdish smugglers eventually, but he wasn't told where or when. Then the attack by the Turkish military on the Kurds at the roadblock took place. Again, he had no knowledge of this, but it must have been planned well in advance.

The wooden boxes were obviously of great interest to Ahmad as they had disappeared after they arrived at the apartment. He had to find out where they were not just for himself but for his men. He followed Mutaz to his bedroom.

"Where are the wooden boxes?" asked Ahmad quietly.

"They are none of your concern, get out," shouted Mutaz pushing him out of the room.

The bedroom door slammed shut behind him. The men were looking at Ahmad and he knew they would not put up with Mutaz and his moods much longer.

"One of his bad days," said Ahmad aloud.

Ahmad was stunned by what Mutaz said, he was the only other person that knew the original location of the gold and US dollars. He helped place the gold and cash into the safes in the floors of the palaces. However, the murder of the workers involved was down to Mutaz. When they recovered the gold and cash, he helped break open the concrete floors and load the wooden boxes with the US dollars and gold bars. There was over three million dollars and a quarter of a million Euros in cash in the large wooden box. A half a million dollars in gold bars was in the smaller boxes. This was only the beginning when it came to the dollars. He knew Mutaz had a Swiss bank account that had over ten million dollars in it. Knowing that there was ten million, he also knew that Mutaz could have put more money into the account or other accounts he did not know about.

Mutaz had promised him that he would get a fair share of the Swiss bank account when they got to Europe, now he was not so sure.

The dollars had come from the US government, sources such as the CIA and special forces. The US government plan was the money would help overthrow Saddam Hussein after the first desert storm raids. Mutaz had an excellent intelligence network of who received money from the US. He had surveillance performed on six high-powered Iraqis which resulted in him finding where they were hiding the cash. It did not take him long to steal it and have it transferred to the Swiss account. He killed three of the six using suicide bombers when they were in their vehicles. They looked like random targets by militants, so the theft of the money never came into question as the men that died couldn't tell anyone where the money was. The gold bars came from a huge floor safe in one of Saddam Hussein's palaces in Baghdad. Saddam trusted Mutaz to transfer them to another palace, which was foolish.

In a private meeting Saddam Hussein told Mutaz, the head of his personal security and the head of his armed forces that he had a plan to hide if the Americans came into the country again. When the Americans and Allied forces left the country, he would come out of hiding and rule again with more of an iron fist. Mutaz knew that his President had hidden much more gold and money, but he did not have time to find out where it was. Mutaz did not like that the President told the head of security and armed forces that he had entrusted Mutaz to hide his gold and cash.

Mutaz had already filtered over a million out of Hussein's cash pile into a foreign account unbeknown to anyone, including Ahmad. Within a month of the last meeting with Hussein the head of security disappeared. He was rumored to have stolen millions in gold and cash from his President Hussein. A rumor that Mutaz had set in motion.

Within a month of the meeting the head of the armed forces was killed in an explosion that was down to a US air strike. The only person left that knew of the location of the gold and money entrusted to Mutaz was him and Ahmad. After the air strike and disappearance of the head of security Mutaz was the only person that the President trusted to keep his escape plan confidential. Mutaz and the President developed a plan to confuse the allied forces that would be hunting him. This plan included using men that looked just like the President that were spread out throughout the country. There would be over a dozen safe houses and hiding places that the President would use. The idea was he would spend a week or two in each place moving around often. They would wait for the Allied forces to raid one area looking for the President and when they moved on, he would hide in the area they had just searched. All the hiding locations were chosen by Mutaz, all were in safe houses or underground. He did not wait for the President to go on the run before he raided two of the palaces where he had hidden the money and gold. The President would be too busy running to find out what Mutaz had done, and he would be long gone even if he did find out.

CHAPTER 14

COLD BLOODED KILLER

It had only been three days since Mutaz had taken Ahmad and the soldiers to the brothel. He was becoming increasingly paranoid since he heard them talking in the apartment. His friend Ahmad was the only one capable of turning the rest against him. He had a shrewd mind and had the loyalty of the men. He had to give him false trust and decided to show him where the money was. They were sitting in the living room area with the rest of the soldiers who were starting to get restless again.

"Ahmad, I'm going to get cigarettes, come with me," he said.

"Yes," he replied.

Ahmad did not realize it, but he still jumped when the general ordered him to do something. It wasn't surprising after spending over twenty years with him in the army.

As always, they left the apartment by the rear entrance. They walked two blocks through trash filled alleyways. At the store they bought a carton of two hundred cigarettes and a disposable lighter. Mutaz handed two packets of cigarettes to Ahmad.

"Let's go to that coffee shop," said Mutaz pointing to a building across the street.

93

Ahmad said nothing in reply and walked behind him across the street.

They sat down at a table close to the road and ordered two Turkish coffees. Mutaz lit a cigarette and offered Ahmad one which he took. He then held the lighter to the end of the cigarette and lit it for him. They said nothing to each other until the coffee arrived.

"Tonight, I want to take you to see where the boxes are hidden," said Mutaz.

"Tonight?" replied Ahmad.

"Yes, we are leaving this place tomorrow night at eight o'clock. We will go to the docks where Riadh has arranged for us to leave on a cargo ship too Marseille, France."

"So, we are really leaving," said Ahmad with a little excitement.

"Yes, we have been here too long. I know you and our men have been struggling in the apartment all this time, but it will all be worth it tomorrow when we leave. Let's finish our coffee and I will take you to the boxes," he replied.

Ahmad was excited at the thought of leaving but he was nervous. Was Mutaz up to something? Was he going to kill him in a back street on the way to where the money was hidden? He walked behind Mutaz as they got up from the table and put his hand on the butt of his pistol, it was tucked into the belt of his pants. Reassured he followed Mutaz past a small market and into a side street.

Mutaz could feel Ahmad's eyes boring into the back of his head, paranoia was starting to build again. He stopped at a wooden door that had seen better days and took a key out of his pocket. He put the key into the lock and turned it unlocking the door with a smooth click, the door swung open.

Ahmad was surprised that the door lock made little noise as it looked rusted and old. When the door opened it did not make any noise either, the hinges on such and old door must have some rust and creak, he thought.

Mutaz stepped through the door into dirt floored courtyard. The only light in the courtyard came from the door he had just opened.

"Quickly come in and close the door," said Mutaz.

Ahmad followed him but very cautiously. It was pitch dark when the door closed, and Ahmad put his right hand on the pistol grip. He quickly and quietly stepped to one side in the hope that Mutaz did not hear him move. If he swung around now, he would not be where Mutaz would expect him to be. He heard Mutaz moving away from him and then a door opened.

The courtyard suddenly filled with a shaft of light from the second door as Mutaz turned on a light. Ahmad let go of his pistol grip and dropped his hand in the hope that he hadn't been seen by Mutaz.

"Come," said Mutaz waving to Ahmad to follow.

He followed as asked but with caution, he was not going to let Mutaz out of his sight. None of the men knew where they had gone so they could not even find him if he was murdered. He saw Mutaz move across the room in front of him, he went through another door. Now he had lost sight of Mutaz he'd gone into a room that was dark, this time a light didn't come on.

"Come in," shouted Mutaz.

Ahmad threw himself up against the wall close to the door, he drew his pistol. He was not going to go down without a fight. This was a loud clanging sound like a metal can being kicked across the floor. He heard Mutaz curse aloud.

"Are you OK?" asked Ahmad.

"Yes, I tripped over a metal bucket," he replied.

As soon as he replied a light came on in the second room.

Ahmad gave a quick bob of the head looking into the room. He saw Mutaz, he had his back to him, he was standing by the large wooden box that contained the money from Iraq.

"Here are the boxes," said Mutaz.

He watched him as he used a crowbar to open the lid on the large box. He slid his pistol into the front of his pants for quick access should he need it and stepped into the room. He gave the room a quick check to make sure there wasn't anyone else lying-in wait. There wasn't the room was empty, it only contained the three boxes that they had brought across the border. He was still nervous and did not trust Mutaz as he stepped towards the box.

"There," said Mutaz pointing into the box.

"The American dollars and Euros," said Ahmad without thinking.

"Yes, what else would be in there?" he replied.

Mutaz then deliberately dropped the crowbar onto the concrete floor, it made a hell of a loud sound.

Ahmad jumped when the crowbar hit the ground, he was so focused on the money. He reached for his pistol.

"You're jumpy my friend," said Mutaz.

"Old habits," he replied letting go of his pistol grip.

"Yes, I would have done the same if I was startled by that noise," he replied.

Mutaz now knew that he couldn't trust his old friend, he reached for his gun.

"All of the training you gave me," he replied trying to recover the situation.

Mutaz stepped up to Ahmad and put an arm around his shoulder.

"This is what we have worked for all our military life, now we will enjoy it together. You have been by my side in good times and bad, I will never forget it," he said.

"We have done a lot together," said Ahmad.

"And we will do a lot more together. Tomorrow, I want you and the two soldiers you trust the most to come here and load a truck with the boxes. I will meet you thirty minutes after you leave the apartment with a car. Both vehicles will then go to the port where we will board the ship to Marseille. You are to be the keeper of the money and gold until we get to Marseille. In Marseille we will do an exchange with Riadh's contact, the gold for Euros. We will stay in Marseille for two days after which we travel to Paris. Riadh has arranged all the transportation and places to stay. What do you think?" he asked.

"You have planned everything for us, I will be glad to leave Turkey," he replied.

"Good, here is the key to the front door. It looks old but it is steel reinforced and well maintained so it does not make a noise. I don't want you to tell the men about the money or this storage location, not even those you choose to bring with you. I want to surprise them all when we set sail on the ship. You will be the one that shows them the money and gold," he said.

He was a little surprised that he would be the one to show the men, but he was happy about it.

"What time do I return tomorrow?" asked Ahmad.

"Nineteen hundred hours. The truck will be parked outside with the ignition key attached under the front wheel arch by a magnet. It is supposed to be full of fuel so check it and of course make sure the engine starts. We do not want something simple like no fuel or an engine not starting to stop us now. I will meet you here thirty minutes after you leave with the rest of the men. When you come here tomorrow, I will brief the rest of our men on the plan and where we are going. I will then drive them here in an SUV that will be delivered to the apartment tomorrow. We will all leave together for the port. It is time to go back to the apartment, it is only three blocks away, you can see the roof of this building from the apartment." said Mutaz.

"I understand, let's go," said Ahmad with a slight sigh.

On the way back to the apartment he was mentally berating himself for doubting Mutaz. He felt a great deal of guilt for suspecting him of doing something untoward. He vowed that he would not doubt him again.

The next day he picked two men that would help to load the truck for the port. He was still a little angry with himself for his actions the previous day. Pulling his weapon out to shoot Mutaz played on his mind. Now he had to move forward and be ready to leave Turkey for a brighter future and support his general.

At 1855hrs he and the two soldiers walked to the storage building, it only took five minutes. When they arrived, there was a truck parked outside as promised. Ahmad felt under the front wheel arch and there was the vehicles ignition key just as described by Mutaz. He opened the door to the storage building and walked in with his men. In the second room were the wooden boxes sitting in the same place. It did not take long for them to load the boxes into the truck. They had forgotten how heavy the small boxes were, but gold is not light.

"I will Lock the front door, wait by the truck," said Ahmad handing the ignition keys to one of the men.

Ahmad sensed something wasn't feeling right about the boxes, it was all going too smoothly. He climbed into the back of the truck and used the crowbar to open the box that he knew contained the cash. The lid came off easier than before. To his surprise inside there was a lot of straw and bricks, but no money. He opened the small boxes they also had straw but a lot of metal bars in place of the gold. He put the lids back on the boxes as he didn't want his men to see that they'd been betrayed. He was furious and threw down the crowbar.

"Is something wrong?" asked one of the soldiers.

"Yes, but I'm going to sort it out, right now. You stay here with the vehicle until I get back, I won't be long," said Ahmad.

He stormed off in the direction of the apartment building with the two soldiers watching. A light rain started to fall but it didn't slow down Ahmad's pace.

"No point in getting wet, get into the truck," said the soldier to his colleague.

They both climbed into the cab and the soldier put the key in the ignition and started the engine to keep warm. The truck engine didn't start as the soldier turned the key, not that he would have known as he was vaporized by the explosion. There wouldn't be much if anything left of the bodies in the truck.

In the early hours of the morning Mutaz wired the truck after he had moved the money and gold. He hid the bomb under the truck next to the fuel tank. It did not take him long to wire the bomb to the ignition. He used the explosives he had brought from Iraq that were supposed to have been for the Kurdish smugglers. He wasn't a true explosive specialist but knew enough to make a simple bomb and wire it to the ignition of a vehicle.

The gold and money took much longer to move than wiring the ignition as he had to move the heavy gold bars on his own.

Ahmad was moving very quickly in his anger not realizing that this would save his life. He pushed through a group of men on the street corner not caring how hard he shoved them. One of the men cursed at him but he didn't hear him. He was two hundred yards away from the truck when it exploded. The pressure wave from the explosion knocked him and the men he had just pushed past violently to the ground. Shrapnel from the buildings and broken windows were carried through the air by the shockwave cutting and slicing anyone and anything in its path. The group of men caught much of the shrapnel, but some shrapnel found Ahmad's back and legs. He was knocked unconscious receiving a head wound and broken ribs from the impact of hitting the ground. The lacerations to his back and legs were mostly shallow.

As Mutaz briefed the remainder of the men in the apartment they heard and felt the shock wave of an explosion. They all rushed to the open window and saw a fire burning three blocks away.

"Stay here, I will check it out," said Mutaz to the men.

As he left the apartment he glanced back and saw them all at the window fixated on the remains of the fire from the explosion. He ran down the stairs and out of the rear doors that they'd been using the whole time. He ran for two blocks through the dirty alleyways before stopping. He looked back at the apartment building and could see the night sky in the distance lit up with the fire from the truck explosion.

He took out his burner cell phone and dialed a number, nobody would answer as the phone he was calling was connected to a bomb in the apartment.

Mutaz had used the remainder of the explosives he had brought from Iraq. Like the truck bomb the apartment bomb was bigger than he expected, much bigger. He had placed the bomb in a large duffle bag that had what the others thought were his clothes for the trip. An assortment of bomb making items were also in the bag with the bomb itself.

Mutaz was again surprised at the power of the explosion as the roof of the apartment building blew open as did the windows. After the initial explosion, the roof collapsed into the building as flames took over. He was successful in killing all that remained of the men that he had worked with and that had protected him for many years. He had no need for them now as Riadh would be his partner and mentor in business. Now he did not have to share the gold or money with anyone, even Riadh didn't know that he had the cash, he told him he just had gold bars.

The local police or military would not find any evidence to identify the men killed in the explosion. Mutaz had left several clues in the apartment that would partly survive the explosion and fire. These items would point the finger at Kurdish rebels. It was also very possible that the explosions would be put down as accidental or a premature detonation. The bomb in the apartment had all the makings of a suicide backpack bomb.

He arrived at the yard where he had hidden the Citroen van from the night before. Inside the van he checked that the four metal boxes were still there. He had transferred the gold and money from the wooden boxes the night before into the lockable metal boxes. He rolled the combinations on the locks and checked the contents; everything was still there. He drove the Citroen van out of the yard and headed to the port.

CHAPTER 15

Mutaz drove through the dock security gate without any problem as the security guard was fast asleep. He turned left and headed along the dock looking for the ship he was to board. The dock came to a dead end with nothing but water in front of him. On the other side of the water, he could see the ship, he was in the wrong dock. He had to backtrack and find his way around. He reversed in between a gap in two containers to do a three-point turn. As he pulled forward a vehicle with its headlights on full beam appeared. He couldn't see anything as the lights were so bright. He put his arm up to block the light to try and see the vehicle. The vehicle stopped and a man got out of the driver's side.

He picked up his Glock and placed it at the side of his seat for easy access. The man was getting closer, he was wearing a uniform, it was the dock security.

"What are you doing here?" said the security officer.

"I got lost I was meant to go to that ship over there," said Mutaz pointing across the water.

"Didn't my colleague at the gate tell you which way to go?"

"No, he was asleep, and I didn't want to wake him."

"Asleep, he shouldn't be asleep, we must check every person and vehicle into the dock. Go back to the gate and check in with him."

"Do I have to? I need to make a delivery to the ship before it leaves tomorrow."

"Yes."

He said yes but his gut was telling him something was wrong with this man.

Mutaz could see the security guard was getting suspicious of him, so he got out of the vehicle, sliding the Glock into the back of his belt.

"Look, I can show you the boxes for delivery," he said walking towards the back of the van.

"Do you have your identity card with you?" asked the security guard as he walked up to Mutaz.

"Yes, in my back pocket," he replied reaching around his back for the Glock.

The guard didn't stand a chance as the weapon came up so fast, it was against his forehead before he could react.

Mutaz pulled the trigger as soon as the muzzle was against the guard's forehead. The bullet went straight through taking out the back of man's head. The gunshot was very loud as the sound echoed around the warehouses and carried across the water.

He ran to the guard's vehicle and turned the lights off before anyone saw them. He then turned his own vehicle lights off and looked for a place to hide the body and vehicle. There was a part of an old anchor chain on the dock, so he wrapped the body in it and dumped it into the dock. After checking a couple of warehouses doors, he found one that he could slide open. The warehouse inside was empty, a good place to hide the vehicle. He walked back to his vehicle to find something to wash the blood away on the dock floor. There were at least a dozen rats already feasting on the brain matter that was scattered on the ground. He left the rats to clean up for him.

He drove cautiously around to the other side of the dock trying not to bring any more attention to himself. It was completely dark with nobody about. He found the right dock and the ship. There on a giant warehouse door were the numbers he was to look for. He slid open one of the doors and drove the van inside. He sat in the front passenger seat and went into a deep sleep.

The next morning Mutaz woke to the sound of workers arriving on the dock. He got out of the van and locked it up. Within half an hour he'd introduced himself to the captain of the ship and the van was being winched into the hold of the ship.

In the back of the van there were two French license plates for the vehicle. Mutaz would put them on before they arrived in Marseille. In the glove box was a forged French driver's license and passport in Mutaz's name. Although forged they were good enough to deceive any policeman and many immigration officials. This was another business that Riadh operated and an extraordinarily successful one it was.

CHAPTER 16

RIADH AL MUSAYYIB

Riadh Al Musayyib was sixteen when he left Iraq and made his way to France using people smugglers. He was a squat five feet five inches tall and two hundred pounds. He looked like he had been hit on the top of the head, and it had compressed his neck into his shoulders. The skin on the right side of his very round face had been severely burned when he was a child, leaving a garish scar.

He and his mother lived in an abandoned factory in the center of Baghdad. His father had thrown him and his mother out of the family home when he was only nine years old. His mother couldn't have more children after she gave birth to him, a fact she kept secret from her husband. After trying for several years to have more children his mother finally broke down and told her husband the truth, this enraged his father. He would lose face with his friends and neighbors because his wife could not give him more children. He quickly took another much younger wife and threw Riadh and his mother into the street with just the clothes on their backs. Living off the street and begging became his life and the only way of supporting his mother, for whom he lived. She was raped on several occasions by men that were also living in the squat conditions of the old factory.

When he was thirteen, he found a man on top of his mother, she was screaming at him to stop. Riadh jumped on the man's back only to be thrown off, he landed face first into the fire his mother had started to keep them warm. The result was the garish scar that he now had on the side of his face. He didn't hide the scar; he was proud of it. He wore it as a medal of honor for trying to protect his mother.

Riadh swore to avenge his mother and pay back the man that had given him the scar. Slowly but surely over the next two years Riadh killed six men that had raped his mother. He stabbed all of them to death whilst they were sleeping. The man that gave him the scar would be the last one to be killed by him. He wanted this one to be special and slow, he had planned it well, but the man disappeared before he could exact his revenge. He was almost sixteen when he and his mother moved again to another derelict building. The factory had been home for four years, but once they left, they didn't stay anywhere very long.

Riadh was strolling through the market, something he did on a regular basis. Unfortunately for him, most of the stall holders knew him and chased him off before he could steal something from them. He always carried his trusty knife that had taken the lives of the six men and wounded several others that tried to tangle with him. Ahead of him there was a scuffle taking place between the local butcher and two boys that he was struggling to hold onto. He knew both boys; they too were orphans and homeless. One of the boys was holding onto a leg of lamb. He was striking the butcher with it trying to get him to lose his grip, it was not working the butcher had extraordinarily strong hands. Riadh saw his opportunity and crept around the back of the butchers stand which was covered on three sides with filthy looking sheets. He crept under the sheet at the rear and reach onto the table on the other side. His hand was searching the table for meat to steal when he hit the jackpot. His hand wrapped around what felt like meat and he slid it off the table. Riadh did not even look at what he had stolen and ran for all he was worth. Thankfully, the butcher and the other stall holders were all focused on the two boys to even notice him. He stopped running after four blocks and finally looked at what he had stolen, it was a three-inch-thick slab of prime beef. The smile on his face went from ear to scarred ear. He was so proud and ran to show his mother. It would feed them for several days when his mother added vegetables to the stew pot, which he also stole.

He ran up the stairs of the derelict house to the third floor where he and his mother had found a corner that was about habitable.

He ran into the room.

"Look, look what I have," he shouted as he held the chunk of meat above his head.

His mother was in the corner her eyes were wide open with the look of death on her face.

Riadh walked slowly towards his mother without uttering a sound. There was blood pouring out of several knife wounds to her body. He knew that this must have just happened, and he wasn't there to save her. Tears started to roll down his face as he slumped to his knees. He was about to start crying when he heard a noise at the rear of the house. He jumped to his feet and looked out of a hole in the wall. Scrambling over the rubble of the house at the rear of the building was the same man that had thrown Riadh into the fire.

The man looked back as he tried to get away through the stones and bricks. There on the top floor he could see the boys scarred face peering through a hole.

He smiled at the boy and shouted, "You're too late."

Riadh gave out a scream that sounded so primal it could have been an animal. He then fell to the floor and wept until he couldn't weep anymore.

Two hours after he found his mother, he'd buried her along with other unmarked graves in a makeshift graveyard. He now had two things to live for, to avenge his mother and to leave Iraq.

It took Riadh a month to find where the man was living that had murdered his mother. He was living with three other men in an old grocer's shop that had been partially burnt out. He watched the man for three days; he was getting to know his routine. On the fourth day he followed the man back to the grocer's shop. Riadh was carrying a can of gasoline. He'd hidden two buckets of water and a fire blanket in the old store earlier that evening.

The man had a habit of smoking Hashish and then falling asleep in the old shop. He was alone, as he was most evenings. He always returned earlier than the other three men.

Riadh followed him into the back of the shop and watched him until he fell asleep. He could hear him snoring loudly, it was time to avenge his mother. He tied the man's feet together and then emptied the can of gasoline very slowly and deliberately over the sleeping body. He didn't want him to wake up yet. He kept his face and shoulders clear of the fuel; he wanted his victim to see what was going to happen to him.

Riadh stepped up to the sleeping body and gave it a massive kick to the right rib cage, quickly followed by a second. The man woke up immediately but could not understand what was happening. As he sat up, he was kicked in the face knocking him backwards.

"Do you remember me?" asked Riadh.

"What, you," he replied.

"Yes me."

"I will kill you just like I killed your mother," he shouted as he struggled to get to his feet.

"Your feet are tied together, you can't stand," said Riadh.

"You idiot you didn't tie my hands," he replied as he reached for the rope to untie it.

Riadh stabbed the man's hands as they reached for the rope, he pulled his hands to his chest.

"You bastard, you are going to be sorry."

"Can't you smell anything?" asked Riadh.

It wasn't until he was asked the question that he realized he could smell gasoline, he quickly realized that he was soaked in it.

"Wait, wait," he said begging.

"You murdered my mother, and you gave me this scar on my face. Now it is your turn to feel the pain my mother felt when you raped her. The pain I felt when you threw me into the fire."

"No, don't please."

It was too late, Riadh stepped back several feet and ignited a cigarette lighter. He watched as the man begged for his life, he was screaming for mercy. The lighter seemed to hang in the air like it was moving in slow motion. Riadh felt a calm come over him as he watched the flame on the lighter. It didn't even get to land on the man as the fumes ignited with a huge flash. He stood watching and listening to the man scream in pain. His body was rolling around, his arms flailing about as the flames rose. He enjoyed the moment but had to put a stop to it. He dumped the buckets of water onto the burning body and then threw the fire blanket over him smothering the flames. It wasn't as easy as he thought to put the flames out be he did manage to do it.

The body was charred more than he'd estimated but the man was still alive and that's what he wanted.

"You will now feel pain like you have never felt before. It will be the last thing you will feel before you die, and I hope it takes a long time."

Riadh walked out of the store with a smile on his face, just one more visit to go before he left Iraq.

At his father's house it wasn't going to be as dramatic as the man that had raped his mother. He knew how to get inside the house and where the bedroom was where his father slept. His father hadn't changed his routine since he threw him and his mother out. He would send his wife downstairs to make him a coffee and she would bring it to him. He'd done his homework on his father just as he'd done on others before he murdered them. His father was still a wife beater and a pig of a man.

Once inside the house he hid under the bed where his father and wife were sleeping. He only had three hours to wait if they woke up at their normal time. He lay under the bed thinking about the happy times he had in the house with his mother. He didn't want to remember the beatings his mother or he got. It was his mother's smiling face as she baked bread in the kitchen that he loved most. She would always touch his nose with a flour covered finger and giggle.

The mattress above started to creak; they were waking up; it was an hour earlier than normal. He saw the women's bare feet land on the wooden bedroom floor and walk out through the door.

He slid out from under the bed on the women's side. His father always slept on the opposite side of the bed facing away from his now wife.

The bedroom door was open, so he walked over to it and closed it quietly. When he turned, he saw his father starting to stir, he was getting up.

"Hello, father," said Riadh.

The shocked look in his father's eyes was all he needed. He plunged the knife blade into his throat until it hit his spinal column. He held the knife hard against the throat so his father couldn't pull it out.

"That is for my mother."

He stood watching as his father grasped at the knife handle, fighting for his life. He was choking as the blood oozed out of his neck. His eyes were bulging in fear and shock. The only sound was from the gurgling of the blood in his mouth and windpipe.

It didn't take long for him to die. He would have suffered longer if Riadh had his way, but he had to leave before the wife came back upstairs. He calmly left the house without anyone even knowing he was there. He was three blocks away when he heard the distant sound of the wife's screams.

CHAPTER 17

Riadh journeyed Northwest through Iraq into Syria and then Turkey where he was employed by people smugglers. The smuggling operation was based in the busy port city of Bodrum in the Mugla province of southwestern Turkey. It was a very strategic port due to its proximity to the island of Kos in Greece. The island was a dumping ground for people being smuggled from Iraq, Iran, and Syria. Once the people landed on the island, they were then the responsibility of the Greek government.

He helped smuggle many people from Turkey. He gained the trust of the smugglers after six months and became an integral part of their operation. His thirst for bigger and better things in his life drove him to steal money from the head of the people smugglers. Fortunately for him at the time he stole the money one of the chief organizers that sourced people to be smuggled went missing. The Head of the operation a man by the name of Ilkin, sent out a hunting party to find him believing he'd stolen the money from him. Ilkin wasn't a man to mess with, he had a very violent background. Many of the boats he used to send undocumented immigrants out to sea weren't fit for a lake never mind the southern Aegean Sea. Scores of boats leaked, sank or the engines failed on route to the island of Kos from the southwestern tip of Turkey.

Riadh's opportunity to get out from under the tyrannical threat of this man came sooner than he expected. After a boat sank in the sea just off the Bodrum peninsula with forty Syrians on board there was an outcry from Greece for Turkey to do something to stop the smugglers. It wasn't until other European countries got involved and threatened various sanctions against Turkey that they chose to do something. There was an organized roundup of smugglers in Bodrum by a newly formed Turkish security force.

He was returning to the office building by the port which the smugglers had turned into living quarters. Next to the office was a small warehouse where they hid the people they would smuggle. They would house as many as sixty people in the warehouse for up to a week without any food or sanitation. It reminded Riadh of the early days after he and his mother were thrown out of the family home by his father.

Riadh wanted to check that his money was still where he had hidden it behind a loose rock in the wall of a warehouse. He stopped to pass the time away with two local fishermen that he had befriended. They liked Riadh and would often give him fish they had caught for his dinner. He sat with them for a minute to talk about the nets they were fixing. It fascinated him that they would be constantly repairing holes in the giant nets. One of the fishermen was showing him how to weave the netting material to make the repairs when two troop carriers raced past them. They were closely followed by two more which stopped close to the fisherman.

Heavily armed troops jumped out of the vehicles and shouted at the fisherman and Riadh to run to safety. They'd mistaken him for one of the fishermen. They didn't need to be told twice and ran along the quay as fast as they could away from the soldiers. He couldn't believe his luck as he ran away. Within a couple of minutes, he could hear automatic gun fire and explosions.

Unlike Ilkin and his small army of men he wasn't going to get into a firefight with the Turkish security forces and hid in the town for a couple of days. News traveled fast about the troops and the people they had targeted. None of the troops were killed but several were injured. The same could not be said for Ilkin and his men as they were all killed.

Riadh had waited long enough for the dust to settle after the firefight and made his way back to the harbor area where he recovered his hidden money. Two weeks later he was living in a squat in the French commune of Villeneuve-Saint-Georges in southeastern Paris. By the time he was twenty he was running a successful business, illegal but successful. His forte was smuggling alcohol and cigarettes in and out of France which earned him a small fortune. At twenty-five he was a millionaire with several properties in France and two in Istanbul. His drug smuggling operation through Turkey raised ten times the millions his cigarette and alcohol smuggling did and in half the time.

He had become well known amongst the underworld of gangsters as someone you did not cross.

CHAPTER 18

AHMAD, ISTANBUL HOSPITAL

Ahmad was unconscious for a week in the hospital in Istanbul. When he started to regain consciousness, he didn't have a clue where he was, in fact he thought that he was in Iraq. He opened his eyes slowly taking in his surroundings. As he became more conscious, he realized where he was, a hospital in Istanbul. There was a window opposite his bed, and he could see lights on the buildings outside, it was nighttime.

The following morning, he was half asleep when he heard voices. He was about to open his eyes when he heard a conversation between two men.

"He still hasn't gained consciousness."

"When he does call the police station, we need to interview him, he may be involved in the bombing in the city," said the second voice.

"I'm his doctor and nobody will speak to him until I think he is able to answer your question."

"We will see about that when he wakes up," said the second voice.

"You can leave the ward now," said the doctor.

"Is that a purple bruise or a birth mark on his right hand?" asked the second voice.

"A birth mark, now leave," replied the doctor.

Ahmad heard the foot fall of shoes walking away on a solid surface. He could not let the doctor know he had already gained consciousness, he had to get fit enough to escape. Another week passed when he was caught by a nurse with his eyes open. She was genuinely excited that he'd regained consciousness.

"Hello, you woke up," she said.

Ahmad had to think quickly.

"Yes, where am I," he said weakly.

"You're in a hospital in Istanbul, what is your name?" she asked.

"Mohamed," he replied.

"Where do you live; do you have somebody we can call?" she asked.

"Tunisia, on business," he replied.

He pretended to lose consciousness again and lay still waiting to see if she got the doctor. He could feel the nurse checking his pulse on his wrist, she then called out to someone.

"Doctor, he woke up," she shouted.

The doctor came over to the bed and checked Ahmad over. The light shining in his eyes made it difficult for Ahmad to make out that he'd passed out again.

"Sometimes this happens when people have been in a short coma, they wake up and drift back into the coma again. It's a good sign that his brain is functioning so he will regain consciousness gain soon. If he wakes again call me immediately, I want to check him out before the police come pounding in here," said the doctor.

"Yes, Doctor," she said.

Ahmad knew now that he had to get out of the hospital, the doctor couldn't hold the police back for much longer. In the night he assessed his mobility again as he'd done the previous three nights. When the nurses weren't around, and the other patients were asleep he stood next to the bed and did simple half squats and leg raises to strengthen them. The ribs still hurt a lot when he moved as did his shoulders and neck. The IVs in his arms weren't a problem, however, he didn't relish pulling out the catheter that was in his penis. He had no choice but to get out of the hospital that night. He would need pain killers to keep him going, he knew where the nurses kept the medications on the ward. They were in a flimsy lockable cabinet on wheels, he could get into that easily. Finding clothes wouldn't be a problem as there were a lot of patients' clothes in a cupboard at the end of the ward. At two in the morning the nurses always took a break and sat in the staff room. They were conscientious and only spent fifteen minutes to eat their food and have a drink. The staff room was outside the ward at the end of a long corridor. His exit would be halfway down the same corridor.

He pretended to be unconscious when the nurse that looked after him made her final round in the ward before taking her break. She stood by his bed checking the vital signs on the machine. She then made a couple of notes on the clipboard at the end of the bed before leaving.

He watched her disappear through the doors at the end of the ward and pushed himself to get out of the bed. Getting out of the bed was painful but he did it, now came the part he wasn't looking forward to.

The IVs came out easily, with little blood leaking out of the holes they left in the skin. The catheter was next, he peeled the tape off his penis that was holding the catheter in place. Then with a sharp intake of breath he pulled the tubing out of his penis. The sensation almost made him pass out as the tube never seemed to end. He didn't realize how long the tube was until it was in his hand. He was surprised at how out of breath he was. He had to give himself a minute to get his breath back.

The wardrobe had a lot of clothes inside, it didn't take him long to find some that fit him. He took a wire hanger out of the wardrobe and used it to open the medicine cart. As he skipped through the names on the bottles, he found one that he recognized as a strong pain killer. Next to the cart was a table with bandages, plaster, and alcohol wipes on it. He grabbed a handful of everything and put it into a plastic bag that was on the cart.

With a great deal of effort and pain he managed to get dressed. He walked through the ward and opened the doors slowly as they creaked. The light in the long corridor was dim, he assumed it was nighttime lighting. He used the wall to support himself as he walked down the corridor towards the fire exit door. The door led straight to the outside parking area. To his left was the emergency room entrance with three ambulances parked outside. He managed to get within twenty feet of the ambulances without being seen, but he was completely out of breath. Once again, he stopped to recover costing himself valuable minutes.

As he stood by the wall one of the ambulance crews came running out of the emergency room entrance. They jumped into the farthest ambulance and drove away quickly. They were followed by a second crew who took off in another ambulance. He was down to one chance and one chance only. He did not have the strength to try and high jack a car in the parking lot, he was so weak an old lady could have fought him off.

It was time to make his move and headed towards the final ambulance. Not surprisingly the driver's door wasn't locked, and the keys were in the ignition. Like the other ambulances it had been reversed up to the emergency room doors. This helped him as he didn't have to struggle doing a reversing move. The engine fired up first time and he was driving away without anyone even noticing.

At first, he didn't know where he was going to go, he just had to get some distance between him and the hospital. As he drove towards the outskirts of the city, he recognized a large mosque they'd passed on the way into Istanbul when they first arrived. Past the mosque was a large market building with many farmers delivery vehicles outside.

He found a quiet side street to dump the ambulance and headed towards the market. It was getting increasingly painful to move but he had to keep going. He stood and watched several pickups and delivery vehicles with canvas backs parked by the delivery doors of the market. Crossing the street unnoticed wasn't a problem as the place was a hive of activity. It was an hour before sunrise and the market was at its busiest before the buyers arrived.

He supported himself against the nearest canvas backed truck. The pain was getting too much, he took the bottle out of his pocket and took two tablets out. Swallowing them without water wasn't pleasant but he did it. Not too far in the distance he heard police sirens, he knew they'd discovered that he'd escaped from the hospital. The other problem was they will also know that he stole the ambulance. He heard voices and moved away from the truck into the shadow of the warehouse door. Two men came out of the market, one wheeling a cart. They both lifted the cart into the back of the truck and walked to the front. As the two men climbed into the cab, he grabbed hold of the tailgate and pulled himself up. He cocked one leg over the tailgate and rolled into the truck just as it pulled away. He gave a quiet cry of pain as his body landed in the bed of the truck. There wasn't anything in the back but the cart and the remains of leafy green vegetables. At the far end of the truck was a pile of burlap potato sacks. He crawled to the sacks and covered himself in them, they would keep him warm and out of sight. The painkillers started to take effect and he fell into a deep sleep.

CHAPTER 19

AL-QADIR JOINS US MILITARY

Al-Qadir became a very accomplished interpreter for the US military forces that occupied Iraq. He was with a patrol close to where Saddam Hussein was found hiding in a hole in the ground and wished he were with that patrol. He remembered how the people of Iraq celebrated when the news of his capture came out. Al-Qadir wasn't one of those that celebrated. He had nothing but hatred for the man and his generals that he allowed to kill innocent people. However, he did enjoy watching him being hung for his crimes. His hanging was all over the internet, and he was surprised at how often it was watched not only by the Iraqi interpreters but the US soldiers also.

His personal mission was to learn as much as he could from the military that he worked for. He watched everything they did and how they did it. He was given weapons training and proved to be a very adaptive learner. He was enjoying everything that he was being taught or that he was learning through the internet. One skill he wanted to perfect was the art of camouflage. The snipers in the military were exceptional at this art form. They even trained against their own soldiers and played a game of how close they could get to them without being seen. The desert camouflage clothing was basic to look at but highly technical at the same time. It was not just the clothing but the camouflage face paint they used.

He was shown how the face paint helped a soldier or particularly a sniper blend in with their surroundings. It also stopped the oils in bare skin from the reflection of the sun. This was particularly important when there was lighter skin against a darker background. The paint could be used for different shades of the desert, jungle or whatever the background was that you were working in. If you did not have the paint with you then he learnt that mud, soil, soot from a fire, juice of wild berries, anything could be used if it supported the background, you were in.

In private he honed those skills to an extremely high level. Through the internet he read as much as he could on warfare tactics and how to be a sniper. He watched the snipers in camp how they were continually cleaning and oiling their weapons. The other soldiers did this with their weapons but not like the snipers. Sand got everywhere and it could be that grain of sand that you missed that could cause your weapon to malfunction. The only weapon that he could see that the sand didn't affect was a knife, but this was kept extremely sharp.

In the early months he'd saved several soldiers on separate occasions from improvised explosive devises or IED's as they had become known. He fought side by side with the soldiers and respected by them for killing those that tried to ambush them. He'd gained the trust of the soldiers he worked for and in return got to see how they did their job up close. Some of the soldiers gave him lessons on hand-to-hand combat and knife fighting skills. He was a great student and became a crucial part of the unit he worked with.

He knew that the soldiers would never trust him one hundred percent and he knew why. Several interpreters in the past had betrayed the soldiers they were working with and had led them into an ambush. Others had turned their own weapons on the soldiers they were working with, so no complete trust was expected. He however trusted them implicitly, he never had a doubt that they would protect him as they would one of their own. He felt like he was one of the team and they always protected the team. The company of the soldiers was something he was getting to enjoy. They had become his extended family, not that he would tell them that.

CHAPTER 20

FIRST KILL

Al-Qadir was enjoying his new job working with the US marines. He had been with the current group of US Marines for a month. A month doesn't sound like much but when you eat, sleep, and walk in their shadow every day and night, it is long.

He'd supported them in firefights when they had been ambushed and proved to them that he could fight and be trusted. They had just entered a small village north of Tikrit hunting for a group of militants that had been targeting US fuel convoys. The villages were helpful in identifying which way the militants had gone. The information showed that they were a day behind them.

He was sat in the shade of a building with three soldiers eating K-rations and enjoying the break. The K-rations were a high nutrient food issued to soldiers by the US military for use in the field. He watched the local villages go past, all of them waived to the soldiers. Hidden from view there was someone also watching them. None of the soldiers or Al-Qadir realized that they were being watched. The man was on the roof of a building three blocks away using binoculars.

Al-Qadir's mind was drifting thinking about his father and mother when he saw a familiar face across the road. He blinked a couple of times to get his eyes used to the sun again. It was him Sergeant Jassim, he was walking into a house.

"Let's go," said the major sat next to Al-Qadir.

Al-Qadir didn't hear him or move, he was going to run across the road and stab the man. The major grabbed his shoulder and shook him, bringing his focus back.

"Did you hear me? Let's go."

"Yes, coming," he said.

He kept his head down as they walked away; he didn't want the sergeant to recognize him. He was becoming calm again and felt a sense of contentment knowing that he'd found his first target.

The major got his troops together in their vehicles and they drove back in the direction of Tikrit. He'd given the last location of the militants and it was passed onto another group of Marines that were further north.

There was a small group of dilapidated buildings close to the road a mile outside the village. The position of the buildings allowed the military vehicles to be hidden from the road and gave shelter to the troops for the night. If the militants doubled back, they would be waiting to ambush them.

As always Al-Qadir volunteered to keep a watch on the road from another position. It was something he had done on many occasions. There wasn't any argument and he walked off into the dark.

It only took him nine minutes to get to the house where he had seen Sergeant Jassim. The house was at the end of a row of houses, all of which had seen better days. There were two window openings in the rear and one to the front. He moved cautiously as he did not want to spook the occupants of the house.

The window openings in the rear, like the front did not have any glass in them. They had wooden shutters at one time, but they too were missing. He listened for any noises inside but couldn't hear any. He climbed through one of the windows and jumped quietly onto the dirt floor. Still there was not a sound inside. There were only two rooms in the tiny single-story house. The one he was in was a kitchen of sorts and the front room had a wooden chair, a table and a tiny twelve-inch television. The house was empty, Sergeant Jassim wasn't home. He climbed back out through the window and made his way to the street. He couldn't spend too much time looking for the sergeant as the Marines would expect him to check-in. He stood on a street corner for ten minutes across from a local café. It was busy with local men smoking and talking which was a favorite pastime of many men in Iraq. There was no sign of the sergeant, he decided to come back another time.

Blending in with the locals were two men, one of them was the one on the roof earlier watching the marines. He took a particular interest in what Al-Qadir was doing.

Al-Qadir walked away from the street corner and made his way back to the marines' location. He'd only gone forty yards when the sergeant came out of a side street. Al-Qadir threw himself against the wall behind him and waited for the sergeant to pass him. He didn't even know Al-Qadir was lying in wait for him until a hand went over his mouth.

The sergeant was tired after spending all day trying to find work. His new life in this shitty little village was a living hell. He wished he'd stayed in Baqubah, but he knew that he couldn't. His betrayal of the policemen's women and children to the mayor had gotten out and he had to run to save his life.

A hand clamped over his mouth and dragged him into the narrow side street. He tried to struggle but it didn't help he was being held hard against a wall.

Al-Qadir quickly shoved a clothe into the sergeant's mouth to keep him quiet. He then took out a small flashlight and shone it on his own face for the sergeant to see.

The face that appeared in the light terrified him; it was General Hadi's son. The young man's eyes looked crazed as they bored holes into his sole.

One of the men from the café ran around the buildings to get a better position to see what the young man was up to. He was only fifty feet behind him as he dropped quietly behind a donkey cart. He was very curious as to what he was up to when the young man dragged another man into an alleyway with swift expertise. He stayed hidden and listened to their conversation.

"You know who I am," said Al-Qadir. "I'm going to take my hand off your mouth, if you try to shout or call out, I will slit your throat, do you understand?"

The man said nothing, he just tried to nod his head.

"What do you want from me?" said Jassim.

"You know what I want, you gave away the location of the safe houses to General Ashkouri," said Al-Qadir.

"No, I didn't," replied Jassim pleading.

"Yes, you did my father told me."

"No, I didn't please, I didn't."

Al-Qadir pulled out his knife and stuck it into Jassim's shoulder blade where it joined the arm. His screams couldn't be heard as the gag was back in his mouth.

"I will ask one more time and then I'm going to cut out your tongue for lying to me."

"OK, but I didn't tell Ashkouri, I told the mayor. I didn't know he was going to betray them."

"In my eyes you told the general and you are responsible for the murders and rapes of the women and girls."

"Wait, what if I tell you the names of the two policemen that told Ashkouri, will you let me go? Please believe my I'm sorry for what I did."

"Give me their names, don't lie and I will let you go."

"Ali and Hamdy, they are the ones you want."

He already knew the names, but Jassim had just confirmed them. He smiled and let go of him.

"OK," said Al-Qadir.

"I can go?" he replied with a smile on his face.

"Yes, straight to hell."

The knife slid across the throat smoothly and slowly. He let the body drop to the floor and watched in the beam of the flashlight as the sergeant slowly bled to death.

"That was for my family and the families you destroyed," said Al-Qadir.

He put his hand into his pocket and pulled out a card, it was his first death card. The hammer and nail did its work, and the card was nailed to the sergeant's forehead.

Feeling invigorated he ran like the wind back to the marine encampment. Thankfully, he hadn't been missed as he gave his flashlight signal to return to the camp from the road. A return flashlight signal told him it was clear to proceed into the camp. That night he had the best night's sleep he'd had in a long time.

The man listening and watching what the young man was doing was extremely impressed. The young man killed without thought or remorse. By the sounds of the conversation, he had every reason to kill the other man. After the man was killed the young man did something to the dead man's head but he couldn't see what. He disappeared back into the darkness as the young man ran into the night. Back at the café he didn't say anything to the local Iraqi where he'd been or what he saw.

The following day the body of the man was discovered by a local. Word spread through the small village quickly. The throat had been cut and a card of some kind had been nailed to the dead man's forehead.

Now the man from the café realized nailing the card to the forehead must have been what he was doing when he couldn't see clearly. It intrigued him and asked the local Iraqi he was with if he could look at the body before it was buried.

There wasn't a mortuary or anything like it in the village, so the body was kept in the local butcher's shop refrigerator until it was due to be removed for burial. With a few coins placed in the palm of his hand the butcher allowed them into the fridge.

He unfolded the off-white cloth that the body was wrapped in just enough to see the head.

"What is that?" asked the Iraqi.

"I don't know," lied the man.

They recovered the head and left.

He knew what the card was but couldn't tell the locals as it may turn the people against the US troops. It was a death card that had been nailed to the forehead of the dead body. Something he had seen before but this one was different; it had been nailed to the body not tossed onto the body. It looked like the printed skeleton and scythe had been patched together from different cards. His gut told him that he would be seeing or hearing about more of these cards. If this were an Iraqi doing this it may be accepted by the people, if it were a foreigner there would be a serious backlash from the people.

He would make it his mission to find who this person was and what was behind the death cards. There had to be a story behind them.

CHAPTER 21

ESCAPE FROM TURKEY

Ahmad woke up in the back of the truck to the sound of machinery, the potato sacks startled him as he threw them off. At first, he had forgotten where he was as he rubbed his eyes, it came back very quickly. It felt like his body was in even more pain than before, he soon realized that the pain killers had worn off. He quickly popped two painkillers into his mouth, swallowing them proved even more difficult than the time before due to his severe dry throat.

Keeping low he crawled to the tailgate of the truck to see where he was. There was a huge wooden structure that looked like a barn and a small mud brick farmhouse. The buildings were encircled by perfectly straight rows of green vegetables. He climbed out of the truck to check if there was anyone around. He could see several people working in one field and an old tractor churning the dirt up in another. He couldn't go to the house as the farmer's wife was most probably inside. He headed towards the barn building, a good place to hide. Next to the barn door was a water trough filled with what looked like clean water. He cupped his hands and scooped a small amount up, it tasted good. He stuck his hands back into the trough and rinsed his face. He didn't notice it at first but there was a gallon sized ceramic pot next to the trough, he filled it with water and went into the barn. The smell in the barn made him gag at first. It was where the farmer kept his cows when he milked them, there was dung everywhere. To one side was a wire rat catching cage with two rats inside trying to chew their way out. Above his head was a loft, it looked like a good place to hide. Unfortunately, there wasn't a ladder to get up into the loft.

After a quick walk around the inside of the barn he found a way to get up to the loft. By using the frame of the barn and the horizontal wooden slats he managed to get into the loft. The effort took its toll on his body, particularly his ribs. There was dust everywhere as beams of sunlight shone through the slats in the barn wall highlighting the dust in the air. In one corner there was a pile of old burlap sacks and what was once a straw bale. He pulled at the sacks and put them in a pile to make himself a bed to lay down. He disturbed at least a dozen rats as the scampered in all directions to get away from the intruder. He jumped back when the rats came out and cursed at himself as he gave out a little scream of pain. He lay down on the straw and covered himself with the sacks, once more the pain killers took effect and he fell asleep.

Without knowing it he slept for twelve hours. He woke up to the sound of the tractor in the farmyard. It was morning and the sun had just started to rise above the tree line in the distance. From under the sacks, he peered through the barn slats to see what was going on outside. The tractor was loading large crates of vegetables into the back of the truck, it was going to the market again.

There was a smell of food drifting into the barn from the farmhouse, it made him realize how long it had been since he had eaten. Hamad's stomach was making so much noise from the lack of food he thought that the farmer outside would hear it. He looked for the ceramic pot of water and realized he had left it on the barn floor. He would have to wait until the farmer drove away in his truck before he could get it.

The voices of a woman and children carried through the barn walls. Looking through the slats he could see them clearly, three young boys, a girl, and a woman. They were all getting into the back of the truck, he could not believe his luck. He watched as the truck drove down the farm road and out of sight. He climbed down from the loft to drink the water in the ceramic pot. He suddenly started to feel the chilly morning air as he was no longer under the warmth of the sacks, he started to shiver. He climbed back up into the loft and found what looked like an old donkey blanket to wrap around his shoulders. He then tore strips out of the old sacks and wrapped them around his hands. He was already getting warmer, especially his hands.

The truck had been gone for fifteen minutes before he climbed back down from the loft. He gave thanks to Allah for the ceramic jug as he drank more water, this time in small gulps. He kept listening for anyone outside, but it was quiet. He slipped out of the barn and walked over to the farmhouse. He knocked on the door just in case someone was still in the home, nobody answered. He opened the door and stepped inside. It was a dirt floored room with a wooden table three chairs and a fire on one side that was still burning. On the table was a metal pot with a lid, it was sitting on a flat stone so as not to burn the wood table. Next to the pot on a wooden board was a pile of Pide ekmek, a type of Turkish flat bread that was partly covered with a cloth. When he took the cloth off it looked just like a bread his mother used to make in Iraq, it made him homesick.

The smell of the bread drove him crazy as did the contents of the pot. He picked up a piece of the bread and ate it like an animal tearing it with his teeth. He was curious as what was in the pot and lifted the lid. It was still red hot from the fire and burnt the tips of his fingers causing him to drop it back onto the pot. He used a piece of the bread to lift the lid off the pot, inside was Orman kebab. The Turkish stew had lamb, carrots, potatoes, and other vegetables that he didn't care about.

He dipped the bread into the stew and grabbed some of the meat and vegetables. He blew on it to try to cool it down, but he still burnt his mouth a little as he ate. He had eaten three pieces of bread and a sizable amount of the stew before he realized what he had done. He looked at the wooden table and realized that he had splashed all over it with stew. He looked for something to wipe the table and try to hide that anyone had been inside. When the family returned, they would soon know that someone had been at the stew and bread. To try to make up for the missing stew he added water and some cut vegetables that were in a basket, it looked a lot better. He placed the pot on the hook over the fire to heat it up again as the water had cooled it down. He hoped that by heating the stew up again he could put it back on the table and the raw vegetables would cook. His problem was the bread he could not hide the fact that three pieces had gone, he had an idea. Within a minute he returned with the two rats in the cage and let them out inside the house, they ran to dark places to hide. There were crumbs of the bread on the floor that he had eaten, and he knew they would come out of hiding to eat them. Hopefully, the woman would blame the rats for the missing bread when she returned. After twenty minutes he took the pot off the fire and placed it back on the table. One last look before he left, everything looked good.

It took him four hours of walking before he came to a town with an oversized mosque. The pain was returning but he did not want to take more pills until he knew he was safe to sleep. He went to the mosque as he had not prayed in weeks. Inside there were only a couple of men praying as he took his stolen sandals off. He looked like a vagrant after sleeping rough in the truck and barn. He hadn't noticed but there were pieces of straw stuck to his blanket and clothing, he smelt strongly of body odor and donkey.

The Iman saw the tramp walk into the mosque and watched him as he prayed. By the look of him the poor man needed a wash, clean clothing, and food. He waited until he finished praying and stopped him at the door as he was about to leave.

"You don't have a home?" asked the Iman.

Ahmad shook his head indicating that he didn't. He couldn't speak as his accent would give him away.

"Come with me," said the Iman.

Ahmad followed the Iman knowing that he was in safe hands, many mosques took care of the homeless. At the back of the mosque was a small building that housed local homeless men. He walked him to the back where there was a room with mats on the floor where they slept. A man approached them which made him nervous.

"Can you make sure this poor sole gets a wash and new clothing," said the Iman.

"Yes, what is your name?" he asked Ahmad.

He held his head down as if he was scared and said nothing. The act he was about to put on was surprising even to him, but he had to survive, or he would be get caught. If he were caught, he knew that the police would torture him until he died.

Ahmad curled his hands up into his chest as if he feared for his safety.

"You are safe here nobody will harm you; do you want to bathe?" said the man.

He nodded his head to say he did but kept his face towards the floor. He was taken into a small room where there was a shower head on the wall. He stood still again acting as if he was scared.

"I will be back in a minute with fresh clothes," said the man.

He had to keep the act up and waited until the man returned before he moved. He hadn't been gone long when he came back into the room with a bundle of neatly folded clean clothes.

"I will leave you alone to bathe, nobody will come in," he said closing the door as he left.

He could not wait to get the dirty clothes off and stood under the cold shower for what seemed an eternity. The block of soap was welcome, but it hurt when he rubbed his sides with it. He checked his body as best he could, the wounds and bruising did not look as bad as he'd expected. The care he had received in the hospital had helped them repair well.

When the man returned, he was standing in the clean clothes with his hands tucked under his armpits for warmth. This also gave the appearance that he was scared. He was shown into another room with bunk beds down one side. Next to the bunk bedroom was a small dining room and open fire kitchen. Gently the man told him to go into the dining room where he was given a bowl of red lentil soup and a huge chunk of bread. He ate it like he had not eaten in weeks as he was being watched by the man that served him. The man smiled as he watched the hungry man eat and walked away.

He took two pain killers and a gulp of water. The fire in the kitchen was giving off the most amazing amount of heat. On the wooden bench next to him was a well-read newspaper, the Daily Sabah. It was folded over and the article looking at him was about the bombs that Mutaz had detonated. The newspaper was old; the article was more of an update on what had happened. He did not pick the newspaper up as he didn't want anyone knowing that he could read. Then he read something that scared him, they were looking for an escaped patient from the hospital with a purple birth mark on his right hand. Without realizing it he covered his right hand and looked around to see if anyone was looking at him, they weren't. This was when he realized that the clothes, he was wearing were a little too big for him and the sleeves were too long covering his hands. He thanked Allah for protecting him and would now have to keep his right hand completely covered. This would not be hard to do as it was winter and a pair of woolen gloves with hole for the fingertips would work.

CHAPTER 22

Ahmad spent months at the mosque paying for his accommodation by cleaning and doing day to day chores for the Iman. His body was fully healed, and he was quietly getting back to exercising to strengthen himself for the journey ahead. He was known by the other homeless men and staff at the mosque as the mute because he never spoke and very rarely raised his head.

It took Ahmad a month before he found out exactly where he was in Turkey. It surprised him to find out that the town he was living in, Catalca, was only thirty-five miles east of Istanbul. Over time he got to know who owned the local shops and who had money in the community. He needed money to get out of Turkey and he was on the lookout for someone to rob.

He had one target in mind that he thought had money hidden away in his shop. He used the same place to beg across the road from his shop, he never saw the owner go to the local bank. Over several nights he watched the shop owner lock the shop door from the inside. He then carried a small cloth bag into the rear of the shop. Ahmad would reposition himself to the rear of the shop and through a gap in the curtain in the rear window he could see the shop owner inside bending over something in the corner of the room. It was always dark when the shop closed so the light inside the room gave him a clear view of what was going on. The shop owner would then go through a door and upstairs to where he lived above the shop. His ritual seemed to be the same when he went upstairs, light on, television on. The television was so loud he could hear everything outside, the must have been hard of hearing.

Ahmad knew that he had to get inside the shop, find the hiding place for the money, steal it, and get out of town and far away before it was discovered. He listened to locals talking about the local police, the roads, markets, and the port of Istanbul. He had located a car he could steal that was in good condition. It wasn't likely to break down as it belonged to the local car repair shop. The car was always parked in the same place outside the garage and was rarely driven. He didn't really need the keys as he could hot wire it. The problem was if the police stopped him, they would know it was stolen. When the mechanics had lunch, they went to one end of the garage and sat next to a workbench. The car keys for all vehicles were kept on a board at the other end of the garage by the roller doors. On the day that he would decide to run he would steal the keys, that day came quicker than he expected.

Two days later Ahmad was walking back to the mosque to eat lunch with the rest of the homeless men. It had become a daily ritual for all of them. As he was about to walk around the corner of the mosque, he saw several police officers. They were dragging the homeless men out of the building where they had met for lunch. He jumped back against the wall in the hope that he had not been seen. A car drove past him and scared him as he did not realize that it was there. He popped his head around the corner quickly to see what was happening.

The Iman was protesting strongly to the police officers' as they pulled the homeless out of the shelter. He could hear him arguing with the police officers that they weren't allowed to remove the men as it was part of the mosque, which technically it wasn't.

Someone tapped Ahmad on the shoulder startling him, it was one of his homeless friends.

"Quickly, follow me into the mosque," he said.

They both ran to the side door of the mosque and stepped inside. After removing their shoes, they headed to the back of the mosque. They knew they were safe inside the mosque as the police would not enter a holy place.

"I heard a police officer say that they were raiding all the places where the homeless stay. Why can't they leave us alone?" he said.

Ahmad knew they were looking for him he had to leave the town that night. He could see his homeless friend watching him, so he started to rock gently back and forward. He held his gloved hands under his armpits making out he was scared.

"It's OK, they don't know we are in here," said his friend putting his arm around him.

Although he wanted to run that night, he could not leave the mosque for fear that the police were watching. He waited until the next morning and walked to the garage. He didn't take the main road which he normally did for fear of seeing the police. Instead, he kept to the side streets and alleys. He watched the garage for thirty minutes before the men went into the back to eat lunch. He stole the car keys from the board without anyone seeing him.

So that it did not look suspicious he ate lunch and dinner at the mosque. He kept to his normal routine so as not to attract attention. Once it was dark, he kept watch on the shop.

Like clockwork the owner locked the shop door from the inside at ten o'clock and turned the lights off as he went into the back. He gave the man time to go upstairs and settle down to watch his television which by the sound coming from it he did just that.

Opening the window was not a problem as the old wooden frame had distorted over time. He slid his knife blade under the catch holding the window closed and flicked it open. He gave a quick look around to make sure nobody was watching and climbed through the window. It was pitch dark inside so he lit a match so that he could see. In front of him on a table was a candle, he lit it.

He couldn't see a cupboard or box of any kind in the corner where the shop keeper bent over every night. There was a small stack of books on the wooden floorboards. He thought that the pile of books must be false, they were hiding a container inside. He grabbed the top book expecting it to be attached to the next one down, but it wasn't. After flicking through the pages of five books he couldn't make out where the man hid his money. Then in the flickering light of the candle he saw a half circle in the dust on the floorboard next to the last book. He went to pick it up, it did not move, so he twisted the book to follow the marks in the dust. As the book lined up with the floorboard, he lifted it. A two-foot section of the wooden floor came away with the book. Under the section of flooring was another piece of wood that turned with the book. It was a primitive but effective locking mechanism. Holding the candle close to the hole in the floor he saw a metal box and lifted it out. Coins rattled inside causing him to freeze. His heart was pounding as he listened for movement upstairs, there was none.

He put the floorboard back in place locked it with the book and placed the remaining books on top as they were before. It all looked exactly as it was before he arrived. He didn't check the metal box until he was a couple of streets away. It had a simple key lock on it which he quickly forced open with his knife. He could not believe his luck; it was full of money.

As he had hoped the car at the garage started first time and he was on the road headed out of the town. He would have a good eight-hour head start before the garage owner noticed the car was missing. Hopefully, the shop owner wouldn't check his cash box until the next night after he closed. He headed towards Greece where he hoped that he could find a way of being smuggled out to somewhere in Europe. He knew roughly where Mutaz would be going in Paris, and he wanted to get his revenge. He knew now that he would have to wait to go to Paris as the Turkish police would have circulated his description to Interpol. He was now a wanted terrorist according to the Turks. He had dumped the original stolen car from the garage into a river and stolen other cars to get him to his destination. He hoped by stealing and dumping different cars the police wouldn't be able to track him so easily.

He worked his way through Greece to the port of Piraeus southwest of the city of Athens. Piraeus was the perfect place for him to find a ship that would go to Egypt, as it was the largest port in Greece and Europe. The port was split into three principal areas, the passenger port for cruise ships, the central port was for local ferries to the Greek islands. The western part of the port formed the third area which was for freight or commercial shipping. It was the western port for which he was aiming.

Talking to some of the sailors on the shore he soon found out the names of two ships that were sailing to Alexandria, Egypt. He got lucky with one sailor who told him that they were shorthanded and needed crew for loading the cargo hold.

The next day he was at work sweating in the cargo hold moving nets of cargo into position. The heat was getting to him and the woolen gloves he was wearing did not help. He felt secure now and discarded them in a trash can on the quay. It only took three days, and the ship was ready to sail. He tried to get a job on board, but the captain wanted photo I.D.'s that he could show to the authorities when they arrived in Alexandria. He left the ship only to return that night before it was due to leave. Working in the hold had proven a bonus for him as he knew the layout and where he could hide until they reached Egypt. He had three bottles of water and a small stack of pita breads to keep him sustained for the journey, with his hiding place located he fell asleep confident nobody would find him. He woke in the darkness of the ship's cargo hold tired and restless after on a couple of hours sleep in the two days on board. He waited until he saw the hold doors opening above him before he moved to another hiding place. He watched as the cargo was gently removed from the ships hold.

The workers were Egyptian, he could tell by their accent and by the clothes they were wearing. His clothes were similar but not the same. He rummaged through the small amount of clothes he'd brought with him and found what he was looking for. With a quick change he now blended in perfectly. He had to leave his remaining items as he would stand out if he were seen carrying something.

CHAPTER 23

AL-QADIR MEETS CIA OPERATIVE

He was on yet another raid with a special forces group from America when he was approached by a CIA operative called Brad. He didn't know he was with the CIA, but he had his suspicions due to the kind of questions the man asked, and he doubted that his real name was Brad.

He took Al-Qadir under his wing and trained him for six months in Iraq and Iran. He was trained in counter insurgency and sniper tactics. Intelligence gathering became one of his many new skills he learnt from the CIA operative. He was a natural and gained people's confidence and trust quickly. Brad knew about the attack on his police unit and the deaths of his family. He offered to help locate the generals responsible for the atrocities committed on his family and those of his small town. There was obviously a catch and that was he had to work with Brad on undercover missions for the CIA first.

It was on a mission on the Iraq-Iran border when Al-Qadir's loyalty was truly tested. He was with Brad heading towards the Iraq border out of Iran in their Safir Jeep. It was an Iranian 4x4 multipurpose military vehicle built by Fath Vehicle Industries. They were cheap to produce and rolled off the assembly line in their thousands for the military. Their Safir was the same color as the Iranian military but didn't have any military markings. Their mission was to gather intelligence on three nuclear scientists that were being held in Iran. Intelligence suggested that they were assisting in the development of Iran's nuclear program. They had located two of the scientists, but neither was being held under duress, they lived in substantial homes and drove their own vehicles. They were moving around freely. Al-Qadir did not understand why they didn't just assassinate them, but Brad told him that was not their call.

Armed with the intelligence they had gathered they drove through the night towards the Iraq border where an extraction team would meet them. It was a bumpy, slow drive through the desert terrain. They had already driven ninety miles and were feeling the effects of being bounced around in the vehicle.

The sun was setting, and it would soon be dark when two military vehicles drove out of a deep dry riverbed or Wadi as they were known. There was a large troop carrier carrying eight soldiers and a Safir like their vehicle with another four soldiers inside.

They initially tried to outrun the soldiers, but their vehicles had two of its tires shot out. It was now down to a fire fight in the desert. They were completely outnumbered and outgunned. Between them they managed to kill four soldiers before the CIA man was wounded. He was shot in the thigh and told Al-Qadir to run and hide in the desert. His job was to get to Iraq and pass on the intelligence they had gathered. With much regret he did as he was told but not before he shot two of the tires on the Iranian soldiers Safir. This meant they would only have the use of the heavier and slower troop carrier.

It wasn't long after he made his escape that the Soldiers captured the CIA man. A group of four soldiers fanned out in search for Al-Qadir. He watched them as they moved in his direction. He knew he would not be able to help his friend and colleague, but he could take out at least a couple of the soldiers. He moved quickly from one desert rock outcrop to another trying to find a vantage point. He found a good place to shoot from between two rocks. He carefully took aim with his sniper rifle picking out the soldiers through his scope. They were easy targets as they were only about four hundred yards away. Due to the sandy and rocky terrain he knew that the minute he fired they would take cover. His goal was to try to kill all four but that wasn't possible in this terrain. The first shot rang out loudly in the desert quickly followed by the second. Two soldiers died instantly but the second two took cover. The remaining soldiers by the troop carrier started firing wildly in the direction of where the shots were coming from. They were shouting at their colleagues to run back to their position. Five minutes later the troop carrier left in a cloud of dust with their prisoner safely inside.

Al-Qadir watched as they left and quickly ran towards the two disabled vehicles. He scrambled to check the spare tire in the military vehicle, to his amazement it was a good spare. However, there wasn't a jack or wheel brace. He went back to his damaged Safir and removed the spare wheel and jack. Within Fifteen minutes he had replaced both damaged wheels on the Iranian military Safir. He decided to use this vehicle and not his own as it had military markings which their vehicle didn't. He hoped this would give him a slight advantage if he came across more Iranian military. He collected the two Jerry cans full of diesel and the medical kit from his damaged Safir before he gave chase. Eventually he saw the lights of the big troop carrier in the distance, they had a good head start on him. He couldn't put his vehicles lights on and drove by the light of the moon, he didn't want the soldiers ahead to see him following.

CHAPTER 24

After two hours of driving, he could not see the troop carrier's lights anymore. This meant that they had seen him following and were preparing to ambush him or they felt it was safe to stop for the night. The nearest military barracks was another six hours drive and a slow six hours through the desert road.

As he came over a rise in the road, he thought he saw a light flicker in the distance. This made Al-Qadir slow down. He could not make out what or where the light was as he drove down into a small valley. He drove slowly for another mile trying to keep the engine noise down to a minimum. Sound travelled a long-distance in the desert especially at night. As he came out of the valley, he pulled off the road before he got to the top of the next rise.

Al-Qadir moved slowly and quietly to the top of a ridge which gave him a good vantage point. There in the distance about three miles away was the flickering light of a campfire. That was all he could see, no men and no vehicle. He moved cautiously on foot keeping to the low ground so not to create a silhouette for the troops to see. When he could he jogged for a hundred yards and then stopped to listen for any telltale sounds of the troops or someone waiting to ambush him. An hour later he got within a few hundred yards of where he thought the campfire was. He tried his best to keep moving in its direction but staying in the lower levels of the desert meant he couldn't see the fire.

Al-Qadir was sweating profusely even though the desert was starting to get very cold. He kept low and moved to a high point behind an outcrop of rocks. He now had a good vantage point and could see the campfire clearly. He could also see the troop carrier parked behind a rocky outcrop. He could make out the images of four soldiers sitting around the fire that meant there were two others somewhere, on guard. He spent another fifteen minutes getting closer to the campfire trying to see if he could locate the two missing soldiers. He was now within thirty feet of the soldiers sitting around the fire. He could hear them talking about the prisoner and what they had done to him. They had beaten him but not enough to kill him as they needed to keep him alive.

He had to find the other two soldiers; he could easily kill the four around the fire but the remaining two may kill his colleague if they heard shooting. He spent another ten minutes moving towards the troop carrier when he saw movement in his peripheral vision. It was one of the soldiers he was relieving himself into the sand.

Al-Qadir still could not see the second soldier, but he had to deal with this one swiftly. He crept up behind him just as he was buttoning up his pants. The move was swift and deadly as he expertly grabbed the soldiers head and turned it one way then quickly the other snapping his neck. He lowered the lifeless body to the floor so as not to make any noise.

Al-Qadir was on the move again this time towards the troop carrier. He kept low as he approached the vehicle, he hoped Brad was being held inside the vehicle. As he got to the front of the vehicle he heard a voice, it was the other soldier, he was taunting his prisoner.

The soldier was cursing the prisoner in very broken English. He was enjoying stepping on the wound on the prisoner's hip. The prisoner never cried out in pain, he just gritted his teeth and made a guttural groan. This angered the soldier as he wanted to hear him scream and beg for mercy. He raised his fist to punch the CIA man again, but it never did strike.

The soldier was too pre-occupied to see his enemy approaching. Al-Qadir moved in for the kill with his knife in his right hand. He placed his left hand over the soldier's mouth and slit his throat with the knife.

Brad couldn't see his partner due to his eyes being swollen shut from the beatings, but he knew he was there.

"We have to move," said Al-Qadir as he cut the rope tied around his wrists and ankles.

Brad just nodded that he understood.

He lifted him to his feet and placed one arm around his shoulder for support. He was moving very slowly due to the wound on his hip and the injuries from the severe beatings he had been given. This was going to take too long trying to get him across the rocky terrain back to the Safir. He lay Brad down in the sand in a slight hollow.

"Keep quiet, I will be back soon," he said.

Al-Qadir had to get Brad into the troop carrier and drive back to the Safir. First, he had to take care of the other soldiers. He made his way around the troop carrier to get a better view of the campfire and the soldiers. To his surprise he only saw three of them, one had moved, this was when he heard the crunch of a boot on sand behind him. He dropped to the ground turning towards the sound at the same time.

One of the soldiers decided to give the soldier watching the prisoner a break. He picked up his metal mug filled with hot coffee and walked to the troop carrier. He thought that he saw one of his fellow soldiers moving around the rear of the carrier and decided to sneak up on him to scare him, one of the games he liked to play. He got within twenty feet when he realized it wasn't one of their own soldiers. He drew his side arm quietly and was about to say something to the stranger when the man dropped to the ground.

Al-Qadir knew dropping to the ground would give him a split-second advantage, one that he needed. As he turned on the drop, he saw his target and fired two rounds in rapid succession into the soldier. He watched as he fell backwards his gun still in his hand in a death grip.

The sound of the handgun firing twice alerted the three soldiers by the fire and they ran towards the troop carrier with automatic weapons raised. They fanned out as they approached calling to their colleagues.

Al-Qadir was on the move trying to get a better view of the soldiers as they approached. He crouched down behind a rock as a soldier moved past him swinging his rifle slowly side to side as he aimed at invisible targets. This was the easy kill as he shot the soldier in the head from ten feet. He dropped down behind the rock again as a barrage of bullets hit the rock and sand around it.

The two soldiers heard the single shot and saw one of their own drop to the floor, they both fired wildly in the direction where they thought the assailant was. They now moved more cautiously giving hand signals which way they should move. They each gave another short burst of fire at the rock, they moved to cover both sides as they approached. One of the soldiers changed direction signaling to his colleague that he was going straight to the rock. As he got within a couple of feet, he crouched down listening for movement but couldn't hear anything. The top of the rock was two feet higher than him, but it had several good foot holds. He stepped onto the front of the rock and pulled himself up. He lifted his automatic rifle and fired blindly down behind the rock where the attacker was hiding. He then jumped down from the rock and slid around behind to find the body.

Al-Qadir being on the blind side of the rock used it to his advantage. He crawled on his hands and knees as the barrage of fire hit the rock. He got himself into another position thirty feet from the rock. It wasn't long before he saw the automatic rifle being fired over the rock and the two soldiers creeping forward. As one pointed his weapon behind the rock Al-Qadir had a clear shot. He fired two rounds into one soldier hitting him high on the shoulder the other tore through the side of his neck. Before the other soldier could respond he shot him through the top of his head.

The threats had been neutralized he now had to get Brad to safety and tend to his wounds. They had a long journey ahead, they needed to get to the border before the soldiers' bodies were found.

CHAPTER 25

GERMANY

Al-Qadir had done a respectable job of cleaning and sanitizing Brad's wounds from the gun shot and beatings, but professional help was now needed. It took him a full twelve hours to get Brad across the border to safety and medical care. They were both eventually flown to a US military base in Germany where Brad was hospitalized. This was the first time Al-Qadir had been outside of Iraq or Iran.

Brad ensured that Al-Qadir had a pass to enter and leave the base at any time, he was also given access to the hospital on the base. He enjoyed Germany and took a two-day side trip to France in a car he borrowed from the base carpool while Brad recovered. He enjoyed this newfound European life.

It was just over two weeks after their arrival in Germany that Brad was to be relocated back to the USA for further medical care. This news did not sit well with Al-Qadir as his future was now uncertain. He walked into Brad's hospital room; a doctor was visiting him. From the expression on Brad's face the doctor's visit was not going well.

"Thank you, Doctor," said Brad.

The doctor turned and smiled at Al-Qadir as he left the room.

"What is going on?" asked Al-Qadir.

"They are sending me back to the US. The doctors here have done all they can for me. The wound was worse than we thought, and the infection got into my hip bone," said Brad.

"You will be OK, won't you?" asked Al-Qadir.

"Yes and no. I will be medically OK, but the doctor said there is a strong possibility that I will have limited movement in my hip and leg."

"What does that mean?" asked Al-Qadir.

"It means that I will most probably be taken out of deep cover field work and placed behind a desk somewhere. Brad saw the shock and now uncertainty in his friend's face. "I have made a couple of phone calls on your behalf. I asked for you to be allowed to return to the USA with me, but my request was denied. I fought hard for you but the powers in Washington refused point blank. They did however tell me that you will be returned to Iraq to continue to work with the US troops on the ground," said Brad.

"What if I don't want to return, I have done everything you have asked of me. You gave me your word that you would help me locate the General's and soldiers responsible for the deaths of my family." He could feel the anger and hatred building inside at the betrayal of his friend and his country. "I will go back but I won't work for your government anymore," he replied storming towards the door.

"Wait, wait I haven't finished telling you everything," shouted Brad just as his friend disappeared through the door.

Al-Qadir stopped in the corridor outside the room, he felt used and betrayed. He could hear Brad shouting from inside the room, he was telling him to go back inside. Against his better judgement he did.

"What now?" he shouted angrily.

"Close the door and sit down. This isn't as bad as you think it is. When I go back to the USA, I will have access to a great deal of intelligence, which I will get clearance for to share with you. That intelligence would hopefully lead you to the men you seek. I have been given the authority to have you continue not only as an interpreter for the military in Iraq but for additional covert operations. These other operations you would perform on your own but sanctioned from the highest levels and under my command."

"Why would I do this, your country has turned its back on me?" he replied.

"The United States hasn't turned its back on you, and I can assure you that you will get US citizenship as soon as I can arrange it. It is a lengthy process even at my level but once they see what an asset you are, they will authorize it. Part of your new duties will be to locate members of the Saddam military regime that have committed atrocities. You will be authorized to bring them to justice by any means. Do you understand what I am saying?" asked Brad.

"Yes, of course I understand. I thought that I would return with you and get out of this war. But I know I cannot get out until I fulfil the promise to my father."

"I take it that you are accepting the position I'm offering?"

"Yes," he replied.

"I have several documents and a map that I need you to read. The map shows three safe house locations in Iraq where you will find not only funds for your mission but arms caches. The funds are substantial, they can be used as you see fit, bribes, purchasing additional weapons, explosives, vehicles. You will also find several satellite phones and localized cell phones, along with many SIM cards. The SIM cards are for one time use only; they must be destroyed immediately after use. There are additional safe houses in France, Germany, Holland, Belgium, and Italy." Brad leaned over to the bedside cabinet and pulled out a brown folder. "Sit down and we will go through the documents together. You must remember all the addresses and information you are about to read. Everything you read in this room will be shredded later and then burnt in the base incinerator."

"Coffee, I need a coffee. Do you want one?" asked Al-Qadir.

"In the corner is a coffee maker, brew some fresh and we will start," he replied.

They spent five hours going through the documents, repeating the addresses and intelligence in the package. Brad was extremely impressed with his friend and colleague as he soaked it all up like a sponge. His memory was incredible as was his intelligence. They were both finally happy that everything in the documents was remembered by Al-Qadir, and Brad shredded the documents in the machine that stood in the corner. Brad made a phone call, and the shredder was removed with the finely shredded documents. He asked Al-Qadir to stay with the shredder to watch it being burnt, which he did.

Back in the room with Brad he was starting to feel like he was going to miss him more than he realized. Since the death of his family, he had not come close to anyone. It frustrated him that he had feelings for the man that had taught him so much. The only other man in his life that had done this was his father.

"Pass me that toiletries bag by the window," said Brad.

"What, you're going to teach me to shave now?" laughed Al-Qadir.

"No, but I have something that may help you one day. It was given to me when I was at the research division for the CIA in Langley. Where is it?" he said rummaging around in the toiletries bag. "Here, take this."

"A tablet, what is it cyanide?" said Al-Qadir.

"No. it is a locator. If you get in real trouble, like abducted, swallow this pill. Inside the pill is a small locator that will last for up to twenty hours."

"How does it work?" he asked.

"The acid in your stomach eats away at the outer coating which then activates the electronic locator."

"Let's hope it works."

"Let's hope you never need to use it," replied Brad.

The next morning, they said their goodbyes as Brad was put on a flight back to the USA.

CHAPTER 26

IRAQ

To his surprise Al-Qadir was flown back to Iraq in a military plane with a contingent of Delta Force. They gave Al-Qadir a Delta uniform for the flight and entry into the military base in Iraq. The idea was he would not stand out when they arrived. He was now working for the CIA and needed to protect his identity. When he arrived at the base, he was taken to one side by an American in civilian clothes. After a short briefing he changed into Iraqi civilian clothing and driven off the base. After the drop he would disappear with only one phone for Brad to call him. He would recover other phones when he found the safe houses. The address he was given at the briefing was in his head and he made his way into the center of Baghdad.

The building was no different to any other on the street, beige looking mud exterior, two stories and a flat roof. At the rear of the building there was supposed to be a single car garage, he checked this out first. He had been given two keys by the man at the military base, one for the building and one for the garage. He unlocked the garage door and walked inside. He gave the beat-up white pickup a quick check. The keys were in the hidden compartment under the center arm rest. He pressed the button under the driver's seat which released the spring-loaded hidden compartment. Inside was a .40 caliber full sized Glock 22, the car keys and knife. He closed the hidden draw after removing the keys.

The engine started first time; it may look beat up, but the engine was new. The tires had plenty of tread but not new enough to bring attention to the vehicle. He closed the garage door and went to the front door of the building. Inside the hallway was a secondary door, the same key opened this one also. The ground floor was only twelve feet wide, and sixteen feet deep, as was the first floor. It was one long room with a well-worn sofa and a small kitchen in the far corner. Upstairs had a bedroom and a room with a toilet and shower.

It took him a few minutes to find and manipulate the three locking mechanisms for the shower wall. As he managed to release each one the shower wall swung open easily. Inside there was an array of small arms, a pump action shotgun, two M16's, and an M24 sniper rifle with a fixed Leupold Ultra M3A 10×42mm power scope. There were multiple extra cartridges for all weapons and additional rounds in boxes. He chose the Glock for his sidearm it was the same as the one in the car. On the side of the false wall were several cell and satellite phones. In a zip lock plastic bag next to them were a multitude of sim cards. He chose one cell phone as instructed and put it in his pocket. He closed the shower wall and secured the hidden locking system that held it in place. He had slept on the flight over from Germany, so he decided to get to know his neighborhood.

After two hours of walking the streets and the area around the building that housed his new home, he felt more comfortable with the area. He had identified several escape routes from his new home as well as good observation points. There were a few local small cafes and mini grocery stores close by which would be useful. He was going to wait for it to go dark before he did his second round of street walking. Many places looked different at night and had a different vibe to them in the dark. The local cafes were much busier with men sitting around smoking, drinking coffee and deep in philosophical conversations. He sat on a wooden chair at one café, ordered a coffee and listened to the local's conversation. This he was told by his father, was one of the best ways to get information quickly. It could be political, local grievances or just men blowing off steam at each other. This café was extremely busy and there wasn't any shortage of information flowing from the conversations. After an hour he moved on to another café and repeated his relaxed coffee surveillance. He learned a lot about the local feeling towards the government and the US soldiers that had come into the country.

CHAPTER 27

PAYBACK

Al-Qadir had enjoyed working with the US military, especially the new skills he'd learnt. He was now a master of disguise and an extremely dangerous killer. As the foreign military started to downsize in Iraq, they slowly returned the country back to the new Iraqi government.

It was time for him to move on also especially as he never did get his clearance to live in America. He was still in touch with his mentor and CIA contact Brad who was still using him for the occasional job, for which he got paid handsomely.

Al-Qadir had numerous resources at his fingertips thanks to Brad. He got to know the best passport forges in Iraq and Turkey, which he used often. He now had a passport for France, Canada, Iraq, and Ireland. He also had a driver's license for the same countries. The passports were so good he'd tested them out in France and Ireland. He had no problem going into and out of both countries. He now spoke not only his native tongue and French that his mother had taught him but English and Spanish fluently. To learn English and Spanish he used the same system that the US armed forces used to train their troops.

During the previous three years there had been two dozen murders around Iraq. Murders that had been put down to one individual or group. The murders were of elected officials, high ranking army officers, police officers and town officials in many districts around Iraq.

In total twenty-two murders had taken place where a Taro style card had been left on the body or at the site of the murder. The card had a black hooded skeleton on it holding a scythe with blood dripping from the blade. At the bottom of the card was the word, Azrael.

Al-Qadir got the idea of using the death cards from a film he watched when he was in the military hospital. A group of young soldiers that were receiving treatment for wounds they had received in battle decided to have a film night. They hung a white sheet over a length of wire that was strung across the ward they were in. They didn't invite Al-Qadir to watch there was no need he could see the sheet from his bed. The film fascinated him, it was a film by a man called Francis Ford Coppola, Apocalypse Now. Even though it was an old film in his eyes, made in 1979, he loved it. At times it was hard to see the film when the sheet wafted around every time a door was open. In the film American soldiers were fighting a war in Vietnam. When they killed the Vietnamese they would throw a card on the body, it was the ace of spades. It was explained to him later by his CIA handler Brad, that the card was used as phycological warfare. The idea was that the black ace of spades put fear into the hearts and minds of the Vietnamese enemy. He watched the film over a dozen times and knew every word and scene.

He couldn't go to a print shop and ask for the cards to be printed for him as this would give his identity away. He saw a set of Tarot cards being used by the same group of soldiers that had put the film on, he stole the cards before he was released from the hospital. With a little cutting and pasting he made his own death card, now he had to duplicate it. He broke into a print shop one evening and made his own cards by using thick card and a photocopier. They came out perfect for him. It was not long before he put his own death cards into practice.

The Iraqi and US armed forces investigated the series of murders but got nowhere as there were very few clues. Most of the murders were up close and looked very personal. A knife being the weapon of choice in many cases with the throat being the main target. Bombing of Iraqi army officers' cars was the second popular method of killing the target. The individual murders had just one card with the body and that was nailed to the forehead of the corpse. The car bombs had several cards scattered around the bomb scene. It was obvious to investigators that the cards were placed so that when the bomb was detonated not all the cards would be destroyed. The killer wanted people to know that he was responsible for the murder.

The death cards had become legendary with the people of Iraq. They praised the man they now called Azrael for avenging the murders of loved ones. They said it was a man because some people stated that they had seen a man dressed in black running away from the scene of some of the murders. It was false but the euphoria of the avenging angel as they saw him had become infectious. He would never allow himself to be seen by anyone as he committed the murders.

Before he left Iraq to find his last two targets in his revenge killing spree, he had one more man to visit. Unlike the other targets he had to hunt down, this one was out in the open.

Baravan Laghmani never got over his embarrassment of being dumped naked outside his home by General Ashkouri's soldiers. The word spread quickly by his neighbors, and he became a local laughingstock. The public were repaying him for all his misdoings and failed promises to the people of the city. They did not even offer him any sympathy for the deaths of his wife and daughters.

He was still the mayor and his corrupt cronies helped cover his position as he grieved for his family. The mayor initially became very insular finding it hard to appear in public but then he found anger. The murder of his wife and daughters at the hands of the soldiers fueled his rage. He could not pay back the soldiers as they were long gone so his target became those that had shamed him.

The mayor had become even more corrupt over the years, something that was hard to do. He ruled the city and its council with an iron fist, if you were not with him, you were out. Several council members had lost their jobs because of the mayor's paranoia. He thought that everyone was plotting against him. Some council members had thugs visit their homes and they were beaten if they did not vote with the mayor, even on the smallest of issues. The iron fist that he was using was being swung by a man that was out of control.

Al-Qadir hadn't been back to Baqubah since he'd left after the funerals of his parents. The closest he had gotten was the military hospital on the outskirts of the city. As he drove into the city he was surprised by the poverty and the number of shops and homes that were closed and boarded up. He called into a small grocery store that also had a kitchen that served local peasant food. Outside on the edge of the road were three tables covered in dust from the road. People would wipe the dust away as they sat down to eat the food they had ordered inside the shop.

As he got out of the vehicle the smell of the food wafted out of the shop door. This made him smile as it took him back to the smell of his mother's cooking.

He knew what the smell was it was his favorite, Tashreeb, a true peasant dish. He walked into the shop and ordered a plate of

Tashreeb and a coffee. Within a minute the plate was on the counter with the steaming pile of food on it. He looked at the thick slices of bread that were soaking up the chicken broth. On top of the bread was lamb and vegetables that were cooked to death. He walked outside and wiped of the dust on the table. He was halfway through his plate of food when a boy no more than six years of age came up to him begging. He looked at the dirty face and tattered clothes on the boy's body, he remembered that was what he looked like after he and his mother were kicked out of their home. He lifted the boy up and sat him on the chair next to him. He pushed the half-eaten plate of food in front of the boy and gave him the rust-stained spoon he had been eating with. He smiled as the boy devoured the food, he was truly hungry.

"What are you doing?" a voice said behind Al-Qadir.

The shop owner had seen what was happening and came out to complain.

"The boy is hungry," said Al-Qadir.

"We don't want his kind in my shop, leave he shouted at the boy."

The boy was very scared and went to get out of the chair, but Al-Qadir stopped him.

"Stay and eat. I would like another plate of Tashreeb and two bottles of water," he said to the shop owner.

"No, leave now," he said angrily and walked back inside his shop.

"I will be back in a minute," said Al-Qadir to the little boy.

Inside the shop the owner was bragging to a man that was stood by the kitchen door. He was telling him how he had told the man to leave and take the peasant boy with him.

Al-Qadir said nothing as the men saw him walk up to the counter. He placed enough money next to the cash draw to pay for the new plate of food he had ordered and the water.

Al-Qadir slid back the oversized sleeveless vest he was wearing over his shirt to expose the handgun tucked in his belt and the knife next to it. He was glaring at the shop keeper with a deep dark look. It had the look of death, and it would not take much for him to act on the look.

The second man disappeared into the kitchen.

"I will bring it out to you," the voice in the kitchen said.

Without saying anything the shop owner pointed at the refrigerated cabinet by the window where the bottles of water were. Although it was refrigerated it had not worked in years it was just a storage cabinet now for water.

He picked out two bottles of water and returned to the table outside. The boy was just mopping up the last of the broth with the tiniest piece of bread. He looked at Al-Qadir with a smile on his face.

Al-Qadir opened one of the bottles and placed it in front of the boy. He snatched it up and immediately started gulping down the water.

"Slowly," he said to the boy.

The next plate of food was brought out by the shop owner, it was larger than the first plate. He placed it on the table a hurried back into his shop.

The boy ate the second plate more slowly, his new friend wanted him to. With the food and water gone he gave the boy just enough money to get himself another meal. If he gave him much more, he would have bragged about it, and someone would take it off him. The boy ran off waiving at his new friend with a dirty face but a mouth that was clean from his tongue licking away the broth. Being given the hearty meal from a stranger would be something he would never forget.

CHAPTER 28

The mayor was leaving his office when Al-Qadir pulled up outside in his vehicle. He watched as he climbed into the back of a sedan helped by a security detail. He did not expect the mayor to have a security detail. If he knew what he had been doing to the local people and businesses, he would have realized why he needed them. He had time to do his surveillance on the mayor and learn more about him.

A week went by before he had enough information on the mayor and his movements. He was surprised at the amount of hatred for the man. The news of the murder of his wife and daughters was new to Al-Qadir but not surprising. He had trusted that General Ashkouri would leave his family alone if he cooperated with him, this was foolish. He had given the location of the safe houses after the general had rolled into town with his troops. He was personally responsible for what happened to the women and girls that were hiding in the safe houses.

For the fifth time in six days, he walked past and around the mayor's new house at a safe distance. Each time he wore a different disguise. It was a palatial home with five bedrooms and a maid's annex. In the garden there were two Alsatian dogs that were allowed to roam free. The dogs made things exceedingly difficult as they were guarding the easiest access to the house, the rear.

The mayor's new wife was a petite woman who left the house to visit friends on a regular basis. She, unlike the mayor did not have a vehicle at her disposal, she walked everywhere. Al-Qadir had even struck up a conversation with her in the street on one occasion. He asked her for directions, which she gave happily. She seemed like a sweet lady to him and was attractive, except for the black eye she was wearing. The mayor was obviously abusing her, another reason to make him suffer.

It had only taken Al-Qadir three days to find the men of the wives and daughters that had been abducted from the safe houses by General Ashkouri's men. All but one of them still lived in the same houses. He left notes at each of their homes stating that the man responsible for the rape, abduction and murder of their wives and daughters would soon be punished. They were all curious who the secretive messages were from and why they had been contacted after all this time. Eight out of the ten men had taken new wives since theirs were murdered, the ninth had lost his mind. His brain and body could not cope with the loss of his wife and four daughters, he had become a blubbering mess in a local asylum. Al-Qadir visited him in the asylum claiming to the doctor that he was a long-lost nephew. When he was alone with the man, he told him who he was and that he was going to kill the man responsible for what happened to his wife and daughters. The man never responded to the news, but Al-Qadir knew that deep down in his brain the message got through.

The mayor's security detail was very professional and looked like they could manage most situations. They went everywhere with the mayor right up to the front door of his house but not inside. Everywhere else he went they were on his shoulder, watching like a couple of hawks.

The driver of the car was the only possible weak link in the three-man security detail. He'd fallen asleep in the driver's seat on three occasions in the last week when the mayor was inside a building attending functions or meetings. The driver only just made it on two occasions when the mayor was coming out of a building. He parked the car under a three-car covered carport to the rear of the office. Only the roof of the carport could be seen from the office building which was a mistake. There weren't any cameras and several blind spots leading to the carport.

To one side of the carport was a chain link fence protecting it from the street. The driver sat reading newspapers and drinking tea a lot of the time. He had a two-way radio that he rested on top of the dashboard. The radio could be heard clearly from the street because the driver had the volume turned up high. Al-Qadir assumed that he had it so loud that if he fell asleep it would wake him up. By sitting close to the fence but out of sight of the driver he could hear everything that was said by the security guards when they called him and when he spoke to them. When they wanted him to drive the front of the office his only reply was yes. He started the car, drove around the corner, and waited in the car by the curb. He never got out of the car at the front of the building.

The two security guards always walked just behind the mayor when they left a building until they got close to the car. This is when guard one would walk forward quickly to open the rear door for the mayor. Guard two would stand over the mayor as he got into the back seat at the same time, he opened the front passenger door. Guard one would close the door once the mayor was inside and run around to the other side of the car and climb into the back seat. This was when guard two got into the front seat.

In the past he thought that it was easier to target the mayor in his own home, but now he changed his mind, the dogs took care of that. He noticed a fatal flaw in the security details routine, and he was going to exploit it. The timing had to be perfect, or it would not work it was a dangerous move.

The next day it was time to put Al-Qadir's plan into action. He had a small backpack slung over his shoulder, like teenagers carried to school. Inside and in the side, pockets were the tools he needed to kidnap the mayor.

He walked quickly but quietly into the rear parking area of the mayor's office building. Using the blind spots, he had identified he was under the carport undetected. As luck would have it the driver was asleep in the front passenger seat. He waited a minute to hear if anyone shouted indicating that he'd been seen, it was all quiet.

He took out a syringe from a side pocket of the backpack and removed the plastic sleeve covering the needle. Swiftly and expertly, he stuck it into the sleeping driver's neck. He hardly moved when the needle went in, and he was now going to sleep for at least six hours.

Within a few minutes he stripped the driver of his clothing and dumped his sleeping body into the trunk of the car. He dressed himself in the driver's clothes and could not help but smell the body odor. He didn't think the clothes had been cleaned in weeks, it repulsed him. His mother and father had always taught him to be clean in his body and clothing. He was ready to put the next part of his plan into action and sat in the driver's seat of the car. He pulled the cap that he'd taken off the driver down slightly covering his eyes. Now he had to wait and hope that nobody came out of the office to check on the driver.

It was an agonizing hour before the call came over the radio. He mimicked the drivers voice and replied yes, just as the driver would have. He'd heard the drivers voice enough times to fool anyone on the other end of the radio. He drove at the same speed as the driver and parked exactly where the driver would have. He kept his hands on the steering wheel together at twelve o'clock, not a good position to drive, but he was imitating the driver.

Everything had to look normal to the security detail. The front door of the office opened and out walked the mayor closely followed by the security detail.

Al-Qadir tried not to look at the mayor or his detail as the driver never did. In his peripheral vision he saw the mayor stop to talk to someone. This made him nervous as it gave the security detail time to evaluate the area around them. Number one security guard was bending down slightly looking at the car, he was looking directly at the car's driver.

Al-Qadir could see that the number one security guard was suspicious about something. It could be his profile as it wasn't the same as the drivers. He put his head back with his hand over his mouth and gave a big yawn as though he was sleepy. The security guard saw what the driver was doing and shook his head in dismay, he was sleepy again.

The ploy worked and the security guard went back to surveilling his surroundings. The conversation with the mayor ended quickly and they walked to the car. Number two opened the rear car door for the mayor as number one stood over him. The protocol never changed as the front passenger door was opened. As soon as the rear door was slammed shut Al-Qadir drove off at speed. Number one security guard had one foot in the car as it accelerated away from the curb. He tried to hang on, but the car swerved quickly to one side. He lost his grip on the top of the door and crashed to the ground. The mayor was shouting at the driver to stop the car.

Al-Qadir have only driven three hundred yards when he slammed on the brakes. The sudden stop caused the mayors body to fly forward into the rear of the front passenger seat. His face made impact first, then his upper body. His nose fractured in two places and poured with blood. He sat back slowly screaming at the driver.

"You're fired, you will go to prison for this," he shouted at the driver.

"Nobody is going to prison," said Al-Qadir as he turned around removing the cap from his head.

"Who are you, where is my driver?"

"He's asleep in the trunk and I'm the man that is going to avenge all the women and children that you betrayed."

"What women and children?" he replied genuinely not understanding.

"You don't remember the safe houses that you identified to General Ashkouri?"

The sudden recall of the memory was written all over the mayor's face, he grabbed at the door handle to open it.

"You're not going anywhere," said Al-Qadir.

He pulled out his silenced 9mm and fired one shot into the mayor's right knee. The screams were unmerciful as the mayor's knee shattered.

In the rear-view mirror, he saw the two security guards running towards the car, they were getting close. With one punch of the accelerator pedal the car sped away gaining distance from the security guards.

He drove to an old apartment building that had been burnt out. It had an eight-foot wall around it and two large metal gates that gave access to the yard. He had chosen this building deliberately as it was the first safe house that had been raided by General

Ashkouri and his men. He put a lock and chain on the gates two days previously to stop anyone gaining access.

The car stopped at the gates and Al-Qadir unlocked the chain and pushed the gates open. Once the car was inside, he rechained the gates from the inside. If anyone had seen him and reported it this would give him time to escape without detection. He parked the car at the rear of the building out of sight from the street or any other buildings that overlooked the yard.

He put a gag over the mayor's mouth and dragged his fat body out of the car. In a room next to where the car was parked was a single wooden chair. He dumped the body next to it.

"Sit in the chair," he said.

The mayor protested under the gag claiming he couldn't because of his injured knee. Al-Qadir stepped forward and raised his foot over the knee. The mayor went out of control screaming as loud as he could under the mask, begging for him not to stand on the knee.

It did not take long for the mayor to put his fat rear end onto the seat. He was sweating profusely and crying from the pain.

"I'm going to take the gag off. If you scream, shout, or make any attempt to make a noise I will stomp on your injured knee, nod if you understand."

The mayor nodded that he did.

The gag came off and the blubbering mayor sat crying. His face was a mess of sweat, blood, and snot. He stood and watched the mayor for a minute enjoying the pain the man was feeling.

"Do you know who I am?" he asked.

"No, what have I done to you?" he replied.

"I'm Al-Qadir Hadi, son of General Abbud Hadi," he replied.

The mayors face gave him away again, he knew exactly who the general was.

"I was a friend to your father," he replied through his tears.

"Do not say you were a friend; you are a friend to nobody except yourself."

"He was made a general because of me," he shouted.

The gag was put back over his mouth after raising his voice, because he was about to make even more noise. The boot did not have to slam into the injured knee just a gentle exacting pressure would be enough to bring a massive amount of pain.

"You had nothing to do with his career he earned everything through his own hard work. He didn't like you or your corrupt friends," he said into the mayor's ear.

He gave him time to regain some composure before he took the gag off again.

"Please stop, I need to go to the hospital," said the mayor.

"The only place you're going is the graveyard."

The mayor tried to shout out hearing this, but the gag was back on in a flash. He cut the clothes from the mayor's body leaving him completely naked in the chair. The names of the women and children were read out to the mayor as he sat in the chair. As he read each name he cut the mayor on the chest, legs, or arms. By design this took four hours with Al-Qadir having to revive the mayor several times with smelling salts. It was getting dark, he had to put the next part of his plan into action, but first he wanted to get some sleep. After three hours heavy sleep he went about the next stage of the plan and returned to the apartment building.

The mayor was awake but barely, he had lost a lot of blood but not enough to kill him. He was fully awake again when the smelling salts were put under his nostrils.

"Water, I need water," said the mayor.

"You won't need water," he replied.

The mayor watched the son of General Hadi walk over to a backpack that was the floor. He was taking something out, but he could not see what it was, it was bottles of water. The man was going to show him some mercy, he was going to get water.

With a bottle of water in each hand he took the caps off with his teeth and walked over to the mayor.

"Thank you, thank you," he was saying under the gag.

With a smile on his face, he poured the water over his body, arms and legs cleaning the dried blood off the open wounds. The water refreshed the burning sensation in the wounds and the mayor was screaming in pain again. He slapped the mayor's chest and flexed his arms and legs to open the wounds completely. Then came the real pain for the mayor as he poured a bag of salt all over his wounds. The mayor was writhing in pain as his body frantically fought the pain surging through it. He convulsed so hard that the chair collapsed under his weight, he passed out.

He repeated the process twice more until the mayor was not feeling anything because his body was in shock. Walking outside he felt that he had avenged the deaths of the women and children and their families. He felt this part of the slate was now clean for the women and girls that had lost their lives and in some small way his parents also. He heard a noise towards the front of the building and cautiously looked outside. As planned, there was a donkey and cart being tied up to the gate. He had paid a local man for the donkey and cart; in fact, he was paid so well the man had enough money to purchase two more donkeys and carts. He waited until the man left and the street was clear before he brought the donkey and cart into the yard. An hour later he had nailed three pieces of wood into a pyramid shape to the back of a chair in the back of the cart. He then lifted the mayor's unconscious body onto the cart and sat him against the pyramid shape with his legs hanging off the back. It was time for the smelling salts again, the mayor woke after two attempts with the salts. He had to be awake the next part.

"You recognize this?" asked Al-Qadir holding up a now famous Azrael death card.

The mayor's eyes almost popped out of his head in fear, he did know the card and its reputation. He was back to fighting and now realized he was tied down with ropes and sitting on a cart. He could not move his head it was firmly tied to something.

The center of the card was punctured with a six-inch nail as it was slid all the way down the nail to the head. The nail and card were only inches away from the mayor's face when the hammer appeared.

Al-Qadir let it sink in for a minute before he placed the nail against the center of the mayor's head and hammered it through his skull and deep into his brain. He stood and watched calmly as the mayor died and covered him with a giant sheet that had been left for him on the cart. The final act before he left was to place a giant sign behind the mayor with the names of all the victims that he had betrayed to General Ashkouri. He unlocked the chain on the gate and dropped it to the floor, he would not be returning.

He was now wearing peasants' clothes like he was one of the local farmer's as he rode the cart into the city center. His face wasn't visible as he held his head down the whole way. As he got close to the police headquarters, he slowed the cart down and stopped it on a small side street. He looked around the corner towards the police headquarters and the crowd that had assembled in the square, they were right on time. There wasn't anyone in the side street, he uncovered the mayor and the sign. He shook the reigns on the donkey signaling for it to walk, and it did out of the side street directly into the square.

The crowd slowly started to see the cart and the body on the back. There was shock and horror at first but then they read the sign and who was responsible for those on the list that had died. Police officers rushed forward to hold the crowd back but there were too many people gathered around the cart.

The shock and horror soon wore off and the spitting started. To a man and woman, they all spat on the mayor's corpse, even the police officers. As if by magic sticks and stones appeared and they started beating and stoning the dead body. His work was done here, time to move on.

CHAPTER 29

EGYPT

Ahmad didn't find it difficult at all to get off the ship, there were so many men working in the hold and on the deck that he just joined in with them and eventually walked off the ship. Going through the port gates into the street wasn't any more difficult than getting off the ship as security at the port was very weak.

He walked along the corniche in Alexandria for an hour enjoying the fresh sea breeze. He had to make his way to Cairo eventually as this was where his cousin lived. He'd never met his cousin but knew of him from his brother who escaped from Iraq before the first bombings by the American air force. His cousin's sister spoke of him fondly and often whenever he saw her in Baghdad. She gave him his address in Cairo four years earlier and told him he should visit. He didn't know why but he kept the address in a small notebook he always carried. He didn't realize how lucky he was when he took it off her.

He'd already exchanged the Iraqi Dinars he'd stolen from the shop owner for Euros. He'd done this in four different money exchanges so that it didn't look strange changing two thousand Euro's worth of Dinars. Now he had to exchange his Euros for Egyptian pounds. It wasn't hard to do as there were tourist exchange locations all over the city. He picked up a tourist map at the bureau de change and found out where the train station was located. He stopped on the way and had tea at a shisha café. The smell of the apple wood burning on the top of the ceramic bowl got to him and he had to try it. With his thirst satisfied he purchased a one-way ticket at the station to Cairo.

He wasn't surprised at how packed the train was but managed to get a seat by a window. The amount of fertile farmland amazed him as the train rolled through the Nile Delta south to Cairo. He was like a young boy again experiencing new and fascinating things. The train stopped suddenly when they were only ten miles outside of Alexandria. Panic started to set in when he thought that it was the police looking for him.

There was a lot of shouting and dismay coming from the other passengers, he could hear them all complaining. It soon became apparent that the train had broken down which was not unusual. He sat back in his seat and waited for the train to start again which it did two hours later. The journey was interesting, but it took five hours instead of the usual two and a half. The train pulled into Ramses station or Misr as it was also known.

The station was named after Ramses the second an ancient Egyptian Pharaoh. In 1955 President Nasser had a statue of the Pharaoh erected in a square close to the train station.

The train rolled to a sudden stop in the station causing some of the passengers to lose their balance. The train doors were thrown open by the passengers, and the mass of people poured out onto the platform. He joined the crowd as they flowed out into the station.

He was amazed at the décor of the station, it had gold-colored walls that were illuminated with lights. In front of him was a giant circular light with a long-inverted pyramid shaped light hanging down from the center. This light had four sides and not three like the pyramids. He imagined that this was what the tombs of the ancient Egyptian kings looked like inside the pyramids. The people in the station seemed to be oblivious to the magnificent surroundings. He wanted to stop them and say look at this, but he couldn't. People kept bumping into him as he stood still looking up at the sight.

He had no idea which part of the city his cousin lived in. He went to the taxi stand outside the station and asked a driver where the address was. The driver offered to drive him there, but it was on the opposite side of Cairo. A costly journey and he didn't want the taxi driver to have time to talk to him or get to know his accent. He walked away without any further conversation, the taxi driver was shouting that he wanted paying for the information, he ignored him.

Across the street was a seedy looking hotel, it was the perfect place for him to stay the night. The reception desk, if you could call it that was a hole in a wall with a wooden counter. Inside an old man was sleeping in a chair with his feet resting on a plastic crate. The tiny lobby was covered in dust as was the room where the old man slept. It looked like the desert sand was covering everything.

Ahmad tapped on the counter twice trying to wake up the old man, but he didn't move. He tried again with the same result, he thought that the man was dead. A young girl no more than eight came up behind Ahmad and walked into the room with the sleeping old man.

"Can I help you?" she asked politely.

"Yes, I need a room for one night, can you wake him up?" he replied.

"No, my grandfather sleeps a lot, I can give you a room. Ten pounds for the night," she said holding her tiny hand out for the money.

"Here," he said handing over the ten Egyptian pounds.

The girl gave him a key that didn't have any room number on it.

"Room two," she said pointing down the short hallway.

"Thankyou."

Ahmad was amazed but not surprised at how efficiently the little girl dealt with his room request. It wasn't uncommon for children in countries in the Middle East and North Africa to help with the family business.

The door to the room couldn't keep anyone out it was so flimsy; he didn't really need a key. As he opened the door the first thing, he noticed was the smell of sewage from the toilet. The plumbing in the hotel must have been ancient or not working. Inside the room was dark and dingy with no windows.

He flicked a switch that was next to the door jamb and a light came on. The ceiling had a wire hanging down from the center with a single bulb at the end of it. The walls hadn't seen paint since the place was built, most probably since the Pharaohs ruled. The bed was a metal frame and a mattress that was no more than two inches thick. There was one heavy woolen blanket on the top of the bed but nothing on the mattress itself. The stains on the mattress were black and brown from years of use. He sat on the bed and felt the whole thing sway to one side. It wasn't going to be easy to sleep in this metal creaking noise machine.

He had to use the restroom but was very apprehensive, he opened the door to what he assumed was the toilet. The smell coming from the restroom was even stronger and he balked hard. There was a small wash basin on the wall to the right and the toilet with no seat was in front of him. The toilet bowl was coated in yellow and brown stains, like the bed it had many years of use and little cleaning. To sit on the toilet, he had to leave the door open, or his knees would have been in his mouth. On the floor was an old newspaper that had been torn into strips to use as toilet paper. It was all very gross, but he had no choice he had to go. Afterwards he regretted turning on the faucet in the sink as the water was deep brown and mud looking. He would have to buy some bottled water to wash himself.

The next morning, he woke up to the sound of arguing outside his room. He couldn't believe how well he'd slept. He listened to the voices, and it sounded like someone didn't want to pay the bill, he couldn't blame them the place was a dump.

He sat on the bed until the argument subsided and the person left. He was very hungry and thirsty, so he left the room to find food, he certainly wasn't going to order room service. Outside on the street it was a cacophony of noise. Every driver in the vehicles seemed to be beeping the vehicles horn, engines roared, and people were shouting different things to each other. He didn't have too far to walk to find food. The street had several food carts serving Ful, pronounced fool, the breakfast of kings and peasants. Ful, was cooked and mashed fava beans with olive oil, cumin, and onion. Each food cart and family had their own version. It sometimes included meat, but not on the vendors carts as the locals couldn't afford it with meat.

Fava or broad beans had been cultivated in the Middle East for over 8,000 years before they were introduced to Europe. Evidence of Fava beans had even been found inside Egyptian tombs.

He went to a vendor that was busy as this told him it was good Ful. He ordered his with a fried egg on top and a piece of flat bread to scoop it up. The Ful came in a small tin bowl with the bread handed to him by the vendor. Some, men stood eating the Ful at a narrow wooden makeshift bar attached to the cart. He, like most of the men sat on the curb with his feet in the road devouring the breakfast. He couldn't tell if it was just because he was starving but it tasted like the best Ful he'd ever eaten. He thought that the atmosphere in the street also helped with different food smells wafting past. The smells were accompanied by smoke from the fires they were being cooked on. He was loving it and felt relaxed for the first time in months.

CHAPTER 30

CIA SAFE HOUSES BAGHDAD

Al-Qadir walked through the streets of Baghdad testing himself to see how he blended in. He was on route to the first safe house address that Brad had him memorize. He had gotten over the thought that his friend and the USA had turned their back on him, he now saw the bigger picture. The building he was looking for was a three-story apartment building with a small basement. He performed his counter surveillance and circled several blocks around the building before he went inside. He had memorized the interior from the plans he was shown and knew it like the back of his hand. The door at the top of the stairs looked like any other door in the building. The exterior of the door was the original door but was attached to a thick steel door on a reinforced frame and hinges. What the normal persons eye wouldn't see was the small hole above the door frame. It looked like a piece of plaster had fallen away, like it had in many parts of the building.

He looked down the stairs to make sure nobody was watching, he was alone. He inserted a long key into the hole in the plaster wall and turned it anti-clockwise. He could hear the mechanism inside the wall working. It was releasing four bolts that were sliding out of the door. He then used his standard Yale style key and opened the visible lock in the door.

He turned the handle and opened the door outward as opposed to inward like a normal front door to a home or apartment. It opened outward as another security measure making it much harder to breach. Should the apartment be raided by the police, military or anyone pursuing the person or persons inside the would have an exceedingly difficult job forcing entry. The steel door was on a strong steel frame which was attached to steel that lined the walls. Even basic explosives used to force entry by the likes of SWAT would fail.

He was surprised at how easy the door swung open considering its size and weight. The first thing he saw inside was a small kitchen and living area with a sofa, coffee table and TV. He closed the door behind him with a quiet thump thanks to the fire-resistant material on the frame that cushioned the noise of the door. He went to work immediately and slid the small refrigerator away from the wall. It was hiding a trap door in the floor that was almost invisible. It was two feet by two feet but just looked like the rest of the flooring. He dialed a number on his cell phone and pressed send. The trap door sprung open jumping up about an inch on one side.

He pulled the twenty-inch square trap door open swinging it on its hinge. There wasn't anything inside it just looked like an old tin box about six inches deep. If it were discovered, it would appear to be just an empty floor safe. He dialed the number again this time the last four digits were all X's. The bottom of the tin box slid open to reveal a fireproof box with a handle on top. He pulled it out and placed it on the kitchen counter. At this point there wasn't any need for secretive gadgets to open the box. If it were found after all the security measures, there wouldn't be any point.

Inside the box were two passports in Al-Qadir's name, one French and the other Canadian. There were two more in Brad's name for the same countries. He was impressed that Brad had these done without his knowledge. There was also an Iraqi I.D. card that he was to always carry with him. This would come in handy if he were stopped at a checkpoint. There were two nine-millimeter handguns and six spare clips. A set of vehicle keys and one hundred thousand dollars in various denominations concluded the contents. He was surprised at how much money there was, and the trust Brad had shown in him. He could very easily disappear in Iraq and live very well with this kind of money.

The only other rooms in the apartment were two bedrooms and a bathroom with a toilet, sink and shower. He was feeling tired and decided to try to sleep for a few hours before he would find the vehicle and go to the second safe house.

Six hours of sleep was more than he'd had in the last two nights. After two strong coffees, a shower, and a change of clothes it was time to go to the next safe house.

The car was in a garage that was part of the apartment building, it was more of a storage unit than a garage. The old Toyota was once a taxi and now just looked like a beat-up old vehicle. Mechanically it was completely renovated with a powerful but quiet V8 engine and suspension to match the newer heavier engine, gear box and drive shaft. He remembered everything that he was told about the vehicle including where the secret compartments where and how to access them.

In the dashboard was a hidden compartment for his sidearm. He pressed the radio tuner button and on/off button at the same time and a section of the dashboard opened on a spring. He put the sidearm into the compartment. It was accessible very quickly if needed. He didn't want to be found with the sidearm if he was stopped by the police or a military checkpoint.

The gear stick looked like any other of its kind. He unscrewed it clockwise and pulled the knob upwards. It had a very sharp knife blade attached to it, he replaced it and screwed the knob back into place. The second safe house was on the far side of the city close to the banks of the Tigris River.

It wasn't a safe house as such it was an old river barge moored amongst several other boats and barges. He spent a long-time performing counter surveillance again to make sure he wasn't being followed; he wasn't. The barge had a heavy padlock and sliding bolt on the hatch that gave access to the inside of the barge. The key to the padlock was hidden under the lip of a side window which he picked up as he past it. To anyone looking they wouldn't have seen the hiding place for the key. He unlocked the padlock and was about to slide the hatch back when he saw a man on a boat twenty feet away watching him.

"Hello, you own that barge?" asked the man.

"Yes," he replied.

"I keep an eye on it as we get some homeless people trying to break into the boats and barges," said the man.

"Thank you," replied Al-Qadir.

"Are you living there?" asked the man.

"For a brief time, I work in Basra but I'm home for a brief time to do some repair work on the barge."

"If you need any help with the work, I know everybody around here, mechanics, welders, electricians all of them."

"I may ask for your contacts names if I can't fix something myself," he replied.

"Good to meet you," he replied.

"And you," said Al-Qadir.

He wasn't happy about having a nosey neighbor, but he stated that he knew everybody so anyone snooping around would stand out to him, this was an asset.

The inside of the barge was basic, galley kitchen toilet/shower and one tight fitting bedroom at the end. He immediately went to work trying to find the hidden compartments described by Brad. He was surprised at the amount of firepower and ammunition stored in the first compartment. A sniper rifle, two fully automatic rifles, four handguns, flashbangs, grenades. The second compartment had C4 plastic explosives and various kinds of timers and fuses/detonators. The third compartment was yet another complete shock. This held almost one hundred and fifty thousand dollars in US Dollars, Euro's, British pounds, and Dinar's. He slumped back onto the floor staring at the money in the plastic bags. There was a little voice in the back of his head that told him to take the money from both safe houses and run. Mentally that voice was silenced quickly as he remembered his father's hatred for corruption. He put a small amount of Dinar into two of his pockets. This would help with food and getting through checkpoints if needed.

He had the rest of the day and night to get to know his surroundings and the area around his barge. He spent a long time evaluating every access and egress point to the barge. He had four escape routes that didn't require him to dive into the river.

He would sleep well that night and wait for the first call from Brad in the morning. A call that he was looking forward to, he hoped that he would get to know the whereabouts of the general's responsible for killing his family and friends.

CHAPTER 31

BIRTH OF AN ASSASIN

Al-Qadir drove five miles away from the barge to receive the phone call from Brad. He was only on the call for three minutes, a great disappointment as he didn't get to know where the men where that he wanted to kill, instead he was given a mission. The mission was to kill an Iraqi minister. He was a double agent and was feeding information to ISIS insurgents that wanted to take over Iraq.

The name, face and addresses of his targets office and home were to be sent through an encrypted message on one of the disposable phones. He destroyed the phone and SIM card immediately. Something didn't feel right about this assassination, why not just kill him at range with a drone missile.

Wherever the minister went outside of his office and home he had a small security detail. These men were former Iraqi special forces now working as private security.

Two weeks had passed since the call with Brad. Al-Qadir had been on constant surveillance of his target. The former Iraqi soldiers protecting him were particularly good, but they left holes in his security. Like any assassination the walk to and from a building was the most dangerous moment for any close protection detail. They didn't have to worry as this wasn't how he was going to die.

The surveillance of his office and home had revealed several loopholes in his security. The easiest way to get to the minister was in his home at night. When he was at the house, only two guards protected him, both of whom were very lazy. There were two house maids and the minister's girlfriend living in the house with him. The girlfriend went out shopping or visiting her friends most days but was always back before her lover. She was also having sex with one of the security guards at the house, another distraction.

The home had a basic security alarm system that was redundant. The maids hated their employer as he was constantly grabbing at their breasts and buttocks. A previous maid was raped by him, which she reported to one of the security team. He reported it back to the minister and she was thrown out of the house. She did do some good as he didn't rape another maid, but he did keep the other sexual abuse going.

Al-Qadir found all of this out after talking to the gardener and asked him if there was any work in the house. The gardener told him not to work for this man as he was an animal. The gardener showed him the small brick hut in the corner of the garden where he lived. There wasn't any running water, power, or even a toilet. He drank water from the garden hose most of the time which gave him parasites in his stomach. He was constantly ill because of it.

He hated the minister as he beat him if he asked for his wages, he would then tell him how he was lucky to have a place to live. The maids would sneak him into the house when the minister was gone and let him wash. They also gave him food and water to help him. They begged him not to drink the water from the hose, but he didn't have much choice.

This information alone made Al-Qadir want to kill the man, now he would enjoy it. When he talked to the gardener, he found out that he went begging in the early evening. It was his only source of money, on most occasions he got less than the equivalent of ten cents. Most of the time he didn't get any money just abuse for begging.

It was Saturday night, and the Minister followed his routine from the previous two Saturday's. He came home escorted by his security detail, once inside the house they took an hour break. This left the two security men inside the house to protect him. The minister would come back out of the house around nine to nine thirty and go out for the night. His security detail would drive him to a local restaurant and then to a not so discreet club in the center of the city. It was really a glorified whore house frequented by rich businessmen. After an evening of excessive drink and debauchery he would return home in the early hours of the morning very drunk.

Al-Qadir watched the rear of the house where the small gate in the wall led to the garden. The gardener had waited as always for the minister to go out for the evening before he left. He walked the same way every time to his favorite begging corner. This only left the two maids and the girlfriend in the house. One of the maids was married and would leave for a few hours to see her husband and children. The girlfriend and her security man lover never wasted any time after the minister left and had sex in his bed.

He waited for the bedroom light to go on before he entered the house. He didn't have to break in as the rear door to the kitchen was never locked, a big mistake by his security team. He walked slowly through the house as he'd done on the two previous Saturday's. He knew the layout and could walk it blindfolded if necessary. The maid was sat in the small room next to the kitchen watching a tiny television. She always had the volume turned up so high she would never hear him. This helped as he had one less person to worry about. He stopped at the bottom of the stairs for a minute listening to make sure he couldn't hear anyone else in the house. He scanned his surroundings paying particular attention to the floor above him. Confident that there wasn't anyone else in the house he walked to the stairs.

As he climbed the stairs to the bedroom level, he could hear the girlfriend and her lover in the bedroom. They were making enough noise to wake the dead. He opened the door to the bedroom next to them which was never used and hid behind a chair in the corner. All he had to do now was wait for the minister to return home.

The front door being slammed shook Al-Qadir out of his struggle to stay awake. He heard someone coming up the stairs, it had to be the minister. The door to the minister's bedroom opened and closed as loudly as the front door. The girlfriend and the minister immediately started to argue with each other. Things went quiet for a couple of minutes when he heard the girlfriend shouting.

"You stink of cigarettes, alcohol and cheap perfume, I'm going to my mothers," she shouted.

Al-Qadir waited for her to leave the house before he went into the minister's bedroom. He was unconscious on the bed still fully clothed. His tie was loosened around his neck which gave Al-Qadir an idea. He rolled the unconscious minister to the bottom of the bed. With the tie still around his neck, he pulled it over a knob on the bed's baseboard. He then gave the minister a swift push off the bed and watched him start to choke on his tie. The minister came around and struggled to get to his feet as Al-Qadir kicked them from under him each time he tried to stand. Within a couple of minutes, he was strangled to death by the tie.

When the body was discovered, the police would put it down to a tragic accident.

CHAPTER 32

Brad had promised Al-Qadir that he would try to find the Iraqi general and sergeant that participated in the murder of his friends at the palace. The third one that was outstanding was the general that abducted and killed the women from the safe house. More personal was the death of his parents because of the same general.

He didn't have much to go on and was struggling to find any of them. He'd been briefed on the two explosions in Istanbul that had been blamed on Kurdish rebels by the Turkish government. The report stated that they were accidental detonations, which didn't seem right to him. Kurds were normally organized and had a lot of experience with explosives. One going off accidentally he could understand but two was a stretch. Something was off in the report, and he wanted to know what it was. He decided to task a CIA operative in Istanbul to dig deeper into the explosions. His name was Connor, and he had a lot of confidence in this agent as he had been a bomb disposal expert with the US Marines for five years. Before bomb disposal he was one of the top snipers for the Marines with many kills under his belt.

His grandfather had moved from Turkey with his wife and their three daughters in the late1950's. His mother was the oldest at the time at eight years of age. When his mother was twenty-two, she married her college sweetheart. His family were Irish immigrants that arrived in the United States 1847. They'd escaped the great potato famine in Ireland which killed over a million people.

His mother and father had two girls and two boys together, Connor being the youngest. His mother kept a lot of the Turkish culture and values alive that her father had passed down to her. She taught all the children to speak Turkish and Kurmanji her Kurdish father's native tongue. This proved to be invaluable to Connor when he joined the US Marines. He'd taught himself Arabic during his ten years in the military and spoke it as he did the other languages without a trace of an accent.

The coded message was sent for him to be ready to receive a call.

"How's things in sunny Florida?" asked Brad.

"Good, I assume you want me to bring something to the party?" replied Connor.

"Yes, it's a main course, not an appetizer."

"Interesting, will you send the menu to me?"

"Yes, I will send it to you now, good luck."

The call was disconnected. The kitchen was a drop point in Istanbul that was for Connor only. By stating that it was a main course Connor knew that it had to be an in-depth investigation. He was intrigued and went straight to the drop point. It would have been much easier to send it to the US Embassy, but Connor had been under cover for six months chasing leads on a gun and explosives smuggling operation. He was getting close to finding out who was behind it. He didn't question the side job, but it would eat into his time for his undercover operation.

Within twenty-four hours Connor had visited both sites of the explosions. The Turkish authorities that had swept the sites hadn't done a very good job of picking through the debris. There was evidence everywhere throughout the rubble. He found two interesting items one from each bomb site. The first was inside the apartment that had collapsed from the explosion. There was part of a cell phone that had a wire connected to it that was out of place. He knew straight away that it was the receiving device for a remote detonation. The wire had been soldered to part of the mother board of the mobile phone. There were multiple parts that would or could have been used in a bomb or in bomb making. In fact, there were too many parts unless this was a bomb factory, which by the evidence it wasn't.

The second interesting find was the truck bomb. He was able to get into the yard where the truck was stored. He was amazed but not surprised that the truck wasn't in a more secure facility. It was put in a yard with all kinds of other vehicles that had been towed off the streets.

All the indications showed that it was a typical car or in this case truck bomb. There was the chassis and part of the cab and engine block still intact, although twisted in places. The steering column was still hanging from the frame of the cab. The seats what was left of them were melted into the springs with human remains welded into them. On the side of the steering column the ignition switch was hanging down on the floor by its wires. It never ceased to amaze him what survived explosions and what didn't. The ignition wiring was one of those amazing moments, they were still intact. There was the clue that this wasn't an accidental detonation, the ignition was wired to detonate a bomb. Quietly he thanked the inefficiency of the investigators that had visited both sites and would pass on his findings to Brad.

Something was eating away at him as he made his way home from the yard. Why would anyone want to kill the people in the apartment and in the truck? What were they doing? Was it connected to his gun and explosives enquiry? He decided to hold off on reporting back to Brad while he investigated a couple of more things.

With the extensive electronic resources, he had access to through the CIA office in London he managed to get answers to his first question. Who owned the apartment, and the buildings close to where the truck exploded? The answers came back reasonably quickly. There was an offshore company that owned the apartment and the building directly next to where the truck exploded. There was something familiar about the company name, but he couldn't put his finger on it. He went back to his own investigation of the gun and explosives smugglers. It was frustrating him that he couldn't remember where he'd heard of the company name before. He had to pass his findings on to Brad at CIA Headquarters, Langley.

It was only two days before his next contact with Brad.

"We are on a secure connection so speak freely," said Brad when Connor answered.

"Have you found something?" he asked.

"Yes, interesting what you discovered. Your predecessor, who was murdered sent a report into Langley about a company that was buying properties in Istanbul. The same company has bought several properties in Paris, Marseille, and London. After he was murdered, we did a deep dive on the company but found nothing suspicious. The company directors all were legitimate. They also had executive positions with highly respected European companies...."

Connor interrupted. "Wait you said had, past tense."

"Yes, we have since found out that each of them has died in suspicious circumstances in the last year."

"How many people are we talking about and in what suspicious circumstances did they die?"

"Five executives, four male and one female. We are looking further into the deaths but two were car accidents and three were killed in what looked like muggings. Here is the interesting part, by investigating them further it appears that they were executives of four other companies. It looks like it was a paper exercise as there isn't any record of board meetings or any recorded documents by any of them. The only time they appeared all together in one company was the one that purchased the two properties in Istanbul connected to the bombings. They were involved with one other company each. There's no record of them as executives of any other company other than the ones they were regularly active with."

"So, they are ghost companies, probably registered in the Caribbean or some other tax haven to make the company look legitimate," replied Connor.

"Exactly, they were paid for their positions with the ghost companies. Their bank accounts show a monthly transfer from a Cayman bank, up until one month before they died. You notice I said up to one month before they died. Each payment from the Cayman bank stopped the month before they were killed."

"So, whoever was paying them had planned to kill them in advance."

"Exactly."

"Being paid for their name and reputation but what went wrong? Was there a falling out?"

"We don't know what went wrong but we are going to find out more about the companies they were connected to. It's a long shot but I have asked our tech geeks to get footage from every camera within a four-block radius of each accident or mugging. We may get lucky and find out what is really going on. There is a strong chance that your arms smuggling operation and the bombing in Istanbul may be connected somehow. I will get back to you when I have more."

"Roger that," replied Connor disconnecting the call.

This latest news from Brad had put another fire under Connor, he knew in his gut there was a connection. He decided to go through his predecessor's files in case he missed something. It may be something that didn't make sense before but now he was armed with new information.

He spent hours going through every document with a fine toothcomb, he didn't find anything. He went to bed and decided to do it all again the next morning with a fresh start. He poured himself a whiskey and started to walk towards the bedroom. There was a piece of paper on the floor, he picked it up. It was a handwritten note that was in the original file, but it only named a town in Iraq, Al Musayyib. He'd seen this before and had all kinds of intelligence on the town but there was never any connection. He put the note back on top of the file and finished his whiskey.

After a restless night he sent Brad an encrypted message about the town of Al Musayyib. There may be something in the CIA archives that connects the dots back to Istanbul and the bombings or his smuggling investigation. He knew it would be a few hours before Brad was in the office, so he asked his CIA desk officer at the Embassy in Istanbul to find out who owned the truck.

The US Embassy had been collaborating with the Turkish authorities after the bombs were detonated. At first, they didn't want any assistance or as they put it interference. The Ambassador reminded them that tourists coming into the country needed to be reassured that this wasn't going to be a new bomb campaign.

With millions of tourists traveling to Turkey every year the government didn't want the flow to stop. Hundreds of millions of Turkish Liras were at stake if tourism took another hit.

The economy didn't totally rely on tourism, but it accounted for almost five percent of the total employment. Almost two million people being directly employed through the tourism sector. The government had put new figures out that tourism income represented almost three percent of the country's GDP with travel exports accounting for over forty percent of total service exports. Their domestic tourism was starting to grow again another area that they couldn't afford a hit on.

The Ministry of Culture and Tourism in Turkey was responsible for its development. With duties to promote, develop, maintain, disseminate, and protect its tourism they had a great responsibility to contribute to the strengthening of national unity and economic growth.

This growth was supported by the Promotion Directorate within the Ministry of Culture and Tourism. They had dozens of overseas offices in over thirty different countries. The Directorate also had Provincial Culture and Tourism offices in that conserved the historical, cultural heritage, and diversify tourism. They organized promotions within the regions through festivals, fairs, and cultural events. The stakes were extremely high for the officials in these tourism offices as they were responsible and answerable to their peers and the people of Turkey.

CHAPTER 33

The information on the truck owner came back very quickly. There didn't appear to be anything untoward, the truck had been purchased two years earlier from a local dealership. The owner also purchased three other vehicles at the same time, this was a little unusual but not surprising. Few companies unless they were large purchased this many vehicles at once. The purchasing company was a transport business located in Istanbul. With the address in hand, he decided to give the company a quick look over. In the meantime, he asked the embassy contact to find out everything they could about the company and the owner or owners.

He found the address the embassy had given him, but it had to be wrong. The building he was standing in front of was a school and according to the faded plaque on the wall outside it was built thirty years earlier. He walked around the block to make sure he hadn't gone to the wrong address. A block away he walked into a what looked like a family-owned corner shop. He showed the address to the man inside and made out he couldn't find it. He confirmed that it was in fact the school. Something wasn't right and the hairs standing up on his neck told him so.

A call came through from Brad on his secure phone.

"Can you talk?" asked Brad.

"Yes, fire away."

"I couldn't find anything remotely connected to Al Musayyib and Istanbul. I had our office run every conceivable combination between the two, including bombings, terrorist attacks and still we got nothing. We were having a brainstorming meeting in the conference room about it. I was talking about Al Musayyib when a young hotshot that we'd just pulled over from the State Department showed up late. After receiving several unfavorable looks for interrupting he cut in on the conversation. In his previous job with the State Department, he told us that he was tasked with collating information on suspected terrorists in France. He was also responsible for cross matching that information with known smugglers."

"People smugglers or arms?"

"People, arms, explosives, and dirty money. He had all this information in his head that just kept pouring out. He is a unique individual with an eidetic memory and photographic memory. He's scary, if the Russians got their hands on him God knows what he would spit out. Once he starts to talk it's hard to shut him up the information just flows out of him.

Here is the interesting thing he produced. He says that we have been looking at this all wrong. He saw the photocopy of the note in the files you have that were left by your predecessor. He says the note doesn't refer to the city of Al Musayyib in Iraq but to one Riadh Al Musayyib. He is an Iraqi that fled to France when he was a teenager. He has built a substantial criminal empire in Paris. He is believed to have operations in not only France but the UK, Turkey, and several other countries. He has legitimate or dirty money property interests in all the countries he operates in. His bank accounts have been impossible to access in France, Switzerland, UK, and the Cayman Islands. Police agencies in each banking location have failed to get the courts to grant them access. He has been on Interpol's watch list for some ten years, but they never get enough evidence against him to make things stick with a court." Brad took a breath to drink some water.

"Can you find out if he or one of his businesses owns the apartment that was blown up here in Istanbul?"

"The brainiac is way ahead of us all on that one. Out of that massive brain in his head he started to tell us what properties were owned in Turkey. He had cross matched the companies Al Musayyib owned with not only the properties but with the executives that all died in suspicious circumstances. They are all connected in one way or another. As we speak I have him sitting down in front of a screen reviewing the several videos we have put together. They are from cameras in the areas where the executives died. I'm sending in an operative to keep surveillance on Al Musayyib."

"Just one operative, which makes it practically impossible for him to keep watch twenty-four seven," said Connor.

"He doesn't have to; we just want to know who he is circulating with and who his security team are? If this proves fruitful, which I think it will I want you to be backup for our man on the ground."

"I will be ready when you need me."

"Speak soon," said Brad.

CHAPTER 34

CORRUPT POLICEMEN

The hunt for Ali and Hamdi was proving to be a challenge for Al-Qadir. Policemen that they had worked with didn't know where they'd gone after the city was taken over by General Ashkouri. Some said that they'd fled the country or gone into the marsh lands to hide. The word was out that the assassin Azrael had killed them. He knew this wasn't true, but he would soon kill them, that's if he could find them. He had to tread carefully as he didn't want people to suspect him of being Azrael.

For the third time in recent weeks, he was visiting one of his father's old colleagues General Nabeel who served with his father. The general was incensed when his father was taken by General Ashkouri. The general responded by rallying other general's and police officers from numerous police stations around the city to move on the town hall. The groundswell of emotion by the police officers emboldened them all. The move had the effect of bringing police officers closer together at a time when they were falling apart. It sent a message out to those that were corrupt to be aware. However, in the police force there was always going to be corruption, it just depended on what your definition of corruption was. Getting a free coffee or sandwich at a reduced rate was corruption in many eyes. Others thought that corruption was the acceptance of money or something more substantial than a sandwich.

Thankfully, when the police officers merged on the town hall, they didn't get into a firefight with Ashkouri or his soldiers. The general knew that his old friend Abbud would produce a solution when he heard how the police officers had reacted to his detention by Ashkouri. The general's health was fading after an attack on a police convoy by militants. He'd lost an eye and walked with a cane due to muscle loss after surgery to remove a bullet. The black patch over his eye gave him a warrior like look and he didn't really mind as he was alive, some of his men died that day.

After the formal greetings and pleasantries, the general made them a strong black coffee each.

"Take them outside," said the general.

They sat in the shadow of the building on rickety wooden chairs outside his humble mud and stone home.

"I think you need two new chairs," said Al-Qadir gently rocking back and forward making the chair squeak.

"They will outlast me," replied the general.

"I don't know so much, you're a tough man."

"Tough but old."

"I see you are walking better with the cane, is the leg getting better?"

"It is a slow process and I'm impatient with my own recovery. The headaches are the worst from the loss of my eye, the pain doesn't stop some days. Sunlight is now my worst enemy and coming from a man that loved the sun and being outdoors it is painful, I'm fine in the shadows."

"My father always said that you and he were the toughest police officers on the street. You both had been in many tough situations together."

"Your father was a good man, an honest man. Why are you here so quickly after your last visit?" he asked.

There was no fooling the old general. "I want to find two corrupt policemen that were passing information to Mayor Laghmani."

"What are their names?"

"Ali and Hamdi, they gave information about the safe houses that my father and you set up. They need to answer for their crimes, and I want them to go to prison for what they have done."

"That's interesting, you say you want them to go to prison, why not let Azrael take care of them?" asked the general.

"I have heard of this Azrael, but I don't think that he is as good as people say he is. I think that the people have built him up to be an avenging angel, he's a myth. I think it is several people doing the murders and they are just using this Azrael as cover."

The general watched him closely as he answered, "That may be the case, it could be more than one person. I happen to think that it is the work of one man and his obsession for revenge."

"That may be so."

A police car drove past with two policemen in front, the passenger saluted the general.

Returning the salute he said, "They still salute me even though I'm retired."

"You are well known, and they have a great deal of respect for you."

"I can say this because I am retired, but I believe in this Azrael and what he is doing. I'm sure he started this trail of death for good reasons, more than likely revenge. I just hope that it doesn't poison his heart and mind and he doesn't lose sight of why he started."

"I think if this is one man, he must be focused and dedicated. I don't think that someone like that loses his way or his reason for doing what he does." Al-Qadir was looking the general straight in the eye. "I'm sure his focus shifts slightly at times but it would appear he has one aim, to crush corruption and punish those that are corrupt."

"That may be so, but he has chosen a very long, slow path to achieve his goals."

"Maybe," replied Al-Qadir.

"I will ask around, see if anyone knows where Ali and Hamdi are hiding, but don't expect a quick answer."

"No, I just hope to find them to put an end to what happened to my mother and father. There are other families that would like them to be found so they can get justice for their families."

"Yes, there are many families that want and need justice. It would be better if Azrael did find them at least they would taste his kind of justice," said the general.

"I'm sure there are a lot of people hoping that Azrael finds them."

"Look after yourself and God go with you," said the general.

"And you." Al-Qadir walked away without looking at the general sitting in his wooden chair.

The general didn't waste any time putting the word out that he wanted to talk to Ali and Hamdi. There were hundreds of police officers on the streets with even more people willing to give information on the two ex-policemen. The story of the safe houses and what they did with the information was well known on the street. Getting information quickly on their whereabouts was not what he expected but it happened. A colonel in the police visited the general in his home and gave him the location of where the two police officers were hiding. As it turned out they weren't really hiding they'd moved to Baqubah where they were involved with the local criminal underworld. They'd become enforces for a local money lender in the city. A man that people feared because of the way in which he got his money back, even when people couldn't pay.

The money lender didn't cripple anyone or hurt them to where they couldn't work. Doing this would be counterproductive as he would never get paid. He did however have his own signature of punishment. He had his minions bring the people that owed him money to his warehouse. In the warehouse he had two things he liked to do to the debtors. The first was a red-hot piece of metal that would be pressed against the persons chest. This would leave a brand with his initials showing that he owned them. The second was always the ownership of any property that the people owned. He only loaned money to people that had something of value, a shop, business, animals, vehicles. He would get them to sign over the property, whatever it was if they didn't pay the debt. In some cases, he even took the young daughters of some of the debtors and sold them to rich men.

CHAPTER 35

Al-Qadir was surprised when he received the message three days after he'd visited the general stating he needed to see him. At first, he thought that something was wrong and didn't think that it had to do with the information he wanted.

As he approached the house, he saw the general sitting on the wooden chair where he'd left him the last time he visited. He smiled to himself as he could see his father sitting next to him in better times. The general stood when he saw Al-Qadir even though it was a real effort to do so. His mobility was getting worse instead of better. They kissed on the cheek and sat in the chairs.

"How are you doing?" asked Al-Qadir.

"I have pain today, but I can take it."

"If you need pain killers, I can get you some."

"I get them from the doctor, but they are weak, I will be OK. I have information for you on Ali and Hamdi."

"That was quick," he replied.

"Yes, but it is good news and bad news, they are working for a man called Zadik Akkad, a money lender in Baqubah. He is extremely wealthy and has numerous businesses most of which he took from people that owed him money. Here is the address where he is located." He handed a piece of paper over. "This man is extremely dangerous and ruthless, an evil man. The police have tried to arrest him many times in the past, but he always gets off the charges because the people get scared to go to court or they are found dead. Ali and Hamdi are working as enforcers for him, collecting debts. Zadik punishes the debtors if they don't pay him on time. If they miss a payment for the first time they will get a small beating, a second time a more severe beating. The beatings are done by Ali and Hamdi, sometimes others he employs also take part. If they can't pay their debts, he takes their property away legally. I say legally but he really steals the businesses or property from them. This is where he gets nasty, he brands the debtors before he takes their property with a metal iron placed onto the chest, his signature move."

"Brands them, the man is sick," said Al-Qadir.

"Sick, yes. He has other men that protect him and his business interests, mostly criminals with violent reputations. Zadik calls himself, 'Sargon the Great' after Sargon of Akkad. He was the first king of the Semitic-speaking Empire of Mesopotamia; this was during the Sargonic dynasty." He paused to take a drink of hot tea.

"I remember being told about him in school, but I can't tell you much about what we were told."

"He is a well-known king in our history, he ruled for forty-five years. He was the illegitimate son of a temple priestess who placed him into a basket and pushed him out into the Euphrates River. The basket was carried by the current until a local water drawer found it further downstream. The man was drawing water from the river to irrigate his crops when the basket drifted towards him with the child inside. From this beginning he grew to be one of the most important and revered kings in Persian history. Today he is a Persian legend whose tales are still celebrated throughout Persia and has the name Sargon the Great."

"You seem to know a lot about him."

"Yes, I was a history major when I went to college, an interest I have to this day. But this man Zadik is no Sargon the Great, he is evil. If you decide to go after Ali and Hamdi you will have to have the full force of the police behind, you."

"I will do my best to include the police."

"Somehow I don't think so." Something caught the general's eye; it was a car that had driven past twice already before Al-Qadir had arrived.

"What's wrong?" Al-Qadir could tell the general had seen something.

"The same car driving past now has done so twice already, if it turns left ahead it is following the same path. I think they may have a problem with me."

"Why you, you're retired?"

"I wanted to find Ali and Hamdi for you and there was only one way to do that, ask a corrupt policeman. I asked Colonel Kassem, you know him he oversaw the training of recruits when you joined."

"Yes, I remember him. We all called him the skull because of his large bald head."

"That's him. If they circle around the back of the shops they will return in about four minutes, go inside the door there is a cupboard with two AK47's in it. Put one behind the door and one inside the doorway. If the car does appear we will have about two minutes before it gets close because of the traffic. They will see us as soon as they turn into this road. I want you to say goodbye to me and walk around the corner."

"I'm not leaving you out here on your own."

"Don't worry, I want the men in the car to see you leave and think that I'm on my own. When you go around the corner there is a window that is unlocked, climb through it, and hide behind the front door. I will give them enough time to get close but not close enough to start shooting. I will walk inside very slowly, that's the only way I can walk anyway. If they are coming for me, they will follow me. If they drive past, it is you they are looking for.

If they have been watching my home, they will know that I always leave the front door wide open. I will make enough noise in the back room for them not to question where I am. I will be waiting with the AK if they start shooting. They won't expect a trap, I'm sure of that. The hallway is narrow, and they will have to walk one behind the other. There is a gap on the hinge side of the doorframe where you will be able to see them clearly. They won't be able to see you as it is so dark inside and their eyes won't have had time to adjust after being in the sunlight.

Take the first one from behind quietly, then shoot or stab the second one or do what you feel is right."

"I think we need to take one of them alive to find out who sent them."

"Yes, you're right. I never went this far with my planning, I'm sure if Azrael were here, he would do what you suggest." He gave a big smile. "Help me stand and leave, the car has turned into the road."

As planned Al-Qadir said his goodbye and walked away.

Nabeel saw a donkey cart was slowing down the car which helped him get into position in the house. Picking up the AK47 he went straight to the back of the house into the darkness of the kitchen, he was a little concerned as he didn't hear Al-Qadir climbing through the window. He suddenly realized that there may have been accomplices of the men in the car waiting around the corner. He had to put that out of his mind and keep to the plan.

Al-Qadir was watching the street through the gap in the hinge side of the door, he had a clear view of the road. The car that General Nabeel had pointed out stopped outside and two men got out. He slid quietly into the dark corner behind the door. His trusty knife was in his right hand ready to strike. He decided to leave the AK47 leaning against the wall in the corner, he didn't need it. The first man moved into the hallway cautiously followed by the second man. The noise in the kitchen the general was making was so loud it could be heard in the street. It sounded like he was cleaning a metal pan.

The second man cleared the doorway and took two steps inside before stopping. Neither man was carrying guns but they both had knives drawn. They moved very quietly towards the kitchen when there was a loud crunching sound. The first man had stood on something that made the noise. They both stopped and the first man looked down to the floor, it was covered in eggshells.

Al-Qadir stepped out from behind the door, clamping his hand over the second man's mouth and stabbed him in the throat. The first man started to turn only to be smashed in the head with the butt of an AK47 through a small window in the hall.

"Here take this," said General Nabeel handing a bucket of sand to Al-Qadir. Lift his head and scatter the sand under it to soak up the blood."

Al-Qadir did as instructed and closed the front door so nobody could see inside from the street. He dragged the unconscious man into the kitchen, realizing he could still hear the noise of the pan being cleaned. Sat on the table was an old tape recorder playing the sounds.

"You, clever old man," he said to himself.

"I will need you to dispose of the dead man tonight or he will stink my home out by morning. You can use my old car which is parked around the back. I suggest dumping his body on the rubbish tip by the river. The wild dogs that run all over that place will chew him up in no time," said the general.

"You didn't mention that you'd recorded the pan noises, so I presume that you have been planning this for some time," replied Al-Qadir.

"Well, since I saw them passing the first time."
"The eggshells were a nice touch, it told you exactly where the first man was standing. You knew he would stop at the sound of the noise and look down, your opportunity to step up to the window opening and knock him out."

"Well, you don't live as long as I do without learning a few tricks. Drag the dead body into the yard out back, nobody will see it there. The gate to the backstreet where the car is parked is locked from the inside. There is an old piece of carpet in the yard, it's just big enough to put under the body to drag it out without leaving a blood trail. Then you can help me put this one in the chair to interrogate."

Al-Qadir put the dead man on the piece of carpet and dragged him into the yard. Getting the second man onto the wooden chair was a little more problematic due to his size. With him securely bound and gagged they sat and drank tea that the general had made.

They were just finishing the tea when the man came around with a splutter and shock in his eyes. He looked around suddenly realizing what had happened, he was tied to a chair. He tried to shout and curse through the gag, but it didn't help him. Sat in front of him was Al-Qadir and General Nabeel calmly drinking tea out of two glass cups.

"Would you like another tea?" Al-Qadir said to the general.

"Yes."

Al-Qadir poured a little tea into the glass and added two sugars to it, stirring the glass with a gentle ping as the spoon hit the sides. He rejoined the general and sat next to him on the chair. Neither of them said anything to the man, they just stared at him.

The man started to get frantic in the chair fighting the bonds and shouting at his captors. He started to sweat the more he struggled with the ropes. He was panicking, the two men never said anything they just sat and starred, they were freaking him out. After ten minutes the man he knew to be a retired general spoke.

"What brought you and your dead partner to my home?" he asked.

The man was trying to speak through the gag, but they couldn't understand him.

"He's not making any sense," said Al-Qadir.

"No, he isn't," replied the general.

The man was now going frantic completely losing it in the chair, shouting louder and louder.

Al-Qadir stood with the knife in his hand and walked towards the man. He started to freak out shaking side to side as he looked at the bloody knife blade.

"This belongs to your friend." Al-Qadir wiped the drying blood off the knife blade on the man's leg. "When we take the gag off you will tell us everything we want to know, or I will start to skin you very slowly until you do."

Al-Qadir slipped the gag out of the man's mouth and slid it down his chin.

"Please, don't kill me."

"Who sent you?" said General Nabeel.

"A man we work for, he is crazy he will kill me if he finds out I told you."

"I will kill you if you don't," said Al-Qadir.

"We will let you go if you cooperate," said the general.

"Remember if you lie, I will skin you alive, it will take a few days for you to die, and it will be incredibly painful." Al-Qadir tapped him on the head with the knife blade.

"His name is Hamdi."

"What did this Hamdi want you to do?" asked the general.

"We were to kill you because you were asking questions, trying to find Hamdi and Ali."

"Who do they work for?"

"He is the crazy one, Sargon the Great, that's what we must call him. He will kill me now that I've told you, his name."

"Was I the only one that you were supposed to kill, what about him?" said the general pointing to Al-Qadir.

"Just you, I don't know who he is?"

"Am I supposed to believe that?" asked Al-Qadir.

"It's true I've never seen you before today."

"Where is this Sargon the Great?"

"He has several places in Baqubah. His house is like a fortress and his office is always protected by armed security guards. I will give you the addresses if you let me go."

"Write them down." The general gave him a pen.

Without untying his hand, he held a notepad under the point of the pen as the man wrote two addresses. The man started sobbing and crying at the same time, mucus drooled down his mouth and chin, dripping onto his legs.

As the general moved away, he clutched his chest and fell to the floor, he was having a heart attack.

"General, general," said Al-Qadir as he leapt to his side.

He put his ear to the general's chest to listen for a heartbeat, there wasn't one. He immediately started CPR trying to revive him. After five minutes he knew the general was gone, he gave up and sat on his heels. He closed the general's eyes and said a prayer over him.

The end of the prayer was broken as the man in the chair had loosened the ropes while Al-Qadir was doing CPR.

An arm went around Al-Qadir's neck in a choke hold trying to cut off the blood to his brain. He reacted by throwing his head backwards smashing it into the man's face. He had to do it a second time before his grip loosened. He gave two elbows to the rib cage and sank his teeth into the man's bicep. He screamed aloud but not for long as the knife blade pierced the side of his neck.

Al-Qadir was furious with himself for allowing the man to get free, now he had two bodies to dispose of. He took the general to the local hospital emergency room making out he didn't know if he was dead or not. He admitted that he tried CPR and the doctor praised him for at least trying.

That night he drove the bodies to Baqubah and left them near the office of Sargon the Great. Both bodies had the signature of Azrael, a death card nailed to the forehead.

CHAPTER 36

SARGON THE GREAT

The news of the two bodies in Baqubah traveled fast throughout the city, Azrael had struck again.

"Zadik, two of our men have been murdered, their bodies were found by the office," said Ali.

"What did you call me?"

"Sorry, Sargon the Great." Ali bowed his head like the man was a king.

"You call me by that name again and I will gut you."

"It won't happen again."

"So, who were the men?"

"The ones I sent to take care of General Nabeel, he'd been asking a lot of questions about us."

"About us, you mean you and that idiot partner of yours Hamdi. This must be dealt with quickly; people cannot see that I won't respond. Kill the general yourself and bring his head to me, tonight."

"Yes, Sargon the Great."

"Get out."

Ali and Hamdi drove straight to the general's home to kill him, something they regretted not doing themselves. When they arrived at the house there didn't seem to be any lights on. They went around the side of the house to get in through a window. They figured the general was asleep. This would be an easy kill for them, they'd even brought a saw to cut his head off.

The house was pitch dark inside, so Ali turned on a small penlight to see where they were going. The room was small with a two-seat sofa and a television to one side. On one wall was a selection of photographs in wooden frames showing the general in uniform over the years. The bedroom was opposite, and they crept inside careful not to make a noise. There was a loud metal ring like a gong as the pan hit Ali on the head and a second one when it hit Hamdi's head. Both men were knocked unconscious.

Al-Qadir reversed the general's car up against the side gate to his house. He then put both bound and gagged men into the trunk. He drove the car for an hour into the wastelands outside the city. He was five miles from the nearest farmhouse and any kind of civilization.

He unceremoniously pulled the now conscious men out of the car and dumped them onto the rocky ground. One of the men lashed out at him with his feet, a reasonable attempt thought Al-Qadir. He cut the gags off their mouths with his knife not caring that the blade cut their faces at the same time. He then removed their boots and slung them to one side.

"So, which one is Ali, and which one is Hamdi?"

"You can go to hell, I know who you are, the son of that shit Abbud the do-gooder," spat one man.

Al-Qadir kept his cool even though the man had disgraced his father. He stepped up to the man and stepped on his legs that were bound tight. Slowly and deliberately, he pulled the knife out from behind his back.

"That knife is too big for you little boy, be careful you don't cut…"

He didn't finish the sentence as the blade slid between his toes, slicing down through bone and sinew. The man wasn't so cocky now as he screamed in pain and passed out. The knife stopped when it reached his ankle, it now looked like he had one giant big toe covered in blood.

"You now," he said to the second man.

"He's Hamdi, I'm Ali, please don't do this," said Ali.

"Ah! So, your Ali, OK you and I need to come to an agreement, or you can be stubborn like your friend. Tell me why you sent the men to kill General Nabeel, don't lie because the men you sent told me. I want to see if you can tell the truth."

"It was Hamdi, he wanted to kill the general because he'd been asking some police officers if they knew where he was. It was his idea, not mine. When the men failed, and Azrael left their bodies by his office Sargon the Great sent us to bring back the general's head."

"Good, who is this man that calls himself Sargon the Great?"

"He's an animal, a money lender. He doesn't have any feeling for anyone or anything just power and money."

"Tell me about his home and his office, what are the ways in and out, how many men guard him?"

Ali didn't shut up for ten minutes giving him a lot of information to work with. Hamdi woke up part way through but didn't make a sound, other than groaning in pain.

Al-Qadir sat them both up in the dirt so that they faced each other. He then walked behind Ali and draw his knife one more time.

"Hamdi, this is what I'm going to do to you."

He slid the knife across Ali's throat causing the man to go into a panic as he choaked on his own blood. Hamdi tried to turn away, but Al-Qadir wasn't having any of it. He held his head back so that he could watch his friend in crime die. Hamdi started to weep as Al-Qadir walked over to the dead body and cut the head off. It wasn't easy to do but cut it off he did, Hamdi was next. With the severed heads of Ali and Hamdi in the trunk in a plastic bin bag he drove to Baqubah.

Ali had given him a real breakdown of the office, he even drew a design of the building and its layout in the hope it would save his life, that obviously didn't work. To the side of the office was a garage where Sargon the Great parked his car, or at least his driver did. He never got out of the car until it was parked inside the garage, a big positive for Al-Qadir. The driver remotely operated the garage steel roller door when they drove up to it. The warehouse was only small and protected by two of the security team from the outside. There was one steel connecting door that led from the warehouse into the garage and then another into the office.

As he drove to the city, he formulated a plan of attack on the garage and warehouse. For his plan to work he had to make sure that the car went inside. This would give him a fighting chance against the six-armed security guards. Four were located on the outside of the building, when the car drives inside, he would only have the armed driver and his partner riding shotgun to contend with. He stopped at the general's house and managed to get a few hours' sleep. After the sleep he made one more stop on his way, he had to collect a few items he needed to complete his plan.

He parked the car three blocks away from the office he was targeting. It was almost five in the morning and the streets were quiet. He left everything in the car for now and changed into his vagrant's outfit. He looked just like a homeless man by the time he added a little brown and black to his face, it looked like dirt. The outer clothes he was wearing smelt bad of stale body odor. As he walked past the garage door entrance, he noticed that there was a camera above the door. On the corner was a man sat in a chair fast asleep with a sidearm that was holstered. From the corner he was supposed to watch the garage entrance and the front door to the office. Like the garage the front door had a camera above it, but this wasn't fixed it was a pan tilt and zoom camera. As he shuffled past the sleeping man, he picked up a plastic water bottle from the edge of the road. He put the bottle to his lips and tilted his head back like he was drinking the contents. He could see the camera over the door, it hadn't moved so there was a good chance that nobody was monitoring it at night. But then something caught his eye, movement on the roof. He kept shuffling until he was out of sight of the office.

The movement on the roof made him curios, why have someone up there at night? He took the stinking outer clothes off and dropped them into a trash can. He looked for a building that would give him a clear view of the roof of the office building. Unfortunately, there was only one and that was directly next door. He found a way to the roof and crawled over the edge to get a better view of the office building. There was the movement again, one man pacing backwards and forwards smoking a cigarette. It was only another minute, and he threw the stump of the cigarette onto the roof and walked to a door. It looked like it led to a stairwell into the building this was the one described by Ali.

He returned to the car and took out the plastic bag with the heads inside, an assortment of weapons, flashbangs, night vision goggles, which he put on his head and a ball of heavy string. He knew exactly where he could access the roof of the office which was via an old fire escape ladder on the side. However, the ladder didn't go all the way to the ground, it stopped ten feet short. There was a wall next to the building which ran close enough to the ladder for him to grab a hold of the bottom rung.

With the plastic bag containing the heads tied around one shoulder and the kit bag on the other he scaled the wall and ladder quickly. He paused before climbing onto the top of the roof and listened for movement, there wasn't any.

Climbing onto the roof he flipped down the night vision goggles allowing him to see in the dark. He slid the Glock with suppressor and rail guard laser attached out of the side pouch of his backpack. He headed straight to the door where the smoker had earlier disappeared, it was wide open. Inside he negotiated the metal stairs slowly and cautiously, stopping to listen for movement inside. At the bottom of the stairs, he could smell coffee and food cooking. These security guys were very lax as the door at the bottom of the stairwell was also left open. He waited a minute listening for noises and clues as to how many men he had to deal with.

There it was the sound of men talking, they were discussing the soccer game that was playing on the television. The sound of the television would mask any slight sound that he made as he approached the room, they were in. He swept side to side with the Glock as he walked towards the door looking for any hidden targets. He flipped the night vision goggle up again as the light from the television would blind him when he went inside the room. Just as he was about to go into the room one of the men came out, almost walking into him. He shot him twice in the head and stepped into the doorway quickly shooting the second man who was rising out of a chair. He swept the rest of the warehouse and went through the door into the garage. The garage and office were both clear, he'd taken care of the internal security threat.

Al-Qadir took his time getting a feel for the layout of the inside of the warehouse and garage. He jammed a metal bar into the door that led into the office so that nobody could come through it into the garage. There were two other doors in the warehouse, one a giant double delivery door and a pedestrian door. Like the office he fixed these two doors so that they couldn't be opened from the outside. Feeling comfortable he went back to the roof and tied a rope to a metal pipe on the only side of the building that didn't have a window or door. He had the rope coiled up ready for a quick abseil down the side of the building. Any security people left would go straight to the ladder on the side of the building that he'd climbed up. They would think that this was the only escape route from the roof, giving him valuable seconds to escape unnoticed.

Back in the warehouse his next job was the severed heads of Ali and Hamdi. He tied the thick heavy string to the hair on each head and tied the other end to the top of the garage door. He set his weapons out in two locations in the building, one hidden in the warehouse and one on a shelf above the stairs leading up to the roof.

CHAPTER 37

He sat next to a large window by the garage door that had iron security bars on the inside. It looked like it opened outwards, he quietly checked that it would open, and it did. The sun was rising quickly, and it would soon be daylight. He stayed next to the window letting his eyes become accustomed to the daylight outside. Now all he had to do was wait.

According to Ali, Sargon the Great arrived every day at eight o'clock. His driver would open the garage door and they would drive inside. The garage door would then be closed immediately after it closed the great man left the car. His bodyguard went everywhere with him except into the office. His office lady arrived at eight thirty even though she wasn't paid until, nine. At ten minutes past eight there wasn't any sign of the car it was getting close to the office lady's arrival and Al-Qadir was thinking that he may have to abort. It was at this time that he heard a car pulling up outside the garage and the garage door started to open.

Sargon was berating his driver for getting stuck in traffic.

"Next time you can't find your way around a traffic jam I will fire you. You must know that it is dangerous for me to be waiting in the car like a sitting duck."

The garage door was half open as the driver drove it forward slowly, that was when he saw the heads.

"What is that?" he said not believing his eyes.

"What? Drive in," said Sargon.

"Look," said the bodyguard in the front passenger seat.

"That's Ali and Hamed, get me out of here, reverse," screamed Sargon.

Al-Qadir waited just long enough for the car to be committed into the entrance of the garage. He opened the window and threw two flashbangs to the rear of the car, they exploded as soon as they hit the ground.

The explosions behind the car shocked Sargon and his bodyguards.

"We're under attack drive in quickly close the door," said Sargon with panic in his voice.

The car tires screeched as the vehicle lurched forward into the garage, the door closing closely behind it.

The security guard sitting on the corner jogged down the street when he saw Sargon's vehicle. He stood at a safe distance as always and would wait until it went inside before he returned to the corner. He walked closer when the car didn't go all the way inside, there were two explosions. He threw himself against the wall next to the window.

Al-Qadir saw the guards head bounce against the wall outside as he jumped at the sound of the explosions. He shot him twice in the head and moved quickly to where the passenger would get out of the car.

The bodyguard flung his door open to jump out of the passenger seat, he only got one leg out when two bullets decimated his head. The driver didn't even get out as two more bullets found their target.

Al-Qadir had moved quickly dispatching the bodyguard and driver. He then opened the rear passenger door to get Sargon out. The man was sitting on the seat screaming his head off as he stared at the dead body of his driver.

"Sargon the Great I presume," said Al-Qadir.

"Who?"

He dragged the overweight pompous bastard out of the car and dropped him onto the garage floor.

"You sent two men after General Nabeel, because of this he had a heart attack and died. Those are the heads of the men you sent." He pointed at the decapitated heads hanging from the string.

He looked up at the heads as they swung from side to side. That's when he realized the heads had something attached to them, they had death cards nailed to them.

"You are Azrael. I can pay you anything, I'm extraordinarily rich, I can make you rich."

He very quickly tied Sargon's hands and feet, he had eight minutes before the office woman arrived. Out of his backpack he produced a hammer and nails, he pounded a nail and card into the foreheads of the two bodyguards.

Sargon was screaming for help and looked like he was about to lose his mind.

"Be quiet or I'll shoot you, where do you keep your money?"

Sargon had lost it, so he slapped him across the jaw twice to bring him back.

"In the corner over there, a safe."

"What is the combination?"

"It doesn't have one, just a key, it's in my front pocket."

Al-Qadir put the muzzle of his gun against the man's head and dug his fingers into the pocket, there was the key. He opened the safe and removed all the money and legal documents that were inside. He put them into another plastic bag out of his backpack and went back to Sargon.

"You are a fat greedy man, and you chose the wrong general to mess with."

He walked behind Sargon and clamped his head between his knees so that he couldn't move it.

"Please, please," sobbed Sargon.

"This is for General Nabeel and all of the people that you have ruined."

He held a nail in front of Sargon's face so he could see what was about to happen. He pushed a death card down the shaft of the nail and placed the point against Sargon's head. The first strike with the hammer was just enough to make it pierce the skull, then came a second, a third and finally a fourth strike. The strikes of the nail head were slow and deliberate, this man was going to feel every strike of the hammer. The nail was now buried deep into the brain of the twitching head.

Al-Qadir stood and watched for a minute as the body of Sargon twitched and then became still in death. He left the building as planned by the rope on the roof, he didn't want to walk out of a door into a policeman responding to the explosions.

The city was buzzing when the bodies of Sargon and his men were found. Many of those whose lives he'd ruined cheered and chanted Azrael's name in the street. Three weeks later the deeds that had been recovered from the safe mysteriously appeared at the homes of the original business and property owners. Money was left with other people that had been abused and used by the now not so Great Sargon.

CHAPTER 38

Brad was having a difficult day in the office, he got them every so often when he was missing field work. He envied his protégé Al-Qadir as he was living the life that he did when he was his age. He was due to check-in with him but was ten minutes late.

He was going through some old files on terrorist attacks looking for some connection with his current investigations. The bombings in Istanbul over a year earlier had led to nothing. The only lead that had potential was the man on the run from Istanbul hospital with the purple birth mark on his right hand. With the many thousands of cameras around he felt sure that one day he would show up. He'd tasked one of the hotshot geeks to go through new and old footage for the man with the purple birthmark. He knew that if he participated in the bombing he wouldn't stay in Turkey. He couldn't believe that the police involved in the investigation didn't take a photograph of the man when he was unconscious. They had really dropped the ball on that one.

As part of a counter-terrorism initiative facial recognition was used on videos and still shots of about every camera that was on the streets of Europe. Likewise, cameras at banks and bureau de change offices were also run for facial recognition. The system at Langley also allowed other features to be added to the recognition system. Brad had a good description of the purple birthmark and its unusual shape. This was put into the system as they had no other leads on the man.

The difficult day Brad was having was about to be turned into a fantastic day as he got a knock on his office door.

"Come," he shouted.

"Sir, I think I have something on the man with the purple birthmark," said an excited young woman.

"What is it?"

"This," she replied handing him a picture.

It was a picture of a man at a counter with his hand under a glass partition, he was pushing Euro notes to a cashier. The camera was obviously behind the cashier as all you could see was the back of her head.

"There," she said tapping the man's hand in the photograph.

"A birth mark, where and when was this picture taken?"

"A month ago, at a bank in Cairo, Egypt, but it isn't the first time he has visited the same bank."

"Have you run facial recognition on him yet?"

"That was my next step."

"Good, do it and excellent work," said Brad as she left his office.

He was grinning from ear to ear, he knew they were finally getting close to some answers on the Istanbul bombings.

He was brought back from his daydream when the phone on his desk rang.

"Yep," he said answering the phone.

"Checking in," said the voice of Al-Qadir.

"How are things?" he asked.

"Good, I would like some work, I'm getting bored."

"I'm sure you are but rest is also a good thing," said Brad looking at the picture the female agent had left.

"Anything going on?"

"No, not really. I may finally have a lead on the bombings in Istanbul."

"Sounds interesting but I don't know much about it," he replied.

"No, you were busy with other things. It's just a photograph of the man who us and the Turkish have been looking for. It's a good one and it shows the birth mark on his right hand," said Brad.

"What birthmark, what man?"

Brad could hear the anger and excitement in his voice, "Do you know something about this?"

"I told you the story of what happened at the palace in Iraq and what the general did. I told you the name of the general and the description of his dog of a sergeant. I didn't know the sergeant's name, but he had a purple birth mark on his right hand."

"Let me send you the photograph, it's a bit grainy but you may be able to tell if it's him. Call me back when you have looked at it."

Al-Qadir couldn't wait for the photograph to come through, it took a long time. The picture was grainy, but it was the sergeant, he had no doubt about it. He had surfaced at last, now he would kill him. He was staring at the photograph when the satcom phone rang.

"Well?" asked Brad.

"It's him, where is he?" he asked excitedly.

"Cairo, Egypt. I want you to sit tight on this information for a few days so that I can gather more information."

"I'm going to Cairo."

"Not yet, we will send you in as soon as I have enough information for you to locate him quickly. There is a lot riding on this and not just your thirst to avenge your family and friends. I promise you that you will be the only one that hunts this man down."

"Two days, that's all I will wait."

"You will wait until I tell you too. This must be done properly, and I can't have you going in all guns blazing. I give you my word this man is yours." He waited for a response but didn't get one. "Listen to me, there are hundreds of banks in Cairo that he could have gone into. It would take you years to stake them all out and you may still never get to him. Let the team here locate the exact bank and see if there is a pattern of him visiting the bank. Let us do our job so that you can do yours."

He was trying to quell the anger he had inside for the sergeant, he hadn't felt it this bad for a long time, but he knew Brad was right.

"OK, I will wait for your call."

"Good, don't blow this after waiting so long. Check in tomorrow as planned and I will update you on anything new."

"Yes," he said disconnecting the call.

He paced up and down for ten minutes trying to calm himself. This was the closest he'd come to finding the sergeant and General Mutaz. He knew that Brad was right, and he had to do this right. The sergeant could lead him to Mutaz who he wanted more than anything.

The four-day wait was almost too much for Al-Qadir but when Brad called the news was good.

"OK, this is what we have. The bank is the National Bank of Egypt in a place called Al Hawamidiyah on the west bank of the Nile. I will send the address and what other details we have. He has a pattern, and this will be in the documents, read and destroy as always. I want you to fly into Cairo tomorrow. Included in the information I'm sending is a safe house and a vehicle, an old Cairo taxi. When you get to the safe house there will be other instructions for you. Remember we need to know as much as possible from this man relating to the bombings in Istanbul."

"Yes, I got it," he replied.

"You are close my friend, don't mess it up now by being too anxious to kill him. Get the information first on the bombings, obviously any information on Mutaz and then you can do what you want with him, understood?"

"Yes, understood. I won't let you down you know that I'm calm now and ready to do my job for you and then my job for my family."

After hanging up the phone he was so excited at the prospect of finally coming face to face with the sergeant. He couldn't sleep all night and ended up going for a run at three in the morning to clear his head.

CHAPTER 39

AMIR FAIZ

Amir Faiz left the Iraqi special forces not long after the arrival of the US and British forces in 2003. He, like many of the Iraqi army had seen enough of the death and carnage that Saddam Hussein and his elite guard had caused. He'd served ten years and put his heart and soul into the army.

He started a security company with one of his army colleagues recognizing that there was a need for private security. This would be especially true after the coalition forces left the country. Their business was slow to start but eventually they had a good business developed. He worked with a US company that specialized in protection of convoys and high-risk targets. They subcontracted him for a lot of work in Iraq and several close protection details of Iraqi politicians. He'd travelled to Paris, Frankfurt and Rome with the politicians and built a nice network of security and intelligence contacts in each location. The politicians liked having him close to them as his scarred face scared most people.

He had become interested in the mystery assassin known by the Iraqi people as Azrael. He was giving politicians and the wealthy of Iraq the jitters. Corrupt heads of large companies and banks were using more private security to protect them and their families because of Azrael. If he could ever meet the killer, he would shake his hand. He like many believed that Azrael was ridding the country of the corrupt political system that was in place. The man was not only assassinating corrupt politicians but corrupt former members of the Iraqi military and police. Whoever he was he'd not only targeted those that had turned their backs on their people for financial gain but those that had given up people in hiding to the Iraqi military. People like General Mutaz and General Ashkouri, two blood thirsty sociopaths.

Amir had followed the attacks by the killer Azrael with great interest. He admired the man's skill, it could have been a woman, but he doubted it, his Muslim bias showing. His service in the Iraqi special forces came to a sudden end when the invasion took place. He wanted to fight but he knew that it would be futile.

His real reason was he didn't believe in his own government or the generals that ran the military. He especially hated Saddam's National Guard. The previous year his cousin told him about the meeting in the desert when General Mutaz appeared with a group of his soldiers. He felt that something was very wrong as the general was heading away from the main fighting and not in a direction that he would expect. That was when he knew that the coward was running and heading towards Iran.

He'd tried through many of his army and air force contacts to find out where the general was, but nobody knew anything. He wanted to give the general a taste of his own medicine and leave his face in worse condition than his was. He touched the scar on his face without realizing it as he thought about the day, he was slashed by Mutaz.

Through his enquiries he had found out about a group of Iraqi's that were found in Iran, they had been slaughtered. The theory was that they had paid smugglers to get them out of Iraq. The smugglers then murdered them all and hid their bodies in a box canyon. It didn't feel right when he dug deeper with his contact in Iran. The vehicles that were left at the scene of the murders weren't the kind that smugglers used. He found out that they were in fact vehicles that had been stolen from farmers by a group of Iraqi soldiers in a small village close to the Iranian border. The description that the villagers gave of the soldiers and the general in charge fitted Mutaz perfectly.

Although the Iranians were normally very secretive his contact was extremely helpful due to their long-standing friendship. They had collaborated with each other in a secretive program between Iran and Iraq. They were trying to stop the flow of arms going through Iran to the Turkish Kurds in the Northwest of Iran on the Turkish border. The Iranian military had lost many soldiers in firefights with the Kurds especially at checkpoints. The collaboration was only known by a few extremely high commanders in both countries and of course the soldiers involved.

He found what he thought was a trail of death and destruction that had Mutaz's fingerprints all over them. At times he doubted himself, thinking he was just wishing these events were connected to Mutaz.

There was one such incident that stood out to him when he was told about it by his friend. A very unusual firefight between Kurdish smugglers and a Turkish military unit. The firefight was very suspicious with too many bullet holes in the vehicles and blood in places were there weren't any bodies. The bodies of the dead had been moved and this didn't make sense. The thing that raised his suspicions more than anything was the report that one of the Kurds had been shot in the head at point blank range. This was Mutaz, this was his signature he now knew that he was on the run most probably heading to Istanbul. He wanted to track him down and have him thrown into jail for the rest of his life. Well, that was the legal solution, he really wanted to cut him up and let him die slowly in the desert somewhere.

He used all his contacts in Istanbul, Rome, Frankfurt, and Paris to locate Mutaz, but nothing materialized. He did talk to the American company that subcontracted him, but they claimed to know nothing. Then came a break, another assassination by the man called Azrael in Baqubah. A notorious money lender and smuggler that called himself Sargon the Great was murdered in his own garage. There were several bodies, all but one that was in the street had the death cards nailed to the foreheads.

The more he dug into this man's background the more he got interested. He was connected to another evil Iraqi that had left the country many years earlier and started a criminal enterprise in Paris. They were in business together not just in smuggling but laundering money by purchasing properties in Turkey.

He went to Sargon's office for a meeting with the lady that ran it for him. At first, she didn't want to share the files in the office even though he claimed to be a Detective, but with the mention of Azrael and the fact he may come back she jumped at the chance to help. There were several files that she showed him that were interesting. The jackpot was a file on a property in Istanbul and another with two properties in Paris. It was time to ask some very pointed questions of the woman.

"In this file for the property in Istanbul it states that he only owns ten percent of it. The file on the Paris properties show that he only owned five percent of them, why is that?" he asked.

"I don't think I should divulge any more information, where is your police identification? I should see it."

"It's in my other jacket at police headquarters but I can get a police vehicle to bring it here." He took out his mobile phone. "I just hope Azrael isn't out there watching, apparently he doesn't like corrupt people or people that don't do the right thing."

"No, wait don't call, forgive me but it has been a shocking time since the murders."

"No, I understand and the quicker we get through this the quicker I will be out of here. So, who is the majority owner of the properties?" he asked.

"It isn't he, but a company which is registered offshore. The company does a lot of business through this office or used to. There was a bit of a falling out between the two of them when the share of the property in Paris dropped to five percent from forty five percent. It was a tough time for all of us during that period, he was like a raging bull. He would smash things on my desk, slap me across the face and threatened to fire me many times."

"Why would he slap you?"

"He blamed me for everything that went wrong with his property dealings."

"So, who owns the offshore company?"

"Please promise me that you won't tell anyone I told you, because I'm not supposed to know who he is."

"You have my word and my protection if anyone does threaten you." He meant that he would protect her but with his own men not the police.

"I found out by accident one day when I arrived in the office ten minutes earlier than usual. He was in the garage on his mobile phone shouting at the man on the other end. I was about to go back out the front door to avoid a slapping when I heard him say, "You don't want to mess with me Riadh Al Musayyib, I warn you," that is the man's name."

"Is there anything else I should know about this man?"

"I don't know anything else, honestly."

He could tell the woman was starting to get upset and gave her a tissue out of his pocket.

"Don't worry you have cooperated fully, here is my card. If anyone comes in here asking the same kind of questions that I have asked, please call me. As you can see there is just my name and a telephone number, no connection to the police if someone sees it. This also applies if someone tries to scare or threaten you, please call me."

"Thank you," she replied.

As he left the office, he felt like he was finally getting closer to Mutaz he booked a flight to Istanbul.

Amir wasn't surprised when he walked off the plane to see his old friend standing in the gangway. They greeted each other and walked towards the terminal building.

"Do you have any luggage to collect," asked Mehmet.

"No, just this small bag I'm carrying," replied Amir.

"Good, follow me."

They walked past the lines of people going through the immigration checkpoint and through a door that Mehmet used a security swipe card on. After a long trek through a labyrinth of corridors they came to a dead-end corridor with a door at the end. To the left of the door was a magnetic card swipe like the first one, a wall telephone and a camera above the door. He watched as Mehmet picked up the phone and punched in a four-digit number. He could hear someone on the other end answer.

"Mehmet. Four, six, four," he replied.

He hung up the phone and swiped his card causing the magnetic lock to disengage.

As they stepped out into the sun it was blinding at first, he followed Mehmet closely to a waiting car. They both climbed in without saying anything, the driver didn't say anything either.

"We will stop at a café on the way, I want you to meet someone," said Mehmet.

"OK."

They talked about nothing much on the short journey to the café. The driver dropped them off outside and parked at a discreet distance further down the street.

Mehmet ordered two Turkish coffee's and waited for the questions to start from Amir.

"What can you tell me about the addresses I sent to you?"

"The first address is not a real address it is a piece of wasteland that hasn't had a building on it for twenty years. The second is more interesting and my colleague will fill you in on that one. Here he comes, he's undercover so don't say anything unless he asks you something."

"OK," replied Amir.

A man approached wearing Sharwall trousers that were typically narrower at the ankle, and a matching dark cream mraxani jacket over his deep brown shirt. The shirt was cinched together around the waist with a pshten fabric that acted like a belt. On his feet he wore dirty handmade fabric shoes called a klash. He blended in with about every other man on the street.

He walked past them and sat with his back to them on a table facing the road. Now the three of them were back-to-back.

The undercover officer ordered a Turkish coffee and a water. They sat without speaking for five minutes. The agent was surveilling the street to make sure they weren't being watched.

"What is your interest in the address you sent to Mehmet?" said the undercover officer without turning.

Amir turned his head towards Mehmet like was talking to him. If anyone were watching them, they wouldn't know they were speaking to each other.

"It came up in an enquiry I was conducting in Baqubah. It was after a man that owned a business there was slain by the one the Iraqi people call, Azrael."

"I have heard of this Azrael through my contacts in Iraq, they say he's a force to be reconned with. Do they know who this Azrael is yet?

"No, he's a mystery."

"What did the Istanbul address you sent have to do with the slain man?"

"His office lady told me that he owned ten percent of the building with another man owning the remainder through an offshore company in the other man's name."
"Who is the other man?" The undercover agent was getting interested.

"His name is Riadh Al Musayyib, an Iraqi that left the country many years ago, he is based in Paris where he's lived for many years. I spoke to a contact of mine in Paris, he stated that Riadh is on the top of their organized crime list. Interpol and other international law enforcement agencies have him on their watch list also, especially for gun running and people smuggling. They have tried many times to take him to criminal court, but the cases always fall apart or the witnesses against him die." Amir sipped his coffee.

"If he's such a crime problem, why don't they send him back to Iraq?"

"He obtained French citizenship several years ago, so it makes things very difficult for the law enforcement agencies and immigration authority to do anything."

"As far as I know his name hasn't come to our attention in Turkey, but I will check it out."

"The address in Istanbul I sent obviously has an interest to you, can you tell me anything about it?" Amir hoped to get an answer connecting Mutaz.

"Confidentially, we are looking into an explosion that happened there last year. It was one of two explosions the same night, the apartment address you sent, and a truck bomb a quarter of a mile away. At first, we thought that the explosions were premature detonations by Kurdish militants. The more I investigated the weaker this theory became. Whoever set the bombs off they wanted us to think that it was a Kurdish group. There were the remains of several bodies in the apartment and two connected to the truck. I'm convinced there were dark forces at work when the bombs were detonated."

"Do you have any leads as to who is responsible?"

"None, I don't suspect the owner you mentioned Riadh, would blow up his own building, it would just bring unwanted attention to him."

"Yes, you're right."

"I get the feeling you have a suspect in mind, who is it?"

"No, it doesn't have any of the signatures of the man I suspect."

"What signatures are you talking about?"

Amir hesitated to give Mutaz's name, he had no evidence. "I don't have any evidence that my suspect is involved. He is an evil, power-hungry animal who likes to shoot people in the head at close range. So, this doesn't look like it has any of his fingerprints on it."

"Wait, you said he likes to shoot people in the head, why?"

"It's what he does, he gets some kind of sick rush from doing it."

"Wait, we had a security man on the docks shot in the head around the time of the bombings. It took a couple of days to find his vehicle as it was hidden in a warehouse that wasn't being used. After the vehicle was found the dock was searched by our underwater search unit, they found his body, he'd been shot in the forehead at point blank range," said Mehmet.

"Are you sure this was around the time of the bombings?" asked the agent.

"Yes, because I was supposed to go to the dock but was diverted to a meeting with the mayor. Another member of my team was sent, I remember it well now. It seemed like it was a robbery but there wasn't anything reported missing from his body or any of the warehouses."

"Who is your suspect?" asked the agent.

"A former Iraqi general called Mutaz, he gave me this scar on my face when he visited our military camp once," replied Amir.

"So, you have a personal interest in this Mutaz, a reason to find him," said the agent.

"Yes, but I want him to answer the many crimes he has committed in my country. I can keep my personal business separate."

"We will speak again if I find anything out, don't leave for ten minutes." The agent got up and left.

Amir and Mehmet sat and had another coffee before they left discussing how they could help each other.

Amir knew what his next move would be, a trip to Paris to find more out about Riadh and his connection with Mutaz.

CHAPTER 40

CAIRO, EGYPT

Ahmad was enjoying his newfound life in Cairo. His Arabic was good before he arrived but now, he was almost fluent speaking Cairo Street Arabic. His cousin was gracious for a couple of months, but his wife wasn't. There was something about Ahmad that she didn't like, she just couldn't put her finger on it. She wanted him out of their apartment a quickly as possible. He couldn't miss the signs from his cousin's wife, she wasn't subtle.

His cousin couldn't throw him out as he thought that Ahmad didn't have any money and certainly didn't have a job. Ahmad kept the money he'd stolen from the store owner hidden and made out he was destitute.

Ahmad had to get himself a new identity as he knew at some point, he would have to get a job and the police were always stopping people and asking for their identification.

All Egyptians were required to carry a national identification card. The card was needed if you required medical help, hospitalization, a job, bank account and for street identification by the police. The card was also needed when passing through police or military checkpoints. If you didn't have a card, there was a good chance that you would be arrested or at least stopped from moving through a checkpoint. The card had the holder's personal details as well as a section for identification of their religion. Islam,

Christianity, and Judaism were the only acceptable religions for the purpose of the card.

The civil registration system in Egypt was centralized in Cairo. There are twenty-seven Governorates in Egypt that are then divided into centers, towns, and villages. Within these locations there are over four thousand localized health offices that registered births and deaths. Once the information of a birth or death is received it is then sent to a department within the Ministry of Interior.

He felt that this government registration system played in his favor as the policeman on the street relied on a visual inspection of an identification card and very rarely had access to computer records.

He went to the far side of Cairo to a registration office to look at the death's registry. When he arrived at the office, he noticed a Sudanese man stood close to the entrance. The fact that he was Sudanese wasn't unusual as they were everywhere in Cairo. This man was paying a lot of attention to what was going on inside the offices.

After a scan through the registry, he found what he was looking for. The death of a man some years earlier he had the same first name, but his family name was Hussein which he found ironic. He was two years older than the deceased but that didn't matter. He wrote down all the dead man's information.

After a short conversation with a desk clerk, he found out that it was easy to apply for a lost identification card. However, there were some pitfalls to this, and one was being found out that you aren't who you say you are. He'd already filled out the application form that was on the information desk and had a passport style photograph of himself for the application. He got nervous and decided to abort.

As he walked out of the office, he noticed the Sudanese man had repositioned himself inside the office like he was waiting in line. He ignored him and walked outside. The Sudanese man followed him and now he thought that he was about to be mugged.

Ahmad stopped by the side of the road and lit a cigarette using the moment to surveille his surroundings. He couldn't see any other Sudanese men or anyone waiting to jump him. He placed his hand on his waistband checking that his knife was still there, it was. He crossed the road towards the market on the far side and picked up his pace. The Sudanese was keeping up with him as he disappeared around a corner.

The street was quiet as he turned the corner as he was at the back of the market stalls. He waited knife in hand for the man to come around the corner.

Ahmad was on the Sudanese as soon as he came around the corner and had him up against the wall.

"Why are you following me?" he said holding knife blade to the man's neck.

"Wait. I can explain," he replied.

"Speak quickly or I will slit your throat."

"I heard you asking the woman about replacing your identification, I can help."

"Help, how?"

"I have friends and we specialize in identification cards and passports. I can get you a new card for a special price."

"A special price just for me I suppose?" Ahmad was no fool.

"Well maybe same price as everyone else. The cards are good, even the police don't know that they are fake."

"How do I know I can trust you?" Ahmad was getting nervous looking all around.

"You tell me details you want on the card, your name, religion that sort of thing and I will have it for you in two days."

"And I suppose you meet me in a dark alley somewhere to collect it?"

"No, I meet you outside the office you were just in, close to a lot of people. One hundred Egyptian pounds is all I ask for the card."

Ahmad looked into the man's black eyes, "Fifty pounds."

"No, I can't do it for this price, I have to make some money."

"No deal then." Ahmad was trying to play the bartering game that went on everywhere in Egypt.

"Ninety pounds, a good deal."

"Eighty and we have a deal, but I must get it in two days outside that office, same time."

"Do you have a photograph with you?"

"Yes, if we do this, I want my name to be spelt correctly, Ahmad Hussein."

"Yes, very important can you write it down?"

Ahmad printed the name on a piece of paper and handed it to the man.

The Sudanese spat on the palm of his hand and held it out. Ahmad didn't shake it and walked away.

CHAPTER 41

The two days went slowly but he was back close to the registration office. Ahmad had been watching the Sudanese man for thirty minutes looking for signs that he had others with him. He was alone but was getting very agitated having waited thirty minutes past the agreed time. He gave up waiting and walked down the street.

Ahmad could see the man cursing as he walked away, he was upset. He followed him for a short distance, when he felt it was safe, he shouted to him.

"Where have you been, I waited?" said the Sudanese.

"I was on a bus, it broke down," lied Ahmad.

"Oh!"

He was a little surprised that the man took his word for it but the buses in Cairo were renowned for breaking down.

"Do you have the identification?"

"Yes, but we walk like we are talking to each other, just in case the police are watching. I will offer you a cigarette out of my packet. Inside you will see the paper you need take it and a cigarette. You then offer to light my cigarette; I will hold your hand to my face and take the money out of it."

He was impressed the Sudanese had obviously done this before.

Before he offered to light the cigarette, he gave the paperwork a quick once over, it was good. They walked for a few minutes and then went their separate ways.

As soon as he felt safe Ahmad unfolded the paperwork to check it out again. He couldn't believe how good it looked, it was an exact copy of a government I.D. He was ecstatic, he could now find a job and not worry if the police stopped him.

It was on a walk to the mosque that Ahmad's luck changed. An elderly woman fell in front of them onto the road, her head hit the ground hard. His cousin tried to save the woman's fall but was just too late. The gash on her head was bleeding profusely, but head wounds always do. Ahmad saw an opportunity to keep on his cousin's good side. He needed to stay a little longer at his house as it was difficult to find a real job, which he needed to support himself.

Ahmad stepped in to help the lady, just as a crowd started to gather around. He kept his head low as he didn't want anyone asking questions about him. With his first aid training from the Iraqi military, he was able to stop the bleeding until the ambulance came. People in the crowd slapped him on the back and praised him for his quick action. His cousin was impressed and told his wife the whole story when they returned home. She was pleased that he helped the old woman, but she still didn't like him. Her mind hadn't changed she wanted him out of their home.

The next day he was walking out of the mosque with his cousin when two men approached them.

"My name is Mossam, you helped my mother yesterday when she fell, I want to thank you," he said.

"It was my pleasure, is she OK?" replied Ahmad.

"Yes, she had six stitches and is being kept in hospital for a couple of days for observation. This is my brother Ali."

The four of them shook hands.

"It looked like a bad wound, I'm glad she is in good hands," said Ahmad.

"If there is anything I can do for you we are in your debt," said Mossam.

"Yes, we owe you a great deal our mother is everything to our family," said Ali.

"No, you're not in my debt," replied Ahmad.

"If you hear of any jobs going my cousin is looking for one, that will help him," said Ahmad's cousin.

"Cousin please," said Ahmad.

"A job we can help with that, we own a ceramic tile business here in town. We have four shops around Cairo that sell them. We have men that do sales and installers," said Mossam.

"I don't know anything about tiles or installing them, but thank you," said Ahmad.

"Would you be interested in working in our warehouse, it is demanding work, but it pays well. If you like it, we can train you for a higher position in the company," said Mossam

Ahmad looked at his cousin who was nodding at him to say yes.

"I would like that, but only if you can train me. As I said I know nothing about ceramics."

"Good, here is my card, the address is on there. Come to the office tomorrow at eight in the morning and we can tell you more about the job and what you will be paid," said Mossam.

"I'll see you in the morning," he replied taking the card.

They walked home talking the whole way about the possibilities of his new job. Ahmad was happy for the work and the prospect of renting his own place. His cousin was happy because his wife would be also especially as he had a job and would hopefully leave their home soon.

The next morning, he was shown the warehouse and the job he had to do. It was simple just moving stuff from one area to another and taking care of orders for delivery. It took him a couple of weeks to settle into the work, but it was easy. A month after starting he heard of a flat that was for rent above a shop close to the warehouse. As soon as the shop owner heard where he worked, he rented the room to him immediately.

It was a very modest place with only two rooms and an external staircase leading to the apartment's front door. The front room was basically a bedsit with a bed, two seat sofa and the smallest sink and microwave he'd ever seen. The second room was a shower room toilet combination. The window in the front room overlooked the busy road outside and there was nothing to stop the constant traffic noise outside.

After a week in the apartment, he purchased a small television from a local TV repair shop. It had become a constant companion for him as he didn't associate with anyone from the warehouse. Over the coming months the only time he saw his cousin was at the mosque. His cousin's wife now had what she wanted, and she wasn't about to ask him to return for dinner.

His life changed dramatically over the following months. He had excellent organizational skills in the warehouse and was moved into a manager position. He opened a bank account for his wages and slowly paid what was left of the two thousand he stole from the store owner. For contingency purposes he kept five hundred Euros for emergencies in cash.

CHAPTER 42

EGYPT

Brad arranged for Al-Qadir to fly on a military flight out of Baghdad to Italy. From the base he made his own way to Rome via train and bus dragging his small wheelie bag along behind him. He would have preferred a backpack only, but he needed to blend in with other passengers on the flight. In the wheelie bag he had an assortment of casual clothes that you would expect a tourist to carry. Also in the wheelie bag was an old copy of a tourist's information pack on Egypt and the Pharaohs. At Fiumicino airport in Rome, he purchased a return ticket in coach class for Cairo at the Alitalia desk. His ticket was for five days with a reservation at the Sheraton hotel in Cairo. It all looked like a genuine tourist visit to Cairo should the immigration and customs people get inquisitive.

The flight went smoothly, and he took advantage of the down time to catch a couple of hours sleep. He wanted to be fresh when he arrived in Cairo as he had a busy schedule ahead of him. Brad had offered him a safe house, but he declined as he wanted to appear to be a tourist as much as possible. He did accept the use of a small nondescript vehicle which would be delivered to the Sheraton hotel close to the airport in the parking garage.

He cleared immigration and customs easily after his French passport was stamped with a tourist visa. As he entered the public area outside the baggage claim he felt like he could have been in any other airport in North Africa or the Middle East. There were hundreds of people crammed into a small area waiting to greet friends and loved ones from the arriving flights. He looked for the sign indicating which way he should go for a taxi. After pushing gently through the crowd, he found the taxi area and took a black and white taxi to the Sheraton at the airport. The taxi driver wasn't pleased as he was hoping for a passenger that wanted to go into the city which was much further away. At the hotel he gave the driver a reasonable tip, not too much that he would remember him.

The reception desk was busy with people checking in, so he sat to one side until it calmed down. Once he checked-in, he was given an envelope by the receptionist that was left for him and went to his room. He did a quick sweep of the room and opened the envelope, inside was the ignition key to the car and the parking space number written on the inside of the envelope. He immediately went to the parking garage to check out the vehicle. It wasn't what he expected as he had asked for a small nondescript car, instead he got a Toyota Landcruiser. Just like other vehicles Brad had supplied there was a hidden compartment with a Glock and spare clips in it. He gave the weapon a quick check and placed it back in the hidden compartment. In the glove box was paperwork from the local Hertz car rental office with his name already on the agreement. He knew that this wasn't a Hertz vehicle, but it was a nice touch if the police stopped him. He decided to take it out to get a feel for the vehicle and evaluate the navigation system.

He drove towards the city center trying to avoid all the suicidal Egyptian drivers. Cairo was like Baghdad when it came to driving and traffic lights, they were only a suggestion especially at night. Before he knew it, he was in the thick of traffic as he crossed the Six October bridge over the river Nile. He now knew why he was given the Landcruiser as there were so many of them and they didn't stand out. He then made his way to the area where Ahmad had been seen at the bank. It was three hours before he returned to the hotel and was ravenous. He ordered a sandwich and coffee from room service as he didn't want to go down to the hotel restaurant. Five minutes later there was a knock on his door with a male voice announcing room service. He looked through the peep hole and it looked like a genuine employee.

"Come in and leave it on the table, please," he shouted in English.

He knew that most of the hotels in Egypt trained their staff to speak English if they didn't already.

He quickly walked into the bathroom and turned on the shower.

"It's on the table sir," shouted the room service waiter.

"There is a tip on the same table for you, thank you."

"Thank you," he replied and left the room.

The next morning, he was up early and headed towards the bank again in the hope that Ahmad would stick to his usual schedule. The traffic was even worse than the night before and it took him almost two hours to get to the bank. He parked across the street and waited for him to appear. According to the bank ATM camera it was eleven o'clock in the morning when he had visited previously. Today Al-Qadir was out of luck as eleven o'clock came and went as did twelve. He was frustrated as this was the only lead, he had to find Ahmad. He decided to walk around the area to see if he could see him working somewhere or sitting in a cafe. He walked for two hours with no luck and returned to the Landcruiser. The traffic was getting busy again as most of the workers were finishing for the day at two in the afternoon.

He was thirsty and hungry again and stopped at a café that was on the next block to his vehicle. It was now three in the afternoon, and he decided to call it a day and drive around in the hope he saw him. He picked up the small slip of paper on the plate that the waiter brought and placed the cash on top of it before returning it to the plate.

He walked to the Landcruiser with half an eye on the bank ATM machine. He was truly frustrated as he had come a long way to find Ahmad and now, he was a ghost again. The traffic crawled past his vehicle as he started the engine. He looked in the side mirror for an opening in the line of traffic in the hope he could get out quickly. His frustration was growing as he now felt that even the Cairo traffic was against him. He could see a bus approaching in the distance and knew from his surveillance that it would stop short of his vehicle. This would be his opportunity to drive out into the traffic.

The bus like many others overshot the bus stop and stopped alongside his vehicle blocking him in. The door for the passengers to get off the bus was right next to his driver's door. Al-Qadir laughed aloud to himself at the irony, nothing was going right. He needed the laughter and the irony of it all to break his mood. He watched the passengers to get off waited for it to pull away. The last passenger to get off was a man, a man he recognized, it was Ahmad. He was shocked and surprised he didn't realize it, but he was staring at him as he turned. Quickly he leaned over to the glove box like he was getting something out. He didn't want Ahmad to see his face just in case he recognized him.

Ahmad waited for the bus to drive away before he took the treacherous walk across the road to the bank. He was having a good day and looked forward to having dinner with the new lady in his life. Like most people crossing the roads in Cairo he took his life in his hands jumping between the lines of cars as they flashed past him. He had worked a little later today at one of the other ceramic stores helping with new inventory. He had been promised a store of his own to manage and today was a test to see if he could do it, he passed with flying colors.

The ATM had two other people waiting in line, so he stood in the line waiting patiently.

Al-Qadir was out of the vehicle and like Ahmad took his life in his hands trying to walk across the road. He was a half block away watching the mans every move, he wasn't going to lose him, not after all this time. He could see him finishing his transaction at the machine and he walked in the opposite direction to where he was standing.

He only walked a couple of blocks and opened a door next to a shop. He could see what looked like apartments above the store, this was where he must be living. On the opposite side of the street was another row of shops with similar looking apartments above them. The building had a flat roof and what looked like a metal ladder on the side wall which went to the roof. He would wait until dark and gain access to the roof to see which apartment Ahmad lived in. In the meantime, he kept the place under surveillance to see if he left.

As darkness fell Al-Qadir climbed the ladder onto the roof and scanned the apartments across the street. They all had light on inside which made it easy for him to see. There appeared to be four apartments judging by the different people inside. He couldn't see Ahmad, but he was sure that it was the second one along as he'd seen men in the others. In this apartment he only saw a woman and it looked like she was setting a table for dinner. The last call for prayer was called out from the many mosques in the area one of which was a block away. A man walked into the room where the woman was setting the table and gave her a hug. He then left the room as did she. A minute later Ahmad walked out of the door to the apartments and headed towards the mosque.

Al-Qadir was down the ladder like a squirrel as he followed Ahmad. Blending in with the rest of the men entering the mosque wasn't a problem. He was two rows back from Ahmad in the mosque as everyone prayed. He walked ahead of Ahmad and collected his shoes by the door, he didn't want to be stuck behind him in the crowd. He followed him through a side street to his back to his apartment, this was a good place to abduct him but not tonight.

Now that he knew where Ahmad lived and had a plan on how to abduct him, he just had to find a veterinary surgery that he could break into. It surprised him how few veterinary surgeons there were in the city. He found one at an animal sanctuary close to an area called Maadi a popular area for expatriates that lived and worked in Cairo. Burglarizing the office was a lot easier than he thought as it had very weak security. It was two in the morning when he returned to the hotel plenty of time for a few hours' sleep.

CHAPTER 43

The next day Al-Qadir parked the Landcruiser in the side street that Ahmad had walked down after the mosque the night before. He double checked the street to make sure that it wasn't a no parking zone and locked it. The street was very narrow and had just enough room for vehicles to squeeze past the parked cars. The Landcruiser wasn't overlooked by any apartment windows as the single-story buildings all appeared to be small businesses.

He sat at a café where he could see Ahmad's apartment door. He wanted to be sure that he returned home before he went to the mosque. If he didn't go to the mosque, then he would have to attack him in his apartment. This would be a last resort as he didn't want to harm the woman that he was living with, she was an innocent.

The melodic call for prayer or the azan as it was known, started from loudspeakers attached to the minarets at the mosques. The loudspeaker measure was the modern way of delivering the call for prayer by most mosques in the city. The more human or old way of delivering the call by men in the minaret had mostly gone.

Al-Qadir sat across from the mosque watching as the hordes of men entered, Ahmad was right on time. He didn't follow him in this time instead he waited for him to come out at the end of prayer. He positioned himself where he could see the doors to the mosque. He would be ahead of Ahmad when he left which gave him time to get to the Landcruiser.

When he saw him leave, he was with another man, something Al-Qadir hadn't thought of. He cursed under his breath as they walked together. At the corner of the side street the man Ahmad was talking to walked in a different direction. He gave a sigh of relief and hurried to the Landcruiser. He positioned the wing mirror so that he could see the street behind him where Ahmad would be walking. He climbed into the back seat and waited for Ahmad to appear. As he got closer to the vehicle Al-Qadir opened the rear door to the vehicle and feigned falling out of the door.

Ahmad enjoyed seeing his cousin in the mosque, being able to talk to him for a brief time was a bonus. He arranged to have coffee with him the next night after prayers so that they could catch up on his new job promotion. His life was better than anything he could have imagined he was in high spirits as he walked back to his apartment. A car door opened ahead of him, and a man got out but fell to the floor. He was clutching his knee as he cried out in pain as he hit the ground. Ahmad was going to ignore him and cross the road but thought that it was wrong he was a different person now, he would help him.

"Are you hurt?" said Ahmad as he tried to help the man to his feet.

Al-Qadir was looking past Ahmad down the street, to make sure they were alone. As he felt the man's hands hold his arm helping him to stand, he struck. In one motion he plunged the needle into Ahmad's neck and pressed the plunger on the syringe full of ketamine. For good measure he punched him in the jaw to make sure he was knocked out. He quickly bundled him into the back seat and climbed in with him. Within a couple of minutes Ahmad was trussed up like a chicken and snoring on the back seat.

AZRAEL

The drive down road number 25 to the farmlands to the South of Cairo was a real mix of city traffic into farm vehicles and small-town traffic. He had chosen the place where he wanted to take Ahmad from his previous drive as he got to know the roads. It was just before Nazlet El Shobk that he turned off the road eventually stopping twenty yards from the Nile River. It was now after midnight and the only buildings around were farmers properties nearer to the main road. He was on a farm track in the middle of a field of a crop of high Maze.

He pulled Ahmad out of the back seat and let his body crash to the ground. He then dragged him to the front of the vehicle and dropped him under the headlights of the Landcruiser. He was starting to wake up from the effects of the ketamine, so he slapped his face a couple of times to hurry along the process.

Ahmad felt like his head was going to explode as he came out of the sleep, he was in. He was completely lost and couldn't figure out what had happened or where he was. There was a bright light shining in his eyes, he couldn't see anything else. Then someone grabbed a hold of him and propped him up against the front of a vehicle. He slowly started to get his vision back, there was someone stood in front of him.

"Who are you? What do you want?" he asked.

"You don't recognize me?" said Al-Qadir.

"No, why would I?"

"Take a long hard look at my face."

Ahmad didn't know what this man wanted; he was totally lost, then the face became clear in his mind. It was the police officer that had struck General Mutaz in the balls at the palace.

"What do you want, I don't have money."

"I don't want your money, I want your life for what you did at the palace, you and your general."

"I was only acting under orders; you don't understand if you didn't do what he said he would kill you. You saw him shoot his own soldiers, he's crazy," replied Ahmad.

"Yes, he did but he also shot and killed a lot of innocent people as you did. You are as guilty as him and when I find him, I will kill him slowly just like you are going to die."

"You don't understand, the man is a lunatic he even tried to kill me and the rest of my soldiers in Istanbul just so he could keep the money."

"What did he do in Istanbul?" asked Al-Qadir.

"He rigged a truck and the apartment we were hiding in and blew them both up. He killed everyone, I only got away because I left the truck to go back to the apartment."

"Where is he now?" he asked.

"I don't know, I ran after the bombings because if he knew I was alive he would kill me. He was supposed to go to Paris to start a new life and business with a man called Riadh Al Musayyib, that's all I know. He lied so much that I don't even know what the truth is anymore."

"Put your hand up to your face so I can see your birthmark."

Ahmad was even more confused now, but he did as he was told as the man took a photograph of him on his phone.

Al-Qadir questioned him some more but realized he had nothing else to offer.

"You want to know who I am?" he asked.

"Yes, but I'm sorry for what happened to you and your friends. I'm not the same man that was in the military, I have changed my life and my ways," he replied.

"You think that is going to help the innocent people you killed, or help kill, they don't have a second chance. My name is Al-Qadir Abbud son of General Abbud of the Miqdadiyah police, some people call me Azrael."

The terror in Ahmad's eyes was immediate he started screaming at the top of his lungs.

Al-Qadir smiled at him and tied a gag around his mouth.

"Now you know what is going to happen to you, but as promised it will be a slow death. I have timed the tides here on the river Nile it is fascinating stuff. The speed at which it changes can be fast and furious or slow and easy. You are in luck as this time of year with the moon in its current phase it will rise slowly."

Al-Qadir dragged him to the edge of the river where it became very muddy, very quickly. At the edge of the river was the remains of an old makeshift pier that the farmers used to put crops onto a boat. It looked like it hadn't been used for many years which suited him.

The river was at its lowest point of the tide change as he tied Ahmad to the wooden post. He struggled the whole time sometimes cursing him and sometimes weeping and begging for his life. He left the gag in his mouth and sat on what was left of the old pier three feet above Ahmad. It took almost two hours for the river to start rising and another two before it got to Ahmad's chin. He was crying and twisting his body trying to pull away from the post he was tied to. As the water got to his mouth, he lifted his chin as if it would save him from drowning.

Al-Qadir took another photograph of Ahmad as the water reached his mouth to show what had happened to him. He could hear him starting to choke as the water entered his mouth through the gag. It was only a matter of minutes before it reached his nostrils and he started to drown. He could see his head swinging from side to side as the brain fought for his lungs to get air, then he went calm.

Al-Qadir waited another two minutes before he untied the dead body from the post and pushed it into the river to be carried away by the current. He resisted the temptation to nail a death card to Ahmad's head as he didn't want it to get back to Iraq. His work was done here, the bonus was he had some answers for Brad and his investigators in Istanbul about the truck and apartment bombings.

CHAPTER 44

AL-QADIR, PARIS

Armed with the information Brad had sent to him Al-Qadir arrived in Paris on an Air France flight from Cairo, Egypt. He moved through immigration quickly and walked out of customs without the need to stop as he dragged his wheelie bag along. He went to the bay on the third floor of the airports multi-story parking lot where Brad said there would be a car waiting for him. As described, there was a Citroen parked in the bay with the ignition key under the rear passenger floormat.

He'd memorized the route to the CIA safe house that Brad had provided. As he drove into Montefermill, a suburb of Paris he couldn't help but see how run down the area was. He'd driven past two blocks of apartments that had many windows boarded up and by the look of the smoke damage on the outside of one there had recently been a fire. He could see why Brad had sent him to this location. There were a lot of Africans on the streets who were most probably asylum seekers. This was the kind of area where people didn't respect or appreciate the police. He'd already seen several drug deals taking place on street corners.

The building he was looking for was at the rear of a row of shops, it had been used for storage at one time. The double doors to the yard blended in so well he almost drove past it. He drove up to the gates and pressed the button on the clicker that was attached to the car keys. Both doors rolled open, and he drove into the yard.

He expected the yard to be open to the elements, but it wasn't. It had a glass wired roof that had motion detectors in each corner. The yard was only just big enough for two vehicles side by side. Directly in front of him was a strong looking reinforced door. He flipped the cover on the combination lock and punched in the six-digit code. He heard an electronic motor and then the metallic grind of bars sliding. The door sprung open about an inch letting him push it open fully.

The single-story room he walked into was sixteen feet wide and about forty feet deep. It had a large three-seater sofa to the right with a television on the wall opposite to the left. At the far end was an open plan kitchen with a refrigerator, cooker, and coffee machine. To the right of that was a door which he presumed led to the bedroom and bathroom. He dropped his wheelie bag next to the sofa and walked over to the fridge. As he'd hoped it was stocked with bottled water and several bottles of beer. The bedroom door was reinforced like the front door as backup for security. The bedroom and bathroom were a saferoom which had independent power and air conditioning. It was designed to hold back even the most determined attackers for at least twelve hours. The closet was small, the back wall of which functioned as a hidden doorway to the weapons and gadgets room.

He immediately went through the assortment of handguns and automatic rifles that were hung on a wire grill on the wall. He chose two Glocks and a UMP Heckler and Koch.40 caliber sub machine gun. One Glock and the UMP would go into the Citroen as backup.

There were several flashbangs and grenades stored with the spare ammunition clips. There was enough fire power for a small army. He chose a couple of knives and a stun gun to go into the Citroen also. He wanted to get started and hunt down Mutaz, but he had to wait for Brad to give him the latest update. He lay on the bed in the hope a getting a couple of hours sleep the operation in Egypt didn't allow him to get much sleep and was feeling exhausted.

The ringing of the mobile phone startled Al-Qadir, shaking him out of his deep sleep. He'd slept for five hours but it felt like it was only thirty minutes ago that he lay down.

He didn't say anything when he answered the phone, he didn't have to Brad spoke as it soon as he connected.

"I have an address for you, I will send it after the call. Your order will be ready to pick up tomorrow but don't be late or it will go back on the shelf," said Brad in fluent French.

"Thanks," he replied and disconnected the call.

He waited for the encrypted address to come through, it was only a mile and a half away. He memorized the map leading from his location and most of the main streets in the Montefermill district. He never could understand why his brain remembered street maps like it did and retained the map like it was in front of him.

He decided to walk to the address Brad had sent. It gave him the opportunity to hone his counter-surveillance skills and get to know the area. He had only walked a quarter of a mile and was asked for the second time if he wanted drugs. Like the previous dealer he just ignored the man and kept walking. There were drugs being dealt out in the open on about every street and no sign of the police.

It looked like the African immigrants had taken over the area. He imagined the apartment buildings he walked past had once been elaborate upper-class homes. The ornate architecture chiseled stone carvings and metal rail balconies fascinated him. The original

black and dark grey roof tiles were now extremely faded. He could
see that many were missing over the arched attic windows. Some
of the buildings were so bad they looked like they were about to
collapse. He was sure that if the original homeowners were alive
today, they would be ashamed of the way the buildings had been
left to rot.

As he turned a corner into a narrow street that he was using as
a shortcut. He stopped suddenly as he faced three tall men. The
lead man asked him in French what he was doing in his street. Not
wanting a problem, he turned to walk back the way he came, by
the accent he knew they were from Somalia. They had a reputation
for extreme violence, and he didn't need the attention right now.

A hand slammed onto his right shoulder and by the feel of the
thumb and fingers it was a right hand. He turned to his right
spinning with his right arm arching towards the arm. His elbow
smashed into the arm at the elbow joint. The man cried out in pain
as his two friends moved towards him.

Al-Qadir didn't want this but now he had no choice. He
kicked the man he'd just hit on the side of the right knee. He felt
the tendons tear as his boot crashed into the kneecap in a
downward direction. The next man grabbed at him, but he was too
slow. The blow to the man's throat was devastating crushing his
windpipe. He fell clutching at his own neck trying to find air.

The third man had drawn a knife and the way he held it; he
knew what he was doing. Al-Qadir pulled out his own knife and
waited for the attack. The knife hand was swift and exacting as the
blade was stabbed towards his body. The slashing started as he
returned the move causing the blades to clash spitting out sparks.
He gave a lightning-fast stab inflicting a small wound to the right
forearm. He kept on his toes like he was in a boxing ring bouncing
around keeping his attacker off guard.

He was doing well until something stopped his left leg from moving, it had gotten stuck or so he thought. The first man had grabbed his ankle attempting to pull him to the ground. He lost balance slightly and pulled his leg free but not before the attacker took advantage of the situation.

He felt the searing heat of the knife blade slicing across his chest. Keep focused he kept telling himself, ignore the pain. To draw his attacker in Al-Qadir grabbed the wound on his chest, making out the injury was worse than it was. The attacker was smiling now as he came in for the kill, a foolish move.

Al-Qadir waited for the attack that was coming. He blocked the attackers knife hand by blocking his forearm with his left forearm, this sent the blade upwards out of harm's way. He stepped into the man's space getting up close and personal. He plunged his knife blade upwards under the Somali's jaw, into the back of his mouth and up into the brain. He twisted the blade feeling the tear of flesh and muscle. The man dropped to the floor like a rock in a bloody mess on the floor.

Turning quickly, he checked that the attackers were all taken care of, and they didn't have others coming to their rescue.

Al-Qadir cursed his luck as he walked away from the three men on the floor. Why couldn't they just leave him alone, but that wasn't the way things worked in this area of Paris. He continued walking to the address he'd been given but with a little more caution. He didn't know if the men he'd attacked had friends or gang members that would go on the hunt if they found them. He didn't want to have to deal with another group of men.

He soon found the address he was looking for. He performed a visual security and surveillance sweep of the building as best he could. Whoever lived in the four-story mid terraced home they were serious about their security. He couldn't see the rear of the house because there was another row of four-story terraced homes backing up to the address.

After twenty minutes of wandering around he saw that there was a for sale sign outside a building that overlooked the rear of the target address. A quick call to the realtor on the for-sale sign and he was inside the apartment within an hour having given a false name.

The realtor was an extremely attractive woman in her mid-twenties and a native of Paris. She was surprised that a single man would want to buy an apartment so large as it was the whole of the top two floors. With four bedrooms, two bathrooms and a large kitchen and lounge. He made out that his wealthy father was going to buy the property. He told her that his father visited Paris on business at least once a month. She wasn't surprised to hear this as many wealthy people purchased or rented a Pied-à-terre in Paris.

The woman was very professional showing him around the inside of the apartment. She then told him that because the apartment was the penthouse it had the garden to the rear for the owners. She asked him if he wanted to see it, but he declined. He could already see two cameras at the rear of the target address. He didn't want his face to be on their system as he was sure that everything was recorded.

On the top floor of the apartment, he had a perfect view of the target address. He could see directly into the rear garden but not into the windows as they looked like they had reflective glass or reflective film on them. Tucked under the gutter was a pan tilt and zoom camera with two fixed cameras further down the wall. It wasn't going to be easy to get inside the building if it was possible at all.

"My father is a very private man. Can you tell me who owns the apartments downstairs?" he asked.

"They are a genuinely nice old couple who used to own this apartment also, it was one big house. Their children grew and left home and started their own families."

"So, a quiet couple then, good. What about the residents of the other buildings either side and at the back?" He was fishing for information on the target address.

"They are all very respectable around here, mostly business and professional people."

"Is this the only house you've sold around here?"

"No, I have sold seven houses in this road alone and three on the other side like that one," she said pointing out of the window.

He looked out of the window pushing his luck he pointed at the target building and said, "Is that a camera?"

"Yes, he isn't a nice man, and his security people are even more rude than him. He tried to get me to go out to dinner with him, gross," she said with a visible shiver.

"People shouldn't be rude, my father always instilled that in me." He was getting on her good side.

"I know, why be rude, he even brushed up against me when I was showing the place to him. He is very creepy and tries to touch me every time I see him."

"You still go over there."

"Yes, unfortunately. He knows the owner of our company; they own properties together. Whenever we have an office event or cocktail dinner the creep shows up." She suddenly realized that she was speaking out of turn about a client. "I'm sorry I shouldn't have said that it was unprofessional of me."

"No apology needed; I totally understand. Who is he anyway?"

"I'm sorry I can't divulge my client's information, please understand."

"No, my bad for asking. Sometimes my curiosity gets the better of me and I ask silly questions."

After a few more boring questions that any would be buyer would ask, he told her that he had to leave as he had another apartment to look at.

They walked out of the apartment, and he shook her hand as they got to the sidewalk.

"One last question, can I see the apartment again if the next one doesn't work out?" he asked.

"Yes, of course here is my business card," she replied handing over her card to him.

"Thank you and goodbye," he replied walking away.

He got what he wanted on the target property but now he had an address for the realtor's office. He now had to plan how to get into the office and search their files for the owner of the target property.

CHAPTER 45

The next day he walked into the realtor's office and asked for the agent that had helped him. He wasn't really interested in the seeing the house again, he wanted to see what the office looked like. He hoped that he would locate where the files were kept and how they were secured.

The realtor walked out of an office somewhere in the back and greeted him. She was stunning and he could see why the creep couldn't keep his hands off her.

"Do you have any other properties in the road that we looked at yesterday?"

"I have one which is closer to the end of the street, would you like to see it," she asked.

"Yes, but is it possible to see it on the computer first as I'm stuck for time today?"

"Sure, come this way."

She walked in front of him and swayed everything she had in the tight-fitting skirt. They went down a short hallway into a tiny office with no windows.

"Please sit," she said pointing at a chair on the opposite side of the desk.

On the wall behind her desk were several small watercolor paintings.

"Nice paintings," he said.

"A pastime of mine, painting takes the stress of the job away. Excuse me while I log into my computer," she said sitting down.

"May I look at the paintings?" he asked.

"Of course."

He played to her ego perfectly and stood behind her as she entered the password to her computer.

He pretended to be looking at the paintings as he looked over his shoulder at her computer keyboard. "Really nice paintings, you have talent." He wasn't paying any attention to the paintings just her keyboard.

"May I use your toilet while you get the information on the computer?" he asked.

"Yes, down the hall on the right," she replied with a smile.

The bathroom was small with a window opening in the top. It was just big enough for him to fit through. He lifted the metal arm keeping the window securely locked in place and opened it. He looked through opening and saw there was a trash bin area at the rear and nothing else, an easy entry. He closed the window but left the metal securing bar resting on the window frame unlocked.

Returning to the office he sat down on the chair opposite her so as not to make her suspicious. She turned the computer monitor around to face him and went through her presentation of the new apartment. After excusing himself and promising to be in touch he left the office with the computer login information in his head. He was pleased with himself as it went a lot more smoothly than he thought it would. Now all he had to do was break into the office and go through the client files.

On his walk through the office and after casually running his eyes over the front door frame he didn't see any real security. The office door had a magnetic contact on it which was most probably connected to an alarm system. By the look of the office, it wasn't a sophisticated alarm system, which he liked, no signs of motion detectors either.

That night he returned and slid through the window easily. The rear office was in complete darkness, not even a computer screen was left on. He sat down at the realtor's desk and took out his tiny penlight, resting it on the desk to illuminate the keyboard.

The password worked first time, he was in. Punching the target address into the system he held his breath waiting for it to come to life, which it did. There was the address, a small picture of the frontage and then a lengthy list of information. It took him a few minutes to find the closing documents for the sale of the building. It was to an offshore company based in the Cayman Islands. There was a local attorney that represented the client in the closing of the sale. The company was obviously a front, most probably using a crooked attorney. He delved deeper into the company name to see if there were any other properties purchased, there were six.

He printed out all the sales documents so that he could study them later. He felt sure there had to be more information that he or Brad could use. He rifled through the realtor's desk trying to find out more on her. Was she really repulsed by the man touching and getting too close to her, he wasn't sure? She dressed provocatively which meant she wasn't as nice a woman as she would want you to think, or that was just his cultural upbringing coming out. In the top righthand draw was a bottle of perfume, spare pens, and a stack of business cards she'd collected from clients and/or businesspeople. There were so many cards, she was obviously a busy woman. He flicked through them making sure that he kept them in the same order as he'd found them. He'd gone through about fifty when one stood out, it was the offshore company in the Cayman Islands that had bought the target address. He scanned over the front of the card and there was a name, Riadh Al-Musayyib. He scanned the card on the office printer and put everything back where it was before. He double checked the desk and chair before he left to make sure they were in the same place as when he arrived.

Once he was back at his newest temporary home, he sent the name to Brad in the hope he could find something out about the man. He didn't know that the businessman was on the target list of not just the CIA, FBI, and Interpol.

The next day he received everything that Brad had found out about the name on the card, Riadh Al Musayyib. He was amazed how much information there was on one man. There was information on him from several different law enforcement agencies across Europe. The criminal empire he had was huge and very profitable by the looks of the property, vehicles, and yacht he owned. It now made sense why there was so much security at the house. There were several pictures taken of him by the different agencies whilst he was under surveillance. It looked like he had at least four bodyguards with him wherever he went. He used three different cars for his day-to-day business, not a bad idea if you're a target.

The list of commercial and residential buildings he owned was expansive with a total value of over a hundred million Euro's. he had several business ventures that on the surface were legal entity's but below the surface they were suspected of various criminal activities. Money laundering, drugs and arms deals being the focus of most of the agencies.

To his surprise he received a call from the real estate agent who told him about an apartment that had come up for rent. She thought that it would be a good place for him to settle while he looked for the property for his father. When he looked at the address on the map he couldn't believe his luck, it was on the opposite side of the street and a block down from Riadh's home. He arranged to meet the agent at the address.

CHAPTER 46

As the taxi drove past Riadh's home he sat in the shadow of the back seat. The taxi stopped about fifty yards further down the street on the opposite side. Stood on the sidewalk waiting for him was the realtor.

"How are you today?" she asked as Al-Qadir climbed out of the taxi.

"I'm good, shall we go in?" he said keeping his face hidden from the cameras on Riadh's home further down the street.

"This is a wonderful opportunity to rent, these properties don't come on the market very often." She was giving her best sales pitch.

She entered a code on the push button access control lock on the front door. They entered a wide hallway that was very ornate. It looked like they'd stepped back in time to the Paris of old. Elaborately hand painted floor tiles, wrought iron railings going up a spiraling staircase to the upper floors. The chandelier hanging from the ceiling had to be worth a fortune just on its own. Then came the ugly mask of modern convenience, an elevator right in front of them.

"It is the penthouse apartment, so we will take the elevator," she said.

He slid the concertina style metal gate open to expose another which he also opened. They stepped inside and she pressed the button for the penthouse. He couldn't help but smell her perfume, it was intoxicating.

The realtor, as before, gave a very professional walk through of the apartment. With three bedrooms, two bathrooms with fittings and wall mirrors that looked like they'd been there since the French revolution. With the addition of an oversized kitchen, it was very grand. She kept emphasizing how lucky she was to find this gem of a property. He didn't care as he was already sold on the apartment and wanted to know when he could move in.

They took the elevator down to the ground floor and walked to the back of the building. Through another key coded door, they entered the rear garden of the building.

"This is a communal garden that all the apartments use, you can even use it for private parties with the approval of the other residents. That gate there in the wall takes you out to the side street so that guests don't have to come in through the lobby entrance. This keeps the interior of the building private," she said pointing to the gate.

"That's a clever idea, I think this would be a good place to rent until we find something permanent. How long would it take to sign a contract and get a key, as you said you were lucky to find this place."

"I can have the rental contract ready for signature as soon as we verify your funds. It is an ugly thing to ask people, but we must have proof of finances to protect our clients," she replied.

"No, I totally understand, I can have that emailed to you today."

"In that case you will have a key or code, within twenty-four hours of the owner accepting the rental agreement."

"Good, but I won't move any furniture in for a few weeks, my father will want to choose which pieces he wants."

"That's understandable. Do you have time for lunch?" She was extremely interested in Al-Qadir, and it had nothing to do with business.

"I would really like to have lunch or even dinner, but I'm swamped today. Can I arrange something with you when the business is settled?"

"Yes, that would be great," she replied giving her best smile.

She didn't have to smile too hard he was already interested.

The rental transaction went very smoothly and as promised he had the code for the access system and a key for the front door should the access system fail.

Al-Qadir set up a sleeping bag, cases of water and non-perishable foods in the apartment. He'd purchased two high end cameras, two tripods and an assortment of long-range lenses. The cameras memory chips had the ability to hold over a thousand photographs each. He set them up so that he could back them up on his laptop. One of the cameras was focused on the sidewalk and parking space at the front of Riadh's home and the other on the front entrance.

With the help of some new motion detector technology from Brad, the front entrance camera had the ability to automatically take photographs. This motion detection would help him tremendously when he wasn't in the apartment or when he was asleep.

The first two days were very boring with little to no movement in and out of the house. There had been a few deliveries of what looked like food from local restaurants. Two security guards took turns to check the perimeter of the building on the hour every hour. This was a mistake to be so predictable with your security checks.

The third day was more interesting as he saw the little man himself for the first time. He was as described by the documents that Brad had supplied from the various law enforcement agencies. His photographs were obviously out of date as he looked like he'd gained another fifty or sixty pounds.

Two bodyguards walked ahead of him, one opening the rear passenger door to the waiting black limousine. The second opened the front passenger door and stood next to it. The little man waddled down the short path to the car closely followed by two more bodyguards. Behind the bodyguards were two very tall, attractive women in extremely short tight dresses. They were obviously expensive prostitutes and it made sense why he hadn't left the home for a couple of days, he had been enjoying their company. Once he was inside the limousine the ladies walked around to the opposite side and got in with him, as did one bodyguard with his colleague in the front. The remaining two bodyguards got into a black Range Rover that was parked behind. This man was profoundly serious about his security, the house was too much of a hard target to get inside.

Al-Qadir rented three different cars on consecutive days to follow Riadh. It was on the third day that he saw one of the bodyguards turning in the rear of the Range Rover to see what was behind them. He didn't know if he'd been seen or if it was just a coincidence, he couldn't follow them anymore it was too risky.

Two weeks of total surveillance boredom was starting to get to him. There wasn't any sign of Mutaz, at the house. He was starting to think that he was going down the wrong track with the Riadh connection. He tried everything he could to find out where the limousine took Riadh, he was hoping it would lead him to Mutaz, but he had no luck. He decided to try and put a locator on the limousine. He couldn't do it at the house due to the surveillance systems. He watched the route the limousine took for a further four days. The route never changed for about six blocks due to the layout of the streets. To get to the main road, they had to follow a one-way system. This was when he had one of his light bulb moments.

Close to the main road was a bicycle courier office with couriers zipping in and out of the traffic. The couriers were carrying mail bags over their shoulders or had wire baskets on the front of the bicycle with a fabric style cooler sitting in the basket. He recognized the logo on the cooler, it was the same meal delivery courier that had been delivering to Riadh's home.

It wasn't unusual for the courier cyclists to get horns sounded at them by the motorists as they took chances to weave in and out of the lines of traffic. Whenever a motorist disrespected them or almost collided with them, they would slap the roof of the car with their hand. All he needed now was a courier bicycle to put his plan into place.

It was far too easy to get the loan of a bicycle with a basket on the front. He told the courier that he wanted to play a joke on his friend for his bachelor party. He only needed the bicycle for about two hours and gave him a hundred Euros, much more than he'd earn in that time. He gave him an additional thirty Euros for the loan of his backpack. He asked for the courier to wait outside the courier office for him to return the bicycle and backpack, which he agreed to.

CHAPTER 47

He put on a slender dark blue track suit and a black wool hat on his head that covered his ears. Next was a worn looking scarf that was wrapped around his face to cover the mouth. All the couriers used this technique to try and keep the car exhaust fumes out of their lungs. He looked in the mirror in the bathroom before he left, he looked just like the other couriers. He looked down at the new black tennis shoes he'd just bought, and they stood out too much. On the way out to the rear garden where he'd left the courier bicycle he would scuff and muddy them up.

The locator was in a small magnetic box frame that would attach itself to any metal it encountered. He slung the battered and beaten backpack over his head slipping his arms through the straps. He put the locator into the front zip pocket of his tracksuit and headed downstairs to the garden.

He stood on the sidewalk next to a busy café where he had a good two block view of the road that the limousine would come down. He was starting to get nervous as the limousine had normally left the house by now. He only had fifteen minutes to return the bicycle and didn't want the courier to walk off thinking it was stolen.

Just as he was about to give up, he saw the limousine turn the corner into the road where he was waiting. He waited for it to pass keeping his head down in case the bodyguards were watching, which he was sure they would be.

He jumped on the bicycle and took off after the limousine, he had to time this perfectly. The traffic was very heavy which he appreciated as this made it easier for him to do what he wanted. Another courier shot past him weaving in and out of cars like a crazed lunatic. He caught up with the courier who was now alongside the limousine. A car pulled across in front of the courier causing them both to pull on the brakes. The courier took a tumble and landed next to the limousine. Al-Qadir went down with him to make it look like they'd collided.

All in one motion he fell off the bicycle rolled on the floor placed the magnetic box under the rear fender of the limousine and jumped to his feet. The courier was cursing in French at the car as was Al-Qadir. One of the bodyguards had rolled down the window of the Range Rover and was shouting at them to get out of the way.

They both rode to the courier office which was only half a block away.

"Check the front of the car," said the driver of the Range Rover.

"We will check it when we arrive at the office, we don't get out unless it's an emergency," replied the bodyguard.

"There was something not right about those couriers," said the driver.

"Watch them see where they go."

Al-Qadir slowed down as he got to the courier office knowing that the limousine was now moving with the traffic. The owner of the bike was stood outside the office as he rolled to a stop. Al-Qadir gave him a high five as he'd seen the other couriers doing this when they got back to the office.

"Thanks, it worked perfectly, do you have a toilet inside?" said Al-Qadir.

"Yes, all the way to the back on the left," he replied.

The driver and bodyguards watched the two couriers as they both stopped at a building. They recognized the courier office and saw one of the couriers high five another man and walk inside the building.

"They are just crazy bike riding couriers, acting like Americans with their high fives," said the driver.

"Yes," said the bodyguard as they watched them walk inside the building.

Al-Qadir gave it three minutes before he walked back out of the building. He turned right and entered a low-rise parking lot where he'd left his rental car. He changed clothes and put on a pair of dark sunglasses. He was only five minutes behind the limousine when he drove out. The transmitter was pinging perfectly on the laptop he'd left under the seat the night before, which was now on the seat next to him. He was about in range of the transmitter as the limousine was now driving fast on the main road. He drove a little faster than he should have to keep within range hoping that the local police did not see him. He hadn't gone more than five miles when the pinging light on the laptop stopped. He slowed down, there was no need to rush now.

He stopped his rental car a mile away from where the ping was indicating where the limousine had stopped and walked the rest of the way. He was a block from the address shown on the transmitter signal but there was no sign of the limousine. It had to be parked there or the transmitter had fallen off or been discovered. He immediately went on high alert, if it had been discovered he could be walking into a trap. He wasn't in the best position to see the front of the building where the ping indicated. The whole block was five story offices and a restaurant across the street from them.

He was about to chance walking down the street towards the office when he heard the screech of a vehicle braking. A van had gotten too close to a local bus which was pulling into the curb to pick up passengers, the driver obviously wasn't paying attention.

He saw an opportunity and quickly walked to the stop forty feet away and boarded the bus throwing the fare into the driver's tray. He sat on the side of the bus that was away from the office building so that he was hidden from view. As the bus drove down the street it stopped close to the restaurant to pick up more passengers. He glanced towards the restaurant and almost slid under the seat. Riadh was sitting at a table outside the restaurant with Mutaz. There was a bodyguard sat behind them facing the road. It took all his control not to jump off the bus and pump six rounds into Mutaz. He looked in the opposite direction to the restaurant to keep his face hidden. He was now looking directly at the office building that had pinged on the locator.

There was the limousine parked in a single car garage next to a glass fronted office building. Sat on the hood of the limousine was the driver smoking a cigarette and one of the bodyguards from the Range Rover was stood by the office entrance. He was elated, he'd not only found Mutaz, but he knew where Riadh's office was. He got off the bus at the next stop and walked back towards the restaurant to see if Mutaz left on his own or if he had bodyguards with him like Riadh. He couldn't see an advantage point where he could observe Mutaz and Riadh. There were so many cameras on the office buildings keeping his head down all the time would stand out to someone eventually. He gave up and walked around the block and headed back to his car. Now what was the plan, he didn't know yet, but he would come up with one.

He needed to perform more surveillance on Riadh's home and somehow find out where Mutaz lived.

The next day Al-Qadir went through the photographs that the cameras had taken of Riadh's home. There were so many that he felt like he'd never get to the end. Then something caught his eye, a van parked down the street. He'd seen it twice now, just out of the view of Riadh's surveillance cameras. He zoomed in on both photographs looking for a license plate, but he couldn't see it for the cars parked in front of it. Then he searched for a company name on the doors or side of the van, there wasn't any. Then it came to him the van was the same color as the one that nearly ran into the bus.

He was nervous about this van as it could be an undercover operation by the local police or some other agency that was after Riadh. There was no way of knowing but he had to try to find out. He made a quick call to Brad and gave him the details of the van. He didn't tell him about Mutaz as he didn't want Brad to call the local police for them to arrest him for the crimes he'd committed. He should have known that Brad wouldn't do that, but he didn't want to take the chance.

The next morning, he had a reply from Brad that as far as the main law enforcement agencies were concerned, there wasn't a surveillance operation in progress. Had there been one Brad would have been told plainly to get his man, whoever he was to back off.

He sat drinking a coffee looking out of the window at Riadh's home. He felt comfortable that they couldn't see him because of the window treatments blocked anyone looking in from the outside. He decided to go for a walk to try to clear his head and eat some breakfast. As always, he left via the rear garden gate as it couldn't be seen from Riadh's home.

The café was a typical Parisian sidewalk café with a few tables outside. He had eaten there several times he wasn't sure how many. The breakfast was also typical for Paris, croissants, and pastries. The coffee was exceptional, much better than the instant brew stuff he was making in the apartment from an electric kettle. His phone rang and the realtors number came up. He felt bad that he hadn't spoken to her since they had lunch a couple of weeks earlier.

"Hello," he said answering the phone.

"Hi, it's Estelle," she said when he answered.

"How are you?" he was nervous about talking to her.

"Good, I thought that you'd forgotten about me, are we still going to have dinner together?"

"Yes, yes, I've been out of the country on business for a couple of weeks. Why don't we meet for a breakfast coffee tomorrow, same place we had lunch and pick a date for dinner?"

"What about eight o'clock?"

"I will see you there, goodbye."

"Bye," she replied.

He felt bad lying to her, but she would never know the truth.

He walked back to the apartment thinking about Estelle, he realized he wanted more than just dinner with her. His mind was racing when he entered the apartment with thoughts of Estelle and Mutaz. He looked through the window and right outside his apartment was the same van pulling up to the curb. He picked up his camera and started taking photographs in the hope he could get a shot of the driver. From the height of his apartment, it was impossible to see his face or anything else. Then came along the scourge of Paris for many motorists, the parking warden.

He watched as the female warden tapped on the driver's window. The window rolled down and a conversation took place between the warden and the driver. She was obviously telling him that he couldn't park in this part of the road. The drivers head came out of the window as he looked down the street to where she was pointing. He followed her and pointed in the same direction with a cell phone in his hand. He was being told he could park further down the road.

He still couldn't see the face but kept taking photographs.

The driver looked like he was cooperating and watched the warden walk away. As he sat straight again in the driver's seat, he dropped his cell phone onto the road. He climbed out of the vehicle, picked up the phone and wiped it on his sleeve. There was a huge scar on his face, it was Amir Faiz. His scar was the talk of many soldiers and policemen after Mutaz had cut him with a knife. He had become something of a legend in the special forces in Iraq. Why was he here in Paris or was it really him, it had to be there couldn't be two men with that horrific scar? He suddenly realized that they may be both hunting the same man.

He watched the van drive away wondering how he could find out what Amir was up to. If they were both hunting Mutaz he could be a huge asset or, he was after Riadh himself. There was only one way to find out and that was to approach him directly. Now all he had to do was find him again.

CHAPTER 48

The breakfast with Estelle took his mind off Mutaz and Amir. He couldn't remember the last time he felt like this about a woman. She told him everything about herself. She was like him, she had no family left alive, her adopted family were the people at the real estate office. Before they both knew it after breakfast they were in bed in her apartment.

The two hours he spent with Estelle were the most unhindered he'd been with any woman. She understood him straight away and he felt the same about her. They arranged to meet again that evening, she insisted on cooking dinner.

It took him a few hours to get his laser like focus back after Estelle but back it was. He drove around the streets where he lived looking for the van but never found it. He had to get to Amir before he screwed up what he was doing. The next day after a late night with Estelle he went back to the area where Riadh had his office. This went on for three days back and forth and then there it was parked close to Riadh's office but this time it had a different paint job.

He pulled the hoody over his head and walked with his head down and hands in his pockets. He kept out of view of the cameras in the street as best he could as he approached the van. The rear doors didn't have any windows, so he felt safe approaching it. He bent down to tie a shoelace and placed a locator quietly and gently under the rear step that went into the rear of the van. He kept walking in the same direction so that it didn't look out of place. As he past the driver's side, he looked into the side rear view mirror to see if Amir was sitting inside. Both front seats were empty which meant he was either on foot or in the back with surveillance equipment.

He sat in his car in the open parking lot four blocks away from where the van was parked. It was now a waiting game to see when the van left and where it ended up. He expected to be a few hours at least but got a surprise as the van was on the move only thirty minutes later. He was in no hurry as the locator was pinging the van's location nicely. Not wanting to take any chances of being discovered he kept a mile back. After ten minutes according to the locator the van had stopped. He found it in a parking lot at the rear of a small hotel four miles away from Riadh's home. He gave the parking lot a drive by trying to see if Amir was around, he wasn't.

He decided to approach Amir as he had to find out what he was doing outside Riadh's home. He knew that he wasn't working for Riadh or Mutaz because why would he be keeping them under surveillance? He decided to come back early the next morning and try to see which room he was staying in at the hotel.

He had a pressing engagement with Estelle to go to and he wasn't going to be late. He spent the rest of the day and night with Estelle something he was torn about. He felt like he was deceiving her all the time, which he was. She asked more about his family and what he did for a living. He was vague as always claiming he was like his father very private and found it awkward talking about himself and his business. She accepted it for now, but he knew that she would eventually press him for more information. He slid out of the bed at six in the morning, dressed and left for Amir's hotel.

He picked up a black coffee on the way to the hotel to try and wake himself up. He was having distracting thoughts again about

Estelle. He got out of the car and walked the block around the hotel to get the lay of the land. He saw a café that was busy with the morning office crowd getting breakfast and coffee before they went to work. He decided to get an espresso as the first coffee didn't wake him up enough, he needed a big caffeine boost. As he got closer to the café, he saw Amir sitting on a table next to the sidewalk. It caught him off guard and he went to turn back the way he came. Amir held up a cell phone.

Amir knew that whoever was following him would show up eventually. The hidden mini camera on the rear frame of the van picked up the placement of the locator. He wanted to speak to the man as he'd seen him getting on a bus a few days earlier close to Riadh's home. He sat at the café knowing that if someone were looking for him, he would sweep the area around his hotel. He wasn't wrong as the man came walking towards the café where he was enjoying breakfast.

The man stopped suddenly when he saw him so he held up a cell phone before he could turn away. He placed the cell phone on the table, then pointed at the chair and walked away.

Al-Qadir walked quickly but cautiously towards the table and sat down. He was checking everyone out sitting outside the café looking for attackers. He sat looking at the cell phone for a couple of minutes when a waitress came over.

"Can I take your order?" she said.

"Espresso."

He didn't have to wait long when the espresso arrived. As the waitress walked away the cell phone rank, he answered it.

"Yes," he said pressing the answer button.

"Answer my questions truthfully or I will shoot you, look at your chest," said Amir.

He looked down and there was a laser dot centered on his chest. "I have questions for you also, Amir."

"Who are you and why are you following me?"

"My name is Al-Qadir Hadi, son of General Abbud Hadi. My father was a general in the police in Miqdadiyah, he died as my mother did after General Ashkouri and his men murdered many of the people in my father's police station."

"I heard of the atrocities by Ashkouri but what has it got to do with me, I never worked with him."

"I know you didn't, I think we may be looking for the same person." He was taking a chance as he didn't really know if Amir was working for Riadh. He knew he didn't work for Mutaz his hate for the man was well known.

"And who would that be?"

"Haider Mutaz, I won't give him the credit by using his military rank he doesn't deserve it."

"What is it you want with him?"

"My turn for a question. Why are you keeping Riadh Al Musayyib under surveillance?"

Amir didn't know if he could trust this man as he didn't know him. He decided to take a chance, he was the one holding the rifle that was pointed at him. "I want Mutaz, not Riadh."

"We have a common enemy by the sounds of it, we should meet."

"Mutaz is mine, don't get in my way or I will kill you," Amir was serious.

"I think we can work together because we both want the end result, Mutaz dead." Al-Qadir paused. "What have you got to lose?"

"Tomorrow morning, same café seven o'clock." He disconnected the call.

Al-Qadir heard the call end and looked at his chest, the laser dot was gone. He had been concentrating so much on the call that he didn't feel the sweat rolling down the middle of his back.

Al-Qadir spent the rest of the day on calls with Brad and his associates trying to find out information on Amir. It amazed him how much Brad and the CIA could find out about people in such a brief time. He had a full dossier on Amir by five in the afternoon and had digested it all by six. He'd arranged to see Estelle again that night but had to cool things off for a little while now that Amir was on the scene. He had a feeling that things may speed up in the hunt for Mutaz.

Estelle was disappointed when he told her that he was going to be out of town for up to two weeks. She was getting strong feelings for him.

"I'm sorry but my father wants me to take care of a business problem he is having."

"I know, I'm just going to miss you," she replied realizing that she sounded a little desperate.

"I will miss you too." It wasn't a total lie, but he would have other things on his mind.

"I have good news about my real estate business, do you remember the huge, terraced house I pointed out to you with the cameras at the back?"

"Yes, I think so, at the back of the first property you showed me, wasn't it?" he knew exactly which property it was, Riadh's home.

"Yes, well he has asked me to sell his Chateau on the outskirts of Paris. It is a huge property with over thirty acres of land with an asking price of forty million Euro's. I have a meeting with him in the morning, isn't that exciting?" She was beaming.

"Very exciting, I'm so pleased for you." He hated the thought of her being anywhere near the stump of a man. He feared for her safety, but he couldn't act on it, not right now.

She showed him a sales sheet on the property and talked about the Chateau for the next ten minutes without taking a breath. To get her off the subject he started to undress her, and she submitted immediately, subject closed.

CHAPTER 49

MEETING AMIR

Al-Qadir sent the latest information to Brad on the Chateau in the hope that he could find something else out. It was his daily check-in anyway, so he put it to effective use. His check-in was normally a coded message just letting him know that all was OK, if he were in danger, he would send a different code.

He'd been at the café for fifteen minutes with no sign of Amir. He'd chosen a different seat this time where Amir wouldn't find it so easy to get a laser spot on him. He contemplated giving up after thirty minutes when he showed up. There wasn't any kind of greeting between them when Amir sat down.

Al-Qadir waived at a waitress putting two fingers up as he pointed at his coffee cup.

They both stared at each other for a minute trying to get the balance of one another. It was Amir that broke the silence.

"I thought about what you said and our interest in the same business. I will be willing to collaborate with you to secure the deal, but I must be the one to execute it."

Al-Qadir thought that this was an effective way to describe what they were both doing, anyone listening would think they were talking about actual business not an assassination.

"That is up for negotiation, I want to execute the deal also," replied Al-Qadir.

"That's not going to happen, you know what I got out of the last deal with this company." Amir tapped the scar on his face.

"I do, but I also have previous dealings with this company and not a good one. They were ruthless on the last deal, and I lost a lot of employees. I don't want to lose any this time."

"I did hear about the employees you lost, and I give you my honest condolences, but I have lived with the consequences of the CEO's past actions most of my life."

Al-Qadir sat back and thought for a few minutes. He had to admit the scar was gruesome and people stared at him even now in the café. He had his revenge for his mother and father when he killed Ashkouri and many others. It wouldn't be so bad to let Amir exact his revenge. By helping him kill Mutaz he would get some satisfaction also.

"I think we can agree on you signing the final part of the deal, but I want to do something at the end to let people know the deal is closed."

"If you can agree to this then so can I, we have a deal Azrael." He said the name quietly so that only Al-Qadir could hear.

"You have me mistaken for someone else."

"No, I know who you are, and I applaud you for what you have done in the past. I found the company we are talking about by following a long trail of events. Those events led me here to Paris. This is what I'm good at following evidence and clues. That is how I know your name and reputation; I followed the clues. It only came to me when you showed up yesterday, that was why I didn't execute our deal before it started."

Al-Qadir knew he meant that's why he didn't shoot him without asking any questions. He felt relieved that somebody knew who he was.

"Like me, you have obviously done your homework."

"Yes."

"So, we are agreed then. I'm quite happy to share my information with you that way we can produce a plan of action."

"Agreed," said Amir reaching forward to shake his hand.

They talked for almost thirty minutes more and left for Amir's hotel. They spent several hours going over the information they both had. Amir was further along than Al-Qadir, his investigation skills showing. He even had the details of a vehicle that Mutaz drove but not an address where he lived, this was where the locators would come in handy. Amir told Al-Qadir to keep hold of the phone he left for him at the café as it was a burner phone. Then volunteered to drive him back to his apartment. At first, he didn't agree as he didn't want anyone knowing where he was living but eventually gave in as he knew where Amir was living. This time Amir was driving a small Citroen and not the van.

"Drop me off ahead on the left, I will walk the rest of the way," said Al-Qadir pointing to the wall ahead.

"Your address is the next road."

"Yes, but I go in through the garden gate at the rear, I don't like using the front door."

"Good idea, I will call you later to arrange where to meet tomorrow."

CHAPTER 50

Al-Qadir was thinking about everything that he'd learnt from Amir and his investigation. He was also thinking about Estelle, but he couldn't see her now until this was done. He unlocked the gate and walked into the yard as another resident was about to walk out. His mind was still distracted when he got to the elevator gate. The elevator wasn't on the ground floor, so he went to press the button to bring it down. He looked up at the old floor indicator that looked like the finger on a clock face. It was stationary pointing at his floor, someone was up there. The penthouse was the only apartment on that floor, he wondered if Estelle had shown up. He went to press the button again and something told him not to, his gut turned over, something wasn't right.

He pulled his Glock out of his belt holster and attached the silencer. He then worked his way slowly up the spiral staircase keeping the weapon pointed up following the wall as he went. He swept the Glock from side to side looking for anyone lying in wait. There was a noise below him and he turned the gun towards the stairs below, it was the ground floor tenant coming in through the front door.

As he got to the penthouse floor, he could see that the door had been forced open. He moved close to the wall and approached the door. He could hear movement inside the apartment and voices, but he couldn't make out what they were saying. He gently opened the door just enough to slide inside.

The door suddenly slammed against him squashing him between the door and frame. He fired one shot towards the back of the door and forced his way inside. He was rushed by the man behind the door and took a punch to side of his head. This was quickly followed by a downward strike to his gun wrist causing him to drop the weapon. A second man appeared and ran towards him arms outstretched. Al-Qadir kicked the first man hard to the chest sending him flying backwards into the window breaking the glass. As the second man got to him, he dropped his shoulder at the last minute and buried it into his stomach throwing him over his shoulder.

Amir was very curious still about this man Azrael. He admired him a lot, he watched him walk away thinking nobody would ever think that he was the Angel of Death. He was looking forward to working with him as he felt they would be a formidable team.

Someone came out of the garden gate that Al-Qadir had gone through, but they didn't close it properly. Not closing doors and gates that were there for security was a pet hate of his. He sat staring at the building wondering how Al-Qadir could afford such a place. It was glorious and smelt of old Parisian money. The open gate was bothering him, so he decided to get out of the car and close it. He was within a few feet of the gate when he heard glass breaking. He looked up and saw a man's back sticking through the broken window, he immediately knew his new friend was in trouble.

Inside the stairwell he bounded up the stairs two at a time as he could hear a fight above him. At the top of the stairs there was an open door and inside the room two men were attacking Al-Qadir.

The first man was attacking Al-Qadir again, but he managed to stun him with an elbow to the temple, he rocked backwards. A third man appeared from the backroom with a handgun. Al-Qadir spun the second attacker around and pushed him towards the gunman. Al-Qadir dropped to the floor rolling as he did and picked up his Glock. He fired two rounds at the gunman only to have the first man jump on his back. The gunman only received a flesh wound to his shoulder thanks to his colleague.

Al-Qadir tried to elbow the man on his back in the ribs, he was trying to get Al-Qadir in a choke hold. This wasn't working so he fired blindly trying to find his attacker's body, both shots narrowly missing. The other men were attacking again he managed to shoot one in the knee before the weight of the man on his back plunged him to the floor.

Amir didn't wait for an invitation to help Al-Qadir he went in very heavy and hard. The first man went down very easily with a left punch to his face and a hard crossing right to his jaw. He swiftly kicked the man in the head that was on top of Al-Qadir just as the gunman pointed his weapon at him. He ducked low in the hope of dodging the bullet, but it was impossible, he knew it. He recognized the sound of a silenced weapon as it spat out two bullets. Amazingly he wasn't hit as he took the legs out from under the gunman.

Al-Qadir felt the weight of the man roll off him onto his side. In front of him he saw Amir fighting like a warrior to defend him. He fired two shots into the torso of the gunman knocking him backwards.

With one dead and two immobilized on the floor they took a minute to catch their breath.

"Well, I have only known you for a few hours and it seems that trouble follows you," smiled Amir.

"Thank you," he replied.

"Who are these men?"

"I don't know but we are about to finds out," said Al-Qadir.

With the front door closed they bound and gagged both men with strips of cloth from their own clothing.

"They both looked like they could be from Iraq," said Amir.

"Who are you?" asked Al-Qadir.

Neither man replied, they just glared back at them.

"You will tell us eventually, so do it now and make it easy on yourself," said Amir.

The way they looked at the scar on Amir's face told him that they feared him and so they should. Both men were shouting expletives behind the gags showing defiance.

"They don't believe you," said Al-Qadir.

"I know, you're Iraqi did Haider Mutaz send you?" Amir dropped the gag on one the men's mouths.

The man spat on the floor and swore at them both in his native Iraqi tongue. He started to shout for help, but the gag went into place before he could raise anyone's attention.

"Wait here a minute," said Al-Qadir as he left the room.

Amir could hear what sounded like floorboards being pulled up and Al-Qadir returned with a small duffle bag. He watched as Al-Qadir opened the bag and carefully and slowly took out a hammer, two six-inch nails and two death cards. The eyes on the two men were now wide open he had their attention.

"Now you know who I am, I can tell you have heard of me. As you can see, I have taken out only two nails and two death cards.

One of you is already dead so he gets the first nail." He walked over to the dead body and hammered a nail into the forehead through a death card. "Now I have one nail and one death card, so whoever speaks first gets to leave." He stood spinning the death card around in his fingers.

One man started to shout through the gag, so Amir dropped it.

"Shout and I will put the gag back on," said Amir.

"It wasn't Mutaz, it was Riadh our boss."

The second man was going nuts shouting for all he was worth behind the gag telling him to shut up.

Al-Qadir wasted no time and walked up to the man. He sat the man up and stood behind him, placing his head between his own knees he drove the nail into his forehead just as he'd done many times before.

The man screamed when he saw what was happening and begged for his life.

"I will tell you whatever you want, please." His eyes had opened so wide at what he'd just witnessed that they looked like they may pop out of the sockets.

"You say Riadh sent you, why?" asked Al-Qadir.

"He was at the chateau this morning with a woman who buys and sells properties for him. As always, he tried to get the woman to go to dinner with him, hopefully with sex after. The woman told him she had a boyfriend, and she was faithful. He wanted to know more about this boyfriend, he's done this before and sent us around to scare the boyfriend off. She told him that her boyfriend had just rented the apartment down the street from him."

Al-Qadir knew that he was talking about Estelle.

"What did he send you here for?" he asked.

"At first it was to scare the boyfriend but when we got here, we found the camera equipment pointing at his home. The place doesn't look like it is anyone's home because of the sleeping bag and no furniture, it was a surveillance point. I called him about it, and he went berserk on the phone. He told us to rip the place apart and find out who the boyfriend was. He said he was sending Mutaz and his men over, but we got here first."

"Where does Mutaz live?" asked Amir.

"Most of the time he lives in an apartment in the basement of Riadh's office."

"What does he drive?" asked Al-Qadir.

"A flashy Black Mercedes, which belongs to Riadh, they are close. He will be here soon."

With that they heard vehicles outside screeching to a stop. Amir ran into the front bedroom and looked through the window, there were two SUV's outside with men pouring out with automatic weapons. He ran back into the living area to see Al-Qadir striking the final blow with the hammer.

"I said he would leave; I didn't say alive."

"We have five or six coming in through the front all with automatic weapons," said Amir.

"Follow me."

Al-Qadir ran to the back bedroom that overlooked the rear garden. "Pull up these floorboards?" said Al-Qadir.

They had several boards up in seconds revealing two backpacks and a rolled-up fire ladder. Al-Qadir opened the window and hooked the fire escape ladder onto it. He then rolled it out and watched it drop to within six feet of the garden below.

"Go down I will join you in a minute," said Al-Qadir.

"My car is where I dropped you off, I will pick you up at the gate."

Al-Qadir ran back into the apartment and waited to hear the men coming up the stairs. There were telltale creaks on the wooden stairs, they were moving cautiously. He knew that they would be moving in a well tried and tested formation the lead coving above and the last man covering their backs. It was standard procedure for any assault team.

CHAPTER 51

Mutaz was curious he wanted to know who this person was that was watching his boss and partner. At first, they thought that it was one of the many law enforcement agencies that were after Riadh. They quickly dispelled this thought when the description of what was in the apartment was relayed to them. This was an individual operating on his own, maybe a freelance press agent. Whoever it was he was going to teach them a lesson.

He brought two of his fiercest fighters with him that had no issues with torturing or killing. In the second vehicle were two of Riadh's henchmen who would watch the front entrance. He'd called the other men that were already at the apartment on their phones, but nobody answered, this wasn't good.

They jumped out of the SUV's all wearing black balaclavas and forced open the front door to the apartment building with a Halligan bar. This was a glorified crowbar with strong prying bends and a spike at either end. The door posed no real problem as it opened on the second attempt. They watched the street to make sure they weren't seen, and they moved inside out of sight quickly.

The sound of the vehicles pulling up so noisily got the resident of the ground floor apartment curious. She lived alone and any bit of excitement she found interesting. She went to the window and looked through the sheer drapes. She liked the drapes because she could see out, but people couldn't see her watching them. She was in shock when she saw the men in balaclavas and carrying firearms, she almost fell backwards over a table in fright. She called the police immediately reporting what she'd seen.

"You stay here," Mutaz said to one of the men. "The rest of you with me."

They moved slowly up the staircase prepared for a shootout. They heard a suppressed handgun being fired from above them. The lead man was just going around the second turn in the staircase when the bullet struck him in the throat. He dropped onto the stairs as the bullet tore through the spinal column as it exited. Mutaz was directly behind the man that was hit and was sprayed with his blood all over his face. The bullet that exited his neck caught him on the side of the head. He was lucky as it traveled downwards across his right temple taking out a piece of his ear. He reacted cupping his ear with his hand. He waived the men behind him forward to move up the stairs.

Al-Qadir waited patiently in the prone position behind the railings of the stairs. He was watching for the first head to appear which it did, he only needed one shot to slow the advancing men down. The shot was perfect as it entered the throat, he was already crawling back into the apartment waiting for a return of fire, he was surprised when it didn't come. He was up and out of the window and down the fire escape ladder in seconds.

As Amir went to drive away as Al-Qadir got into the car, they heard police sirens.

"How did they get here so fast?" said Al-Qadir.

"I don't know but I'm not going to wait around."

Amir performed a three point turn slowly so as not to attract any attention. As they turned the first corner two police cars flew past them into the street they had just left.

Al-Qadir realized that he'd lost his satellite phone in the fight in the apartment. He would have to contact Brad for his check in another way. The phone was of no use to anyone as every call, text or message sent and received erased automatically leaving no trace on the phone. He was already a day behind with his check-in and Brad had tried to call just as he met Amir the day before. The check-in was no longer a priority, Estelle was, he had to find her, and he knew where to look.

Mutaz was screaming fury as his men took over his position, they didn't shoot because there wasn't a target to shoot at.

"The police are coming," shouted the man on the door.

"Everybody out," shouted Mutaz.

They just made it outside and drove away as the police arrived. Mutaz had a lucky escape with the bullet and his luck held out as the police arrived just too late. He was angry that he had been shot but even more angry that this boyfriend got away, he called Riadh.

"I don't know who it was, but he is good, very good. We didn't get into the apartment because someone had called the police, I had to leave one of my men dead on the stairs."

"Come to the Chateau we have a way of making the man come to us, my new girlfriend will bring him here. She has his phone number on speed dial, isn't that cute. I have had an enjoyable time with her, she now knows what it is like to have a real man. Bring the men with you and we will work out the details of what we can do when he arrives." He hung up the call. "Now, let's you and I do it again, see how you fight this time," he said to Estelle touching the claw marks on his face from her nails.

Estelle was lying naked next to him on the bed, bruised and battered. She'd put up a good fight, but it just excited the fat pig even more. He started again, slapping, and punching her until he was aroused enough to perform.

Estelle was in no position to fight back anymore; her body had become numb from the abuse and beatings. She didn't even feel the blows anymore, her body was giving up the will to live. Her brain had shut down to protect itself from further trauma.

CHAPTER 52

Mutaz ripped the balaclava off his head as he got into the SUV, so did the rest of the men, as they drove away from the apartment. They didn't want to be seen wearing them as they drove past the oncoming police cars.

Mutaz held a cloth to his ear to stop the bleeding. It was more painful than he thought it would be to lose a part of the ear. He was gritting his teeth but not just because of the pain but the anger and frustration of not capturing the man in the apartment. He made a phone call and told the security guards inside the office apartment to meet him at the chateau.

Riadh wasn't impressed with the Mutaz and his team for failing to bring the realtors boyfriend back. He'd had his fill of the girl and left her tied to the bed as he put on a silk dressing gown. He walked downstairs and called his personal bodyguards inside.

"Mutaz is on his way back here, he failed on his mission to get the boyfriend. I don't know who he is but to get the better of Mutaz and his men he must be someone special. I will be calling him as soon as Mutaz gets back to arrange for him to come here. I will offer her in exchange for him, the fool may accept, personally I would leave her to her fate. How many men do we have here at the chateau?"

"Six, counting myself," replied his bodyguard.

"OK, with Mutaz and his men plus those on the way from the office that gives us a total of fourteen. What do you suggest we do to fortify the chateau?"

"I will put two of the men in the cover of the trees one at the front and one to the rear. Two more patrolling the outside constantly rotating, they will be a visible deterrent. I will be inside with another to protect you. When Mutaz comes though he will have his own ideas of what we should do," replied the bodyguard.

"Don't worry about him, he has already failed to capture the boyfriend, I will deal with him."

"Why not call the detective with the Paris police and see if he can find out what really happened at the apartment?" replied the bodyguard.

"That's a clever idea, he may be able to tell us more about the boyfriend, always good to know your enemy."

The phone call to the detective didn't last more than five minutes as he already knew everything that happened at the apartment. The description of the three bodies in the bedroom had been circulated to every law enforcement agency in France, not just Paris. It was the death cards that got everyone's attention. Death cards were something Riadh had heard about but in Iraq not France, it sent shivers up his spine.

It was almost two hours before Mutaz and his men arrived at the chateau, an hour over schedule. Both SUVs pulled up directly in front of the chateau on the gravel driveway. Mutaz was first out still holding the now bloody cloth to his ear. The rest got out and stood by the vehicles as they knew this wasn't going to be a pleasant meeting for Mutaz.

Riadh barged through the chateau's main doors in his silk dressing gown, he looked like a round ball on stumpy legs as the silk clung to his body. He stopped at the top of the steps when he saw Mutaz holding the bloody cloth.

"What happened, why didn't you get him?" screamed Riadh.

Mutaz glared at him, he was in no mood to be spoken to this way, he'd been shot. He walked towards Riadh with hate and anger written all over his face. As he got closer Riadh's personal bodyguard stepped forward, warning him not to go any further.

Riadh held his hand up to stop his bodyguard from going any further, he appreciated that his man was willing to take on Mutaz.

"What took you so long to come here?" asked Riadh.

"We had to make a detour as the police had several roadblocks checking vehicles after the shooting at the apartment."

"What happened at the apartment?"

"It was an ambush, he was waiting for us, I lost one of my men and most probably the ones you sent to the apartment," shouted Mutaz angrily.

"But you survived, didn't you?"

"Only just the bullet took part of my ear," he replied removing the cloth for Riadh to see.

"A flesh wound nothing more. Clean yourself up and meet me in the study, we have plans to make." Riadh turned and walked inside.

Mutaz was cursing under his breath as he walked up the steps into the chateau. Twenty minutes later he'd cleaned the wound and put a bandage on the ear. The study was a huge room with a lot of

Louis the 13th furniture inside. It was Gordy and over dressed for his taste but that was what Riadh liked, everything completely over the top. The round man was sat behind the large desk in an equally large leather chair smoking a cigarette.

"Sit down," said Riadh angrily.

"I'm not one of your minions to be spoken down to, do you understand?" replied Mutaz.

"Until you succeed in what I ask you to do I will talk to you as I please, you forget who pays you."

"I'm in business with you and not an employee, you forget that. Don't push me too far Riadh, you know what I'm capable of." Mutaz heard a shuffling noise behind him.

Riadh's personal bodyguard walked up to Mutaz and put his pistol to the back of his head.

"You see, you aren't on your game, my own bodyguard can walk right up to you and put a gun to your head. If I said pull the trigger, he would pull it and be rewarded for doing so. You are slipping Mutaz, and I don't know if I need you anymore." He was bluffing because right now he did need him. "I'm willing to give you a second chance with this boyfriend who, judging by what he's done to your men, he isn't just a boyfriend. I will be calling him and tell him to stand by his phone for instructions to collect his girlfriend. I will suggest it is an exchange, him for her, but they will both die."

"Does he know about this place?" asked Mutaz.

"I don't know I haven't asked her if she told him about it, but I will. Why do you ask?"

"If he knows about the chateau he will come racing over here, I would be surprised if he wasn't already on the way. I want him to think about his girlfriend and what I've done to her, this will put his mind off balance. He will come after us like a raging bull without any real plan of attack, but I want him to think about it overnight." He enjoyed being a sadist as Estelle had found out personally.

Riadh said nothing for a minute and looked at his bodyguard for his approval, he nodded that it was the right thing to do. They strategized for ten minutes with Mutaz glaring at the bodyguard whenever he got chance. He would kill him the first chance he got for putting the gun to his head.

"OK, I will call him and tell him to go to my office in the morning, this will give him all night to think about what I have said."

Al-Qadir and Amir were planning to go to the Chateau as they couldn't think of anywhere else that Estelle could have been taken. This had become a rescue mission but one that was fraught with danger. They were checking their weapons and ammunition when Al-Qadir's cell phone rang. It surprised him at first because the only person that called him on that phone was Estelle.

"Answer it," said Amir.

"Yes," he said connecting the call on speaker.

"You were expecting your beautiful girlfriend to answer and not me?" said the man's voice.

"Who is this?" he replied.

"Oh! Come now you know who it is your girlfriend's new lover, she is incredibly good in bed. She liked me biting her very much it excited her, have you done that?" He was hoping to push the man over the edge.

Amir watched Al-Qadir expecting him to go berserk on the phone, but he didn't, it was like an earie calmness suddenly swept over him.

"What girlfriend?"

"I see, you are playing the game, I don't know what you're talking about." Mocked Riadh. "Let's get down to business because I must go back to biting and abusing your girlfriend, Estelle. If you want to see her alive again, I suggest you do exactly as I say. Be at my office in the morning at seven o'clock, wait outside for instructions. If I don't see you on the surveillance camera outside my office at seven or if you move out of view of the camera until I call, I will kill her. You will receive a phone call telling you were to pick her up. You will then stay with me, and she will be able to leave. I will then do to you, what I have done to her, I like men as much as women. If you try to find us before the call in the morning I will kill her, do you understand?" He waited for a response.

Amir was fuming at the things being said, he wanted to shout out, but he didn't. He was amazed that Al-Qadir wasn't showing any emotion whatsoever, even with the knowledge of what had happened to his girlfriend.

"Have you finished?" he said calmly.

"With you yes but not with her, we have a long night ahead of us together, see you tomorrow." He disconnected the call.

Amir didn't speak to Al-Qadir when he finished the call, he walked out of the room and downstairs to the hotel lobby to give him some space. What was being said on the phone by Riadh upset him, so he knew that it must have upset Al-Qadir.

"That should keep his mind boiling over until tomorrow. One thing is puzzling me, the Paris detective said the bodies in the apartment had death cards on them, why?" Riadh said aloud to himself.

"What did you say?" said Mutaz sitting up in the chair.

"I forgot to mention that I made a call to my detective friend that I pay a lot of money to for information. I asked him what he knew about the bodies in the apartment. He said that the bodies had death cards nailed to the foreheads, whatever death cards are. Do you know what they are?"

"Death cards nailed to the forehead, are you sure he said this?" said Mutaz.

"Yes, I'm sure what does it mean?" snapped Riadh.

Mutaz went on to explain about the man they called Azrael in Iraq who had become something of a folk hero to the people. He was an avenging angel of sorts that had many kills credited to him.

"It seems like this Azrael has come to Paris; he will be given a great reception." Joked Riadh.

"This is not a man to take lightly he is a talented and a ruthless killer," replied Mutaz.

"As am I," said Riadh.

"This changes everything, we need to adjust our plans," said Mutaz.

"Well look at you the Great Mutaz he fears this legend of the Iraqi people, Azrael. You will stick to the plan, there are many of us he has no chance. We will deal with him like any bug and squash him when he gets here tomorrow." He enjoyed trying to shame Mutaz in front of his bodyguard.

Mutaz left the office his brain spinning out of control. First, he had to deal with the idiot Riadh now he has Azrael coming after them. He wasn't scared, he'd never feared any man, but he does respect some men and this Azrael was one of them. He put one of his men who was a good sniper in the woods on the drive to the property, he positioned himself where he could get a good shot of anyone coming into the drive. As the sun rose in the morning, he would put two men on the roof with binoculars where they could see all around the chateau and the tree line beyond. There was already a good clearance all around the chateau itself with two hundred feet of manicured lawns surrounding it. Beyond the lawns were nothing but tall conifers on three sides and an open apple orchard to the right. Being the end of winter, the apple trees were bare of leaves and hiding amongst the trees would be impossible. At the front of the apple orchard close to the chateau was a row of new apple trees. Thick wooden poles were buried in the ground on two sides of each tree to hold them in place until they rooted.

Mutaz had the external patrols of the chateau exchange with the interior security every thirty minutes, he didn't want anyone falling asleep. It was going to be a long night but hopefully an enjoyable morning when Azrael arrives. He was quietly looking forward to seeing who this legend of the people was. He would kill him and let the Iraqi people know that he was the one that did it. He would end their pathetic love for this mystery man, he would become more powerful and feared than ever before.

CHAPTER 53

CONNOR TO PARIS

Brad hadn't heard from Al-Qadir for two days and he was getting concerned. There were new developments between Riadh Al Musayyib and the explosives and gun running that Connor was investigating. The biggest connection came from the GIGN or Group d'Intervention de la Gendarmerie Nationale. They were an elite French counter terrorism team who were investigating several leads that connected to Riadh supplying Islamic militants with explosives. The connection that raised Brad's eyebrows was the number of suspected militants and high-level criminals that had been killed. They had been killed all in the same way, at close range with a bullet to the head. This killing method was in the reports on the former General Mutaz that Al-Qadir was hunting down. He decided to send Connor to Paris to locate Al-Qadir.

Connor was looking forward to getting out of Istanbul for a brief time. The information Brad had given him was exciting. He'd read the portfolio on Al-Qadir and was impressed. He'd done more in six months with the US Marines than most soldiers do in years.

There were several interesting footnotes that Brad had included that were separate from the report. One was the information or lack thereof about the man known as Azrael in Iraq. It didn't take a genius to realize that Brad was letting him know that Al-Qadir could be Azrael. He didn't see this as a problem but a huge bonus, the man had skills far beyond the norm.

The CIA Gulfstream landed at a small private airfield on the outskirts of Paris. Inside the privacy of the hanger, he was met by his local counterpart who gave him a quick rundown of the SUV vehicle and the weapons that were concealed under the floor in the rear. The hidden compartment was the width of the rear of the SUV. It opened by a signal received from a code entered the cell phone he'd been given. The lid popped open on a spring mechanism revealing his mini arsenal of weapons and ammunition. A modified Barret M82A1 .50 BMG sniper rifle with scope, two M16's, two Sig Sauer pistols, his personal preference, a suppressor, flash banks and two knives. His communications were standard for the CIA, non-traceable or trackable cell phones.

His counterpart had already zeroed in the sniper rifle for him, he would have preferred to do it himself, but he didn't have the time. It would have been an immense help if his counterpart could go with him in support, but Brad had unofficially authorized Connor to go to Paris.

The address for the safe house was already logged into the vehicles GPS. He contacted Brad on route to the safe house to see if there was an update on Al-Qadir, there wasn't. This didn't sound good to him, and he stopped short of the safe house at a gas station. He put Al-Qadir's apartment, Riadh's home and the Chateau address into the GPS. He would go to Al-Qadir's apartment first to see if he were there. When he looked at the GPS he realized how close Al-Qadir's place was to Riadh's obviously for surveillance.

He parked two blocks from the apartment and walked the rest of the way. He had dressed in dark clothing that fit in with most of the other men walking around the streets of Paris. As he approached the apartment, he saw a lady and a policeman talking. It looked like the lady was giving him a hot drink in a cup. He remembered the name of the street where he'd parked the SUV and quickly scribbled it on a piece of paper, he was going to ask the policeman for directions. He thought that it was a way of trying to find out why the policeman was stood outside the apartment building.

"Excuse me, can you tell me where this street is?" he asked the policeman.

Before he could answer the woman saw the address on the paper, "You have to go back the way you came and turn left then first right," she said.

"You must be a very important woman to have your very own policeman," he said smiling.

"Oh! No, there was a shooting yesterday in the top apartment, they brought dead bodies out…" she was stopped short by the policeman.

"Madame we cannot discuss this," said the policeman.

"No, of course not."

"Thank you for your help," said Brad and followed the lady's directions.

He had to contact Brad and let him know what had happened, with luck he could find out who was taken to the morgue. Hopefully, it wasn't Al-Qadir but for some reason he didn't think he was one of the bodies. The lady did say bodies and not a body, he was straight on the secure phone to Brad.

It was ten in the evening, so he did a drive-by of Riadh's address and his office building, both looked quiet with no sign of security guards outside. This was contrary to what he'd read in the reports that Brad sent to him. There were normally security guards posted outside the home especially at night.

He drove to the safe house as he wanted to check out the weapons that were in the vehicle. It wasn't that he didn't trust his counterpart here in Paris he had an old habit of stripping and cleaning all his weapons, particularly sniper rifles. As he drove into the garage he received the call from Brad, Al-Qadir wasn't one of the bodies. The interesting thing was there were three bodies in the apartment all with death cards nailed to their foreheads and one body on the stairs with a through and through bullet wound to the neck. It sounded like Al-Qadir had put up a good fight. There wasn't anything he could do right now, so he got a few hours' sleep.

CHAPTER 54

Al-Qadir and Amir brainstormed for two hours putting a plan of action into place. They were happy with it but they both knew that it was very unlikely that Al-Qadir would survive. They both changed into black SWAT style clothing. Amir put on his black wool hat and picked up the heavy coat and bullet proof vest. Once he parked the car close to the chateau grounds he would put on the vest and blacken his face. Getting stopped by the police with black face paint on would certainly cause a problem.

"May God be with you," said Al-Qadir as Amir left the hotel.

"And with you," he replied.

Amir was heading towards the chateau he was the only ace up Al-Qadir's sleeve. Riadh nor Mutaz knew that Amir was collaborating with him, so they had to take advantage of that.

Amir parked the car in amongst some trees a mile from the chateau. He covered the car with broken tree branches and stepped back to see if you could see it, you couldn't. He carried a duffel bag and a backpack that were loaded with weapons, ammunition clips, flash bangs and three grenades. Over his right shoulder he had an M16 with a suppressor attached and a Sig Sauer holstered on his hip. He put the night vision goggles on his head and started his walk through the forest. The goggles didn't show anything, so he flipped them back up and moved a little further. He did this several times checking that he wasn't walking into somebody ahead. The chateau had a wall that surrounded it on three sides, on the fourth side to the rear of the estate was a small river. The main gates were ornate wrought iron painted black and gold that were remotely operated by a clicker in a car or from the house. He flipped down the goggles and crossed the road putting his back against the wall. There was a heat signature moving through the trees where he'd just come from. He raised his rifle and pointed it at the moving target, it was a deer. He took a deep breath and crept closer to the gates.

He knew that the gates had cameras on them, so he kept away from them. Just in front of him was a tree that was close to the wall. He smiled as this would have been cut down if he oversaw the chateau's security, he flipped the goggles up again. He was up the tree in no time which gave him a good view of the inside of the property wall. Once again, the goggles came down as he peered over the wall. He slowly scanned the inside of the grounds to see if there were any guards on the inside. He could see down the long drive, but he couldn't get a clear view of the front of the chateau.

He was about to get over the wall when he saw movement to his left. Someone was stood next to a tree smoking a cigarette. He got lucky as he didn't see him at first. He raised his suppressed rifle and took careful aim. The shot was on target as the bullet entered the side of the head dropping the man to the ground. Even though the rifle was suppressed the sound was louder than he liked. He got lucky as he pulled the trigger a fox sounded off in the distance helping to partially cover the rifle sound.

He sat on the wall for a couple of minutes waiting to see if there was anyone else hidden in the trees, there wasn't. Once inside he slowly made his way towards the chateau going from tree to tree. Twenty yards from the edge of the tree line he had a clear view of the front of the chateau. He could see two armed guards walking clockwise around the building, they were spaced thirty yards apart.

He knew that there would be more guards on the opposite side and on the inside, this is where they would be holding Estelle. He had to find a good hiding spot in the undergrowth, somewhere with good cover to help protect Al-Qadir. He and Al-Qadir were certain that making him stand outside Riadh's office in the morning was just a ploy to make sure they knew where he was.

There looked like a good amount of chest high ferns on the ground to his right, they were right on the edge of the tree line. He moved slowly and quietly towards the ferns to settle down for the night. He'd only gone ten paces when something caught the front of his boot, it was a trip wire. He froze thinking it was attached to an explosive device, it was impossible to tell with the goggles down. He was about to flip them up when the external flood lights came on that were on the roof of the chateau. He was immediately blinded by the lights as the goggles intensified the light.

He dropped to the ground and started crawling to get some distance from where the trip wire was. He could hear someone shouting instructions loudly.

Mutaz was sat in a chair in one of the front rooms of the chateau next to the computer that was monitoring the trip wires they'd set up around the building. He'd staggered the trip wires so that they created a zig zag pattern through the tall conifers. On the river side he put several trip wires hidden on the bank of the river. It was a simple method of detection but effective. He would have used infrared detectors, but they could be seen if anyone were wearing night vision goggles.

The alarm sounded on the computer startling Mutaz. On the computer monitor he could see that sector three in his map of wires was flashing showing it was a break. He hoped that it wasn't just a deer or other wild animal, he knew this was the only real fault in setting up this system.

He ran to the front doors with his night vision binoculars gathering the waiting guards that were sitting around the entrance hall. He scanned the trees where the alarm had been activated and there it was, a heat signature. He watched it for a few seconds and could clearly see someone crouched in the bush. He threw the switch next to the door that turned on the floodlights. Six of his men ran outside with him with fully automatic weapons raised they formed a straight line and advanced towards the trees. On Mutaz's command they fired into the trees where the person was hiding.

Amir rolled behind a tree as bullets started flying and thumping into the trunks of the trees around him. He lay flat on his stomach behind the base of the tree which gave him a certain amount of protection. It seemed to go on for a long time when it suddenly stopped, they were reloading.

He raised himself to the prone position and saw several men in the glow of the floodlights, perfectly outlined as targets. He hit the first man who was closest to him and then a second before moving position. The rain of bullets started again.

Mutaz saw the man next to him go down and then another, he dropped to the ground keeping his body as flat as possible. He and the remaining men returned fire emptying their clips quickly before reloading.

Amir moved again in a crouched position to get behind a larger tree, he took a bullet to the upper arm. Behind the tree he stopped to see how bad it was, he could still move the arm, so he wasn't too worried. The bullet caught his upper arm and hit the back of the bullet proof vest.

Mutaz had crawled on the grass to get a better position on the shooter as his men ran for the cover of the trees. In the beams of light flooding through the trees from the floodlights he saw a figure behind a tree. As the man moved, he fired at him, he was sure he hit him. He crawled forward now directly to the right of the man behind the tree. He raised his rifle just as he stepped on a twig snapping it. He fired quickly as he knew the man would have heard the twig.

Amir heard a noise to his right and turned to shoot he was too slow as three bullets buried themselves into his vest. He was knocked backwards unconscious.

Mutaz moved through the trees knowing he'd hit the man dead center this time.

"Over here," he shouted.

The men dragged the unconscious body into the light of the flood lights. Mutaz was surprised when he saw the face, he recognized it or at least he recognized the scar. They took Amir to the steps of the chateau were Riadh was standing now that the all clear call was given.

"Is this the famous Azrael?" asked Riadh.

"Maybe, he was a soldier in the Iraqi army when I was a general," replied Mutaz.

Amir coughed as he started to regained consciousness, his chest heard like hell.

"He's still alive, good. Take him to the servants' entrance at the back, I don't want his blood inside my house. I will meet you in the kitchen," said Riadh.

Mutaz got his men to carry Amir, but not before they searched him for weapons and stripped him of the coat and bullet proof vest.

In the light of the kitchen, it was clear how bad the facial scar was from the wound Mutaz had given him. Amir was fully conscious now but in a great deal of pain from the bullets hitting the vest. He stared at Mutaz with so much hatred it seemed to burn through him.

"So, you are the famous Azrael," said Mutaz.

Amir didn't respond he just continued to glare at him.

"This is what happens when you mess with me," he said grabbing Amir's face. "I gave this to him to teach him and other recruits a lesson."

Riadh walked in with his bodyguard.

"You did this to him?"

"Yes," said Mutaz.

"Impressive scar, what did he do to deserve that thing on his face?"

"Nothing, it was a lesson to the army recruits at a base I visited."

"Nothing," repeated Riadh. "So, your actions in response to this man doing nothing has brought him here, brought him to my home." Riadh was losing his temper fast. "This is what your stupidity and arrogance has done, he came for you. I have a good mind to let him have you and be done with this. We don't need this kind of attention, we have lost several men because of you," Riadh was frothing at the mouth he was so worked up.

"You don't talk to me like that," screamed Mutaz. "Without me you wouldn't have half the business you have now." He'd lost control and pulled out his pistol.

The bodyguard and two of the other guards pointed their weapons at Mutaz in response. It was a standoff everyone was pointing their weapons at somebody.

"Put your weapons down," shouted Riadh.

Slowly all of them did, including Mutaz.

"Well, what a happy family you are," said Amir.

Mutaz punched him in the stomach as hard as he could.

"Leave him." Riadh was getting tired of the antics of Mutaz. "Sit him in the chair."

Amir was dropped unceremoniously onto a wooden chair.

"I will deal with him," said Mutaz.

"No, he is mine, you have done enough damage. So, are you really Azrael? If you are, I could do with someone like you to work for me? Oh! Wait I forgot, I have your girlfriend, or should I say I've had your girlfriend, several times." He laughed aloud his belly fat jiggled about. He got right up to Amir's face and looked closely at the scar. "Tomorrow I will add another scar to the other side of your face to match this one," he said poking the scar.

Amir spat in his face making him jump back.

Riadh lost control and whaled his fists down on Amir's face. It didn't last long as he ran out of breath.

"Let me take over," said Mutaz.

"No, nobody touches him. Tie him up here in the kitchen and I will deal with him in the morning. Did he have a cell phone?"

"No, just a few weapons and a knife," replied Mutaz.

"Where is the phone? Your girlfriend may want to call you from my bed." He laughed as he walked out of the kitchen.

On the way up the stairs the bodyguard stopped Riadh.

"What if that guy isn't this Azrael person, what if he is still out there?"

"Good question, we will know in the morning if there isn't anyone standing outside the office then we have him, I'm going to bed," replied Riadh.

Mutaz couldn't help himself when they tied Amir to the chair, he just had to get a few punches in.

"I will be the one to finish you off, you wait and see," he said giving a final punch to the jaw knocking him out. "Two of you stay with him."

Amir woke after the beating not realizing at first where he was. Then the pain in the chest and his jaw quickly reminded him. The two guards watching over him were studying him carefully.

"So, what did you really do to get that scar?" asked one of the guards.

"You heard him, he did it for fun, it wasn't even a lesson, he's a sadist and a bully," replied Amir.

"You must have done something?"

"No, nothing. He has done this to other recruits as well as many beatings. He only beat those that he knew couldn't fight back or didn't have the skill to. Any chance of a drink of water for the condemned man?" asked Amir.

"No," said the other guard.

"We're not animals," said the first guard who went to the kitchen sink and put some water in a cup from the faucet. He held it to Amir's mouth as he gulped it all down.

"Thanks."

"You know that Riadh will punish you for spitting in his face. He can be as evil as Mutaz."

"I'm going to die anyway."

"Most probably, but why suffer in the meantime?"

"I'm not dead yet, I will fight to the bitter end."

"You are as crazy as them," said the guard.

"Not crazy, determined to get my revenge, that's all."

Amir knew the end for him was close he just hoped that Al-Qadir was nearby. As he told the guards, he wasn't giving up until the end.

CHAPTER 55

It was four in the morning Al-Qadir just couldn't sleep, he just rolled around in the hotel bed. He thought that by now Amir was somewhere close to the chateau as planned. He drank a full bottle of water and went for a run to clear his head. The run did him good as did the shower he took before he left.

He drove the car towards Riadh's office parking it in the street a block away. He was exactly on time when he arrived outside for the office camera to see him. All he had to do now was wait for the call from Riadh. His mind was jumping around from Amir and the plan they'd put together and Estelle. If what Riadh had said was true she had been abused by him and he didn't doubt that the man had violated her. He could feel the anger building inside himself again, he calmed himself down.

He didn't fear for his own life even now as he stood outside the building. He knew they wouldn't kill him here they wanted to do it slowly, take their time and enjoy watch him suffer.

Mutaz woke early and went down to the computer that was showing the video of the cameras at the office. He realized that it was thirty minutes past the hour when Azrael was supposed to get there but he didn't care. Azrael was downstairs tied to a chair in the kitchen.

He tapped the computer keyboard to wake the screen up which had gone into sleep mode. The screen was split into four showing what the cameras were looking at. He sat forward in the chair staring at one of the pictures. There was a man in his twenties stood outside the office, exactly where Riadh had told Azrael to stand. He waited five minutes to see if he moved but he didn't. He ran up the stairs to Riadh's room and banged on the door loudly.

The personal bodyguard burst out of the room next door with his gun raised.

"Put that down and tell him to come downstairs to the computer," said Mutaz.

Back at the computer the young man hadn't moved out of camera shot, he couldn't believe it. Riadh rolled into the room wearing a silk dressing gown closely followed by his bodyguard.

"What is it?" he said angrily as he tried to wake up properly.

"Look," said Mutaz.

He was seeing the same young man. "If that is Azrael who do, we have downstairs? Asked Riadh.

"I don't know but I intend to find out." Mutaz stormed out of the room almost knocking Riadh over.

"Follow him make sure he doesn't do anything stupid; I'm going to get dressed," said Riadh.

The bodyguard was seconds behind Mutaz when he entered the kitchen.

"What is that on his shirt?" shouted Mutaz at the top of his voice.

"Water, I gave him some water," replied one of the guards.

"What do you mean you gave him water who said you could," Mutaz said grabbing the guard by the shirt.

The guard was in no mood for the Mutaz theatrics and pushed him away hard causing him to fall.

Riadh's bodyguard smiled when Mutaz fell, he knew that his men wouldn't put up with him for much longer.

Mutaz crashed to the floor but jumped back up quickly with his pistol in his hand. He didn't hesitate and shot the guard in the head.

The bodyguard jumped on Mutaz as did the guard's partner. They pummeled Mutaz on the floor with their fists as he tried to fight back.

"Hold him down," said the bodyguard.

He pulled a piece of rope off the kitchen table that they'd cut from the one they tied Amir with and bound Mutaz's hands.

He was kicking out and screaming at them like a mad man. All three men were sweating profusely as Riadh walked in.

"What the hell is going on?" He said still in his dressing gown.

"He shot Pierre," said the bodyguard.

"You are unhinged Mutaz, truly unhinged, why shoot him?"

"He put his hands on me." he screamed.

"If they untie you, can you keep control of yourself?"

He shook his head to get the sweat off his face, "Yes."

"Untie him and if he tries anything like that again shoot him." Riadh needed Mutaz right now, but he would kill him as soon as they dealt with this Azrael.

Riadh got dressed and walked back into the room to look at the computer screen.

"He's still there." Riadh dialed the boyfriend's cell number and watched the screen.

The man took a cell phone out of his pocket and put it to his ear.

"So, you are Azrael I presume, we have a friend of yours here," said Riadh.

"You have already told me that you have my girlfriend."

"No, I mean your other friend with the wonderful scar on his face."

"Who are you talking about?"

"You know who, your partner in crime, the man you're working with to get me."

"I work alone, I don't need anyone else to help me kill you. Then I will kill Mutaz and go on my way or you can give me my girlfriend and Mutaz and I may let you live."

Riadh burst out laughing. "You think that I don't know that you and this scar faced mongrel aren't working together, he told us everything."

"Then for someone who I obviously haven't met he told you whatever you wanted to hear under torture. Where are you, so I can come and kill you?"

"You can come here but it is you that is going to die. You know my chateau's address leave now; you have one hour and fifteen minutes to get here."

"It takes ninety minutes to get there from your office, you know that."

"Then you had better get a move on if you want to see your girlfriend alive. When you get here drive with your car windows wide open, enjoy the breeze." He disconnected the phone.

Riadh was starting to get doubts about this man he sounded very sure of himself. He had his bodyguard, Mutaz and nine other guards, all heavily armed. He sat and thought for a few minutes, he was trying to figure out what this man could do when the odds were stacked against him.

"Put one of your men down by the crossroad where he must turn to come to the estate. If any other vehicles show up, he is to call you and take care of the other vehicle. Put another man by the main gate on a motorcycle, when he drives in here make sure he follows the vehicle." He said to Mutaz.

"We...." He was cut off by Riadh.

"Do it," shouted Riadh with fury in his eyes. "You get the girl from my bedroom and the scarred one, take them out to the apple orchard and bring some rope." He said to his bodyguard.

The bodyguard went to the bedroom for the first time since the girl was taken in there. At first, he couldn't see her, then he saw the hand ties to a bed post. She was hanging off the bed her naked body half on the floor and half hanging by the arm. Her body had bruises all over it as did her face but what repulsed him were the deep bite marks on her breasts and back. He lifted her as gently as he could, she was barely breathing. Her eyes were just round puffed-up balls of red flesh they were so swollen.

"Come in here," he shouted.

Two guards entered the bedroom and stopped in their track when the saw what was left of the girl he was carrying.

"Is she alive?" asked one of the guards.

"Barely, take her down to the orchard and treat her with respect, at least we can do that for her." He said throwing a towel on her that was on the floor.

Riadh had the guards strip Amir of his shirt and tied him between two of the trees support posts by his arms. He had them do the same thing when Estelle was brought to him. The ropes were pulled so tight that Amir's toes would only just touch the ground. Estelle was in the same position with her head down and chin resting on her chest, she was remarkably close to death. The sexual and physical abuse she'd endured had taken its toll. She had survived without any food or water to this point, but she was beyond saving.

The guards were disgusted at Riadh had done to the woman. They had seen some terrible things in their careers but this one was one of the worst.

CHAPTER 56

The guard sat at the crossroads on his motorcycle, he could see a car coming about half a mile away, it pulled over to the side of the road. He watched the man in the front seat through his binoculars, he was looking at a map, a lost tourist. A second vehicle approached and went around the one at the side of the road. After he inspected the car who would send it to the chateau, and call Mutaz to let him know it was on the way.

All the windows were open on the car as instructed; the driver stopped by the motorcycle. The guard held his weapon on the driver as he looked behind the rear seats for any hidden passengers, there were none.

"Open the trunk," he said.

"I have to get out to do that, it's not released from inside the car."

"Get out, hands in the air," said the guard.

Al-Qadir opened the trunk with the key and the guard looked inside, his eyes opened wide at what he saw. Al-Qadir's knife blade was swift and deadly as it slammed into the throat of the distracted guard. He kept hold of the man's weapon as he fell and wiped his blade on the dead man's shoulder. He dragged the body into the trees out of sight and rolled the motorcycle on top of him.

He got back in the car and drove down the dirt road before stopping for ten minutes. He was already dressed in all black but now he put his body armor on and strapped his Glock to his leg holster and a second into his belt holster. Hanging from the body armor were two grenades and two flashbangs, in short pockets were several fully loaded clips for the Glocks. He threw the guards rifle onto the backseat and placed a third Glock with a suppressor attached on the passenger seat. He drove on to the gate which was a quarter of a mile away around the bend in the dirt road.

The security guard sat on the motorcycle heard the car coming and steadied himself pointing his AK47 towards the open metal gates. A car slowly crawled alongside him.

"Which way?" asked Al-Qadir.

The security guard made a fatal error and for a split second he looked in the direction that he was indicating. The two bullets fired by Al-Qadir tore through his head exploding it open on the opposite side.

He sat for another minute and then drove slowly along the driveway to the chateau. On the roof he could see one man standing with a rifle that was pointed at his car. Outside two double doors that led into the chateau were two-armed men and a group of armed men to his right by some small barren trees. To his left were three Mercedes SUVs parked neatly in a row.

As he drove towards the front of the chateau, they all raised their weapons and pointed them at him. He deliberately drove closer to them than they wanted as Mutaz shouted repeatedly for him to stop. He stopped the car at an angle the same way that police stopped their cars when doing traffic stops. The front of the vehicle was between him and Mutaz and his men.

The man he knew as Riadh waived two men away as he moved to one side revealing the two people strung up to wooden posts. He couldn't deny he was shocked when he saw Estelle and Amir, especially Estelle. She was hardly recognizable her naked body was so bloodied and beaten, his blood boiled but he knew he had to keep calm. He put his hands up to the windshield to show that didn't have a firearm. Pulling the guards AK47 across from the passenger seat he slowly lifted it out by the strap. He could see that some of the security men were extremely focused, especially the one stood with Riadh. He looked a lot more professional than the rest. Mutaz walked towards him as Al-Qadir swung the AK47 onto the hood of the car.

"This belonged to your security man on the road, you will find the one on the gate in the grass with two holes in his head."

Walking towards Al-Qadir Mutaz said, "Take the guns out of the holsters and drop them to the floor."

"No, you come and get them if you want them," replied Al-Qadir.

Mutaz stopped suddenly and started walking towards Estelle and Amir.

"This is what you came for," shouted Mutaz lifting Estelle's head back by her hair.

He paused as the shock of her disfigured face registered on this man, Azrael.

Amir mouthed that she was dead, Al-Qadir didn't flinch, didn't show any emotion, or react.

"Leave her alone," said Riadh moving towards Al-Qadir.

"No. I want him to see this," said Mutaz as he put his pistol to her head and pulled the trigger.

Riadh stopped dead in his tracks when the gun was fired, he couldn't believe that Mutaz shot the girl.

"Enough," shouted Riadh as his bodyguard stopped him moving towards Mutaz. "We are going to take our time with you Azrael. I released all my staff from the chateau for a week, so you know how long it is going to take for you to die."

Mutaz turned his gun towards Amir.

"He is next," said Mutaz.

Al-Qadir took two steps backwards towards the trunk of the car, he wanted to get Mutaz's attention.

"Stop, what have you got in the trunk? You two check the trunk," said Mutaz to the men standing closest to the car.

Al-Qadir feigned disappointment and stopped.

"It's locked, where are the keys," said one of the guards.

"In the ignition," replied Al-Qadir.

"Pass them to him, very slowly," said Mutaz.

He did as he was told and removed the keys from the ignition passing them to the guard. One guard stood with his AK47 pointed at the trunk just in case someone was inside, the second put the key in the lock and opened it.

The explosion wasn't massive, but it did the job it was supposed to do. Al-Qadir made a directional bomb with all the explosive force aimed to the rear of the car. The ball bearings flew out shredding the two guards.

Everyone except Al-Qadir ducked when the bomb detonated. He immediately tore one the grenades off his vest and threw it towards the group of guards to his left, it exploded killing two more. Riadh said on the cell phone that there were fourteen altogether, by his count they were now down to eight, he didn't know about the one Mutaz had murdered in the kitchen.

The guard on the roof was about to fire down on Al-Qadir when the top of his head exploded. His body fell over the edge to the ground ten feet from Riadh. A second guard stood next to Riadh was hit in the head splattering him with blood and brains.

"Sniper," shouted Mutaz as he opened fire on Al-Qadir.

Al-Qadir dropped down behind the car using the engine block for protection. He drew two Glocks and fired over the top of the car towards Mutaz.

"Let's go," shouted Riadh's bodyguard as he pulled him around the corner of the building towards the kitchen at the rear.

Mutaz got two of his men to run with him towards the building, they didn't realize it, but he was using them as shields against the sniper. The first man went down before they'd taken half a dozen paces, the second fell within seconds but was only winged. He and Mutaz dove towards the corner of the building and out of the line of sight of the sniper. They ran as fast as they could to the kitchen entrance where Riadh and his bodyguard had gone.

Al-Qadir kept his Glock pointed towards the corner as he ran forward. He got to Amir and cut the ropes that were holding him to the wooden post. He picked up the AK47 that was with the dead body of the guard the sniper had killed and gave it to Amir.

"Cover me," he said running towards the building.

The kitchen door was open, and he knew that one or more of them were just waiting for him to come running in. He fired several rounds through the kitchen window to draw their fire. It worked the window and frame was destroyed by the bullets that tore through it. He tossed his second grenade in through the now broken window and ducked down.

The explosion caught the last of the guards as he tried to run out of the kitchen, it took one of his legs. Al-Qadir went in through the door sweeping for any potential attackers, there weren't any.

The guard was writhing on the floor in pain holding his upper leg like that would stop the pain.

"Where will they go?" said Al-Qadir.

"Go to hell," he replied.

Al-Qadir stood on the top of the leg where the explosion had severed it. The guard screamed as the pain surged through his body.

"OK, those bastards left me here, I owe them nothing, they will go to the study. Next to the fireplace there is a secret door that leads to a hidden cellar. They can get out through the cellar next to where they park the SUV's."

Al-Qadir shot him once in the head ending his pain.

Amir was leaning against the chateau trying to get some circulation back into his arms and legs. Thankfully being as fit as he was it was returning quickly. He wanted to go after Mutaz but couldn't move properly yet. He saw the movement in the shrubs by the SUV's, it looked like Riadh's bodyguard. He fired at him forcing him to go back down the hole he was trying to crawl out of. He heard four shots in quick succession from the sniper, he was shooting out the tires on two of the vehicles.

He moved a little closer to the hidden exit in the shrubs and fired a short burst into the small doorway. He knew this would keep their heads down, Al-Qadir wouldn't be far away from them now.

Al-Qadir moved very slowly and quietly through the narrow corridor towards the main area of the chateau. He could hear gunfire outside and hoped Amir was OK. The corridor was an extremely dangerous place to be as he had nowhere to hide. It was twenty feet long and a trap if they started firing on him. To his surprise they didn't shoot which meant they had moved further into the chateau. He got to the door leading into what looked like a large circular lobby. He stopped in the crouched position and listened for a minute; he couldn't hear anything.

As he entered the circular lobby area, he heard an AK47 being fired outside again, this time he was sure it was Amir. There was a room to his right with a lot of bookshelves on the walls, it had to be the study. Sweeping his weapon up the stairs and down towards the study he moved quickly. The study looked empty as he entered, the fireplace was to his left and an open wooden panel on the opposite side, the secret door.

The bodyguard returned to the cellar when he was shot at by someone outside. He had to get around them and help his boss get out through the hidden cellar. He returned to the study and stepped through the hidden door just as a shadow cast on the floor by the study entrance. Someone was approaching, he hid behind a large leather chair close to the desk. He listened for movement, and it came, it was one person by the sound of the soft boot noise.

The blow to Al-Qadir's temple was severe knocking him to the ground. He rolled onto his back with his feet up and planted them squarely into the chest of his attacker, it was the bodyguard. He was angry at himself for not seeing him first.

The bodyguard jumped from behind the chair on the man's blind side and hit him in the temple with the back of his fist. As he fell, he flung the heavy chair out of his way to get to the man, it was the one they called Azrael. He dove on him to plant as many punches as he could. He didn't make it as two feet hit him in the chest and threw him off.

Al-Qadir was up and on his feet, he lashed out with a roundhouse kick to the head of the bodyguard. He followed through with a side kick to his right knee, which didn't connect. He took a fist to the face and another to the ribs. He returned with his own punches to the torso when he saw the flash of a knife blade. He leapt back just as the blade cut him across his right upper arm.

He drew his own knife and blocked another strike by the bodyguard. Al-Qadir made a move like he was going to his left to draw the bodyguard in to that side. As the man stabbed at him, he grabbed the bodyguard's knife hand and pulled him in towards him. With a clean thrust he buried his own knife under the man's right rib cage. Al-Qadir received a headbutt in return splitting the top of his left eyebrow. He twisted his knife and plunged it into the ribs again. The bodyguard started to cough up blood as the blade had pierced the lung. He let him drop to the floor and stepped back. Even though he was coughing up blood he wasn't done as he reached for his sidearm in the holster. Al-Qadir admired him for fighting to the end and stepped on the hand as the man took his last breath.

Amir stripped one of the security guards of his body armor and extra clips of ammunition. Now wearing the vest, he walked up to the hidden exit under the bushes and emptied a magazine into the cellar below. He quickly put in a fresh magazine and kept to one side.

"I'm coming for you Mutaz," he shouted.

There wasn't a reply, but he knew better than to go down into the cellar, it would be suicide. He heard two shots shortly followed by a flashbang going off in the cellar and the sound of someone in pain further inside. He banged the cellar door as if he were coming in to draw fire, but nothing happened. Cautiously he made his way into the cellar below. The only light was coming from the entrance he'd gone in through. He waited for his eyes to get used to the dark and moved slowly forward. He could hear someone cursing, it sounded like Riadh, then the lights came on in the cellar. He threw himself against the wall expecting to see Mutaz, it was only Riadh. He was kneeling on the floor in a prayer position holding his ears. There was someone at the far end of the tunnel it was Al-Qadir.

Al-Qadir went to the false panel that led into the cellar, it was only open a couple of inches. He threw the panel open on its hinge, two shots from inside the cellar rang out immediately.

"You give yourself away Mutaz."

"Come down and we can talk about your girlfriend, Riadh liked her very much. You could see what he did to her, but I was the one that finished her in front of you."

Al-Qadir pulled a flashbang off his vest and tossed it into the cellar. He rolled to one side and covered his ears and closed his eyes. The boom of the flashbang was intensified by the narrow cellar walls and low ceiling. He heard two people both reacting in pain to the flashbang, one was Mutaz and the other hopefully was Riadh. He entered via the six steps and could see the two men on the floor holding their ears. He flicked a switch on the wall next to him turning on the lights. At the other end of the cellar was Amir wearing a bullet proof vest, which he knew must be hurting due to his injuries. He waived for him to move forward to join him.

They quickly checked Mutaz and Riadh for weapons and tossed them out of their reach. Mutaz wasn't going to give up without a fight and grabbed the inside of Al-Qadir's leg.

Al-Qadir felt a hand grab his leg, he was waiting for something from Mutaz and sliced the forearm deep to the bone. He watched as Mutaz screamed in agony, cursing him. They got both men to their feet and moved them into the study. Riadh was begging for mercy the whole time, he never stopped whining, even Mutaz told him to shut up.

They tied Mutaz to the same leather chair that the bodyguard used to hide behind. They stripped Riadh of his clothes and tied his fat naked body to his desk chair. Amir then shoved a gag in his mouth to muffle the constant whining.

"As much as I'd like to kill you, I think that honor should go to Amir here," said Al-Qadir.

"You can't kill me because you haven't got the guts to," replied Mutaz.

Amir left the room and returned a few minutes later with a roll of duct tape from the kitchen. He wrapped it around the forehead of Mutaz securing it tightly to the back of the leather chair. He slapped his face a couple of times; the head didn't move.

"Do you have your knife?" he asked Al-Qadir.

"Yes, here," he replied handing it over.

He unscrewed the top of the handle and emptied out several small items. It was a basic survival kit inside the handle including a needle and sutures for stitching up wounds. He took his time checking the length of the thread as he fed it through the needle.

"I don't think I will need the alcohol wipes, do you?" he said to Al-Qadir.

"No, why bother." He had no idea what Amir was about to do.

"The first cut will be for me, and the second cut will be for what you did to Estelle," said Amir smiling.

Riadh was sweating profusely watching what was going on. The fear in his eyes could not be hidden and it would only get worse.

Amir licked the length of the six-inch blade on both sides and then held Mutaz by the jaw.

"This will sting a little," he said.

He stuck the point of the knife inside Mutaz's mouth and slid it in an upward direction towards his ear. The screams filled the chateau as the knife did its work. Mutaz tried to shake himself out of the chair the pain was so bad.

"As you saw I cleaned the blade first, but I think the alcohol wipe would do a better job." He stuck the wipe into the gaping smile that Mutaz now had on one side of his face.

Riadh couldn't believe what he was seeing, it was gruesome even for him, he threw up, but the gag kept most of it in his mouth forcing him to swallow it.

Al-Qadir didn't show any emotion watching Amir go to work, if anyone deserved it, he did.

"Now we have to close the wound, we don't want you to get an infection, do we?" said Amir.

He stitched the wound shut and enjoyed every scream that Mutaz let out. The stitches were deliberately big twisted and ugly.

Amir wasn't done and went to town on the other side of his face and repeated the entire process. He held a mirror up in front of Mutaz so he could see what he'd done to him, his face looked like a Halloween mask.

Riadh couldn't look anymore and sat in the chair weeping.

"Your turn," said Al-Qadir as he cut the gag of his mouth.

"No, wait I have millions, I will make you both rich men, please don't," he said sobbing.

"Millions, what do you think Amir?"

"Sounds tempting," he replied giving Riadh hope.

"What if I said I was interested, how would we get our money?" said Al-Qadir.

"The computer on my desk, I can show you my offshore account. I will transfer the money to your personal accounts. Untie me and I will prove it to you."

"OK, let's see if you're telling the truth. Amir, do you have your account details?"

"They are engraved in my memory, what about yours?"

"The same," replied Al-Qadir.

Amir checked the desk drawers and underneath for weapons, there weren't any.

He untied Riadh's hands only, he had his account open in no time, they were shocked to see he had fifty million in the account. He set up the transfer page and all he had to do was put in the account details. Both transactions went through faster than they expected, twenty-five million into each account.

"Well, that's good, now we can share this money with the people of Iraq that have been harmed and made homeless by the likes of you," said Al-Qadir.

"I have one more question for you, who is your contact in Turkey for your illegal drug and weapons operation?" asked Amir as he started to record the conversation.

"I don't work with anyone, just my own people," replied Riadh.

"Oops! He failed the test, I know the name of your contact that was my way of giving you a chance," said Amir.

"He wants to see if you are holding out on us, if you aren't we would discuss letting you live," said Al-Qadir.

Amir held Riadh's right hand flat on the desk and stabbed it with his knife pinning it to the desk. The screams were a joyous noise to Al-Qadir as he knew that Riadh had made Estelle scream in pain.

"It is the Minister for tourism, he ships out the drugs or weapons as tourist information, so does the Minister of culture they are both on my payroll. It's so easy as most of the goods go out as diplomatic boxes. Now I have told you take the knife out of my hand."

"Who else?"

"Nobody, I only deal with them, please I need something for the pain."

"He has been truthful, should we let him live?" asked Al-Qadir.

"No," replied Amir.

"You said you would let me live," shouted Riadh.

"No, we didn't, you are going to die," replied Amir.

"OK, now we take care of the last bit of business, Estelle's revenge," said Al-Qadir.

"Wait we had a deal," said Riadh the fear returning to his eyes.

"Yes, we had a deal, but Estelle didn't, she never stood a chance, you like expensive Brandy, don't you?" he picked up the decanter off the table by the window. He poured two glasses out and gave one to Amir.

"To Estelle," he said.

"To Estelle," Amir repeated clinking the glasses together.

They both drank the Brandy in one go and threw the glasses into the fire.

Al-Qadir then poured the remainder of the Brandy onto Riadh's crutch.

"What are you doing?" said Riadh panicking.

"This," he replied striking a match from the cigar box on the desk, he tossed it onto the Brandy-soaked crutch.

Like Mutaz before him he was trying to scream the chateau down as the fire ate away at his genitals. He tried to put the flames out with his hands, but they caught fire as some of the flaming brandy transferred from his crutch to the hands. He passed out with the pain but was soon brought around by Al-Qadir. They lifted him out of the chair and dragged him outside face down. His face hit each step at the entrance on the way down and then was greeted by the stones of the driveway as they dragged his body towards the river.

They left Riadh staked to the ground next to the river in long grass where he couldn't be seen. His body formed a perfect X, stretched out to the maximum by the ropes.

"At night down here by the river the rats come out to feed, but don't worry too much when the foxes show up for their turn, they chase the rats away." He Placed a fresh gag on Riadh's mouth and put a hood over his head. "You will be able to hear the animals, but you won't see them, not until they start chewing at your arms, legs, and body. The birds are the nosiest, but you won't see them either not until they poke their beaks through the hood to get to his eyes.

Back at the chateau they untied Mutaz and repeated the dragging journey that Riadh had just experienced, except his ended at the stakes where Estelle had been tied. They tied Mutaz's naked body to the posts in the same manner as Estelle.

Mutaz was still trying to be defiant but the pain his face was unbelievable.

Amir went back to the chateau and brought out a full-length mirror that was on a stand. He placed it in front of Mutaz so that he could see what he looked like. He then stitched Mutaz's eyelids open so that he couldn't close them, he wanted him to see his own face until he died.

Amir pulled out the knife that he'd used on his face and stepped right up to him.

"Each one of these is for the people you have scared or killed over the years."

He slowly dragged the sharp blade across his chest and abdomen. When he'd finished there were thirty long shallow cuts in his skin. They were long and shallow so that he wouldn't bleed to death.

"I'll be back in a minute," said Amir walking towards the kitchen door.

Amir returned with a sheet and a bucket of water. He handed the sheet to Al-Qadir.

"To cover Estelle," he said. "This is salt water." He threw the water onto Mutaz.

The screams were so loud they both thought for sure that someone heard them.

CHAPTER 57

Al-Qadir picked up Estelle's lifeless body, covered it with the fresh sheet and carried it to the Mercedes at the front of the chateau. Stood next to it was Connor wearing camouflage clothing and cradling his sniper rifle. He opened the rear of the Mercedes as Al-Qadir placed her in the back gently. With love he kissed her on the cheek and closed the door.

"Amazing, that tracking pill you swallowed really worked, who'd have thought," said Connor.

"Brad wasn't sure it would work when he gave it to me, thanks for the help," replied Al-Qadir.

"What now?" asked Amir.

"We take care of Estelle's body, cold storage somewhere and then a funeral," said Al-Qadir.

"I will make a call to someone that will take care of her, then the three of us are going to get drunk," replied Connor.

That night they did get drunk, very drunk but not without reason. Connor made good on his call to a high-ranking contact with the Paris police. Estelle's body was recovered and taken to the city morgue. The police told her colleagues at the Real estate office that she'd been abducted and the man who abducted her died in a shootout with the police.

The funeral was taken care of by Al-Qadir, and no expense spared. The real estate office was given invitations to attend but were advised that there wouldn't be an open casket. It was a small and very private service and burial. Al-Qadir, Amir and Connor kept their distance at the burial and let her friends at the office grieve for them.

On the fourth day after they'd left the chateau one of the grounds keepers discovered the carnage. When the police arrived, they found Mutaz tied to the tree stakes, he was still alive, with a death card nailed through one of his hands. Once they removed him from the tree stakes shock set in and he died on route to the hospital. It would be three more weeks before they found Riadh's body when the tractor mower was cutting the long grass down by the river. There wasn't much left of the flesh as the wild animals and birds had eaten their fill.

The horror scene found at the chateau was news all over France and Europe. It was put down to drug gang rivalry but when the death card was mentioned the people of Iraq knew what it really was.

Amir sent the information and recording of Riadh's confession about his conspirators to his contact in Istanbul. It sent shock waves through the government when they were arrested. A full-scale investigation was launched into other possible corrupt officials. The ministers both agreed to a deal if they exposed who else was involved. However, before they could talk, they were both found hung in their police cells under suspicious circumstances.

Over the following months many people in Iraq that lost loved ones, homes, and businesses to Mutaz and Sargon received anonymous donations of money. The word spread quickly about the demise of Mutaz, and many Iraqi families gave thanks to the people's protector, Azrael.

Six months passed without a single corrupt politician, police officer or military officer being killed. The people were beginning to fear that their protector had forsaken them, then it happened. A cruel trader of young girls was found strung up to the iron gates of his home with a death card nailed to his forehead.

The man was known by locals as an abuser of young girls but every time someone got the police involved, they died suddenly. He was extremely violent and thought that he was untouchable.

Word spread quickly about his body hanging from the gate. Locals came from all over the area and spat on the body and stoned it. They were shouting that they hoped he went straight to hell. Then all at once the people started chanting, Azrael, Azrael, Azrael. Their guardian angel and protector was back.

MICHAEL J. BENSON

MORE NOVELS

BY

MICHAEL J BENSON

TERRORIST HARVEST
RADICAL ELIMINATIONS
HOME GROWN TERRORIST
HARD TIMES LIVERPOOL
LIVERPOOL'S CIVIL WAR

Made in United States
Orlando, FL
05 June 2022